The Keeper of Secrets

Maria McDonald

Copyright © 2024 Maria McDonald

The right of Maria McDonald to be identified as the Author of the Work has been asserted by her in accordance with the Copyright, Designs and Patents Act 1988.

First published in 2024 by Bloodhound Books.

Apart from any use permitted under UK copyright law, this publication may only be reproduced, stored, or transmitted, in any form, or by any means, with prior permission in writing of the publisher or, in the case of reprographic production, in accordance with the terms of licences issued by the Copyright Licensing Agency.

All characters in this publication are fictitious and any resemblance to real persons, living or dead, is purely coincidental.

www.bloodhoundbooks.com

Print ISBN: 978-1-916978-65-2

Dedicated to the memory of my mum and dad who taught us the importance of love, life and family.

Beth: Florida, 1976

My grandma died when I was seventeen. I loved her dearly. Born in County Cork, she had no intention of ever leaving Ireland until the American navy landed in her hometown and she met my grandpa Ed. They both said it was love at first sight and they married in 1918. When the war ended, she moved to the States to join him, leaving everything she knew behind. She was a wonderful, caring Irish woman. Full of quaint sayings, and the smartest person I knew.

When she died, she left me her tape recorder and a series of tapes. After the funeral, I played the beginning of the first one. She had addressed the recordings directly to me as if she were reading out a letter. They were numbered and dated so I could listen to them in order. I was so upset to hear her voice I turned it off and put the whole lot in a drawer, promising myself that I would listen to them when I was in a better frame of mind. But life got in the way. School and boys took all my interest, then college beckoned and before I knew it, I was packed up and living in a dorm with several other girls. When I went home for Christmas break, my mom said she had packed them into a memory box tucked away in my wardrobe. Dad said it was important that I listen to them but not until I was ready. But I was still nowhere near ready to hear my much-loved grandma's voice.

After college came work. Accountancy is not the most creative profession, but I loved it. Then my father died. I went home, back to my old room which, other than a fresh coat of paint, looked much the same as I had left it ten years earlier.

That's when I found the tapes. Every evening I listened to my grandma's voice. Every morning I relived the things my grandma had said. Maybe it's just as well I hadn't listened to them when I was younger. I would never have understood. Now I hope I'm older and wiser. My grandma taught me to always listen to both sides of every story. She'd told me several times growing up how lucky she was. But I don't think I understood fully until now.

Act 1

Lizzie

Chapter 1

Knockrath Manor, 1912

It was Da who nicknamed me Lucky Lizzie. I was born in the first minute of the first day of the 20th century. Da said that I brought luck and joy to the whole family, but mostly luck, for it was after I was born their fortunes changed for the better. Our family was offered a cottage on the grounds of the big house Ma and Da both worked in. Primrose Cottage sat at the edge of the woods, its half door permanently open, slivers of smoke trailing into the sky from the open fire which always had a pot of soup or stew bubbling away in preparation for the family evening meal together. My mother insisted that we always ate together. She swore that the family who eat together and pray together, stay together. So that's what we did.

The Haughton family were in residence in the big house during the summer months and during those months my ma, Catherine McCarthy, spent her morning baking bread and cakes for the family then hurried home to cook and clean for her own family. My da, Mick McCarthy, worked on the estate. He was a large man, hands like shovels they used to say, which everyone continued saying for years afterward, the one abiding memory of Mick McCarthy, big hands, big heart. He would arrive home in the evenings and grab Ma, the two of them laughing as his hands encircled her narrow waist and he danced her around the table, before whisking his children to join in, his rich baritone booming out, warm and engulfing everyone. Our home was a happy one, full of love and laughter.

My sister Maggie and I are what was known as Irish twins: born in the same year, me in January, Maggie in November. Maggie was the pretty one, dark hair, slim figure, everyone said so. Da used to say that she'd steal hearts when she was older. Jimmy was the baby, three years younger than Maggie. Blond, bonny and smart as a whippet, us girls treated him like a doll. We walked the two miles to school in the village every morning and back to the estate in the afternoon. Then after we'd finished the jobs set out for us by Da, we frolicked in the woods, gathering flowers in the spring and berries in the autumn. Da taught us how to grow vegetables in a plot to the side of our cottage and Ma taught us how to make preserves from the berries we picked in the autumn. It was an idyllic life.

I'll never forget my first interaction with Lord Haughton, the landowner and master of the estate. It was on a summer afternoon when I went to the kitchen door of the big house with Ma's coat. She had left it on the hook on the back of the door on that bright sunny morning, but the afternoon had brought dull and persistent rain. We had spent the morning picking strawberries. I left Maggie and Jimmy washing them for Ma to make jam when she got home. It was a short ten-minute walk to the back of the big house, and I could feel the rain soaking through my outer clothing as I reached the kitchen yard. I turned to look back but from that vantage point all that could be seen of our home was a wisp of smoke blending into the grey sky.

"Good afternoon."

The strange voice came out of nowhere. I stepped back

abruptly, my hand to my chest. The outline of a tall, thin person stood in the open doorway of a small building to the left of the yard. Recognising Lord Haughton, I recovered my composure, nodded and curtsied in his direction.

"Hello, sir."

"And what are you doing, sneaking around the backyard of Knockrath Manor?"

"My mother's coat, sir. I thought she might need it."

He beckoned me and, with a glance at the firmly shut kitchen door, I stepped towards him. He lunged forward and grabbed my hand, pulling me forcefully into the shed. It smelt of butter and cream and I realised that it was the outhouse used for making and storing cheese.

"And your mother is?"

Stunned, I stared into the face of the master. He was towering over me, taller than my da even, but thin like a rake, with thin pale lips drawn in a straight line.

"Mrs... Catherine McCarthy, sir." I stuttered over my mother's name as if I had never said it before.

"And you are...?"

"Lizzie, sir." And I curtsied again.

"Well, well." He spun me around. "Quite the young woman now, Lizzie McCarthy. You certainly have grown up since I saw you last."

I tried to free my hand from his grasp, but he held it tighter.

"Sir, my mother is expecting me," I said, my voice a hesitant whisper.

As suddenly as he had grabbed me, he let me go.

"Get out of here, child," he growled.

I didn't need to be told twice. Turning on my heel, I ran towards the kitchen door, nearly tripping on the cobblelock in my haste to get away. The kitchen door opened as I reached it and my mother's voice echoed out into the yard.

"Good girl, Lizzie, I'm going to need that coat... What? What is it?"

I stumbled across the threshold stuttering, "Lord Haughton collared me."

"What did he say, child?"

"Nothing much, he just asked me my name, but he frightened me, that's all."

"Silly goose."

I was soon cocooned in the warmth of my mother's embrace and treats from the cook, Mrs Short. She was a short stout woman, an ambassador for her profession. Her apron started each day pristine and by evening carried remnants of every meal prepared in her kitchen. Mrs Short was a good friend to the McCarthy family, often sending home leftover meat and pies. With no children of her own, she took pleasure in sending little treats home for us, chocolates and cakes, the likes of which we would never have seen let alone tasted.

"Can't abide waste," she would say as she placed the remains of a large chocolate cake in Catherine's basket. "Lady Haughton wanted chocolate cake for her tea and her with the tiniest appetite I ever saw. She only ate a sliver of it, and the rest of it'll spoil, even in the pantry. Take it home for the kiddies. A little bit of chocolate will do them no harm."

Every evening Ma's basket unveiled some treat or other. All in all, the McCarthys were the best-fed children in the whole of Cork. Da worked long hard hours, same as every worker on the estate. We had our vegetable patch and the whole of the woods to run wild in. The Haughton estate was as good a place to work as any other. Mr O'Sullivan, the estate manager, was in charge when the Haughtons weren't there, and he was a fair man. The Haughtons' main residence was in England somewhere, while their children attended boarding school. The eldest, George, was in Trinity College Dublin, the daughter, Amelia, in a finishing school in Paris and Ralph, the youngest, attended boarding school in Dublin. Ralph Haughton was roughly the same age as me but there the similarity ended. As the youngest, he was bullied by his brother and laughed at by his sister, so he sought out the uncomplicated comfort of us, the McCarthy children.

Chapter 2

The Village Fête

In late August every year, in the week before the Haughton family dispersed for the winter, the Haughtons hosted the village fête on the extensive lawns to the front of Knockrath Manor. Mrs Short and Ma were busy for days in advance, preparing for it. Da and all the other men were called in from the fields to set up tents and long tables and on the morning of the fête, the women of the house set out trays of food and jugs of lemonade around vases of cut flowers from the gardens. It was an amazing sight.

The weather for the fête that year was perfect. Azure skies with warm sunshine. Bees flitted from table to table, swatted away by the serving girls. It was mostly local girls hired from the village wearing white aprons and hats above rosy cheeks flushed from the heat and the effort of keeping the trays of food full and the jugs free of insects. When Ma told me that I would be helping that year I was over the moon. It made me feel so grown up. I was so ready to take on this first adult task, rather than looking after my younger siblings. Maggie was left in charge of Jimmy as I donned my white apron and cap and took my place at the last tent at the bottom-left of the lawns. Ralph sat on the grass hidden behind the linen tablecloth and folded his gangly legs in under the table.

"Pass me down a sandwich, Lizzie."

"What are you doing? You'll get me in trouble."

"No, I will not, Lizzie. I doubt if they will even notice I'm gone."

Sometimes Ralph's self-pity irritated me. While I could sympathise with him, he really didn't realise how good a life he had, despite his bully of a brother. George was the eldest and his parents treated him like a demigod. Tall and broad in a way Ralph would never be, George was sure of his place in the world, but had a mean nature. Ralph often fell victim to his loutish pranks, brought home from boarding school and practised on his younger brother. The cruelty of it had surprised Maggie and me, for we thought the Haughton boys were brought up to be gentlemen and should know better. Every school holiday George had another mean trick to practise on his brother. Ralph went to his parents with cuts and bruises, evidence of the ill-treatment meted out to him by his brother but every time his parents told Ralph to take it like a man. On that day Ralph was limping. His shin was mottled purple from the kick George had given him, when Ralph had inadvertently got in George's way during cricket practice.

"You must stand up to him, Ralph," I scolded him. "And I don't mean, take whatever he dishes out. I mean don't let him hit you. Don't fall for his silly tricks."

"It makes no difference, Lizzie. George takes pleasure in hurting me. I swear he does. I've tried talking to Papa about it, but he insists that George doesn't mean any harm. That it is all simply good old-fashioned boyish fun. He said I need to grow up, that I need to learn to be more like George... and less like Amelia."

Ralph's voice tapered off into a whine.

"Shush, we have company." I hurried to the other side of the table as Master George approached.

"Afternoon, sir, may I pour you some lemonade?" I said.

"Yes, thirsty work this," George said.

He smiled at me and to my surprise my heart gave a little leap. I didn't know whether it was fear or anticipation, for the look he gave me left me in no doubt that he liked what he saw. Master George may have been his brother's tormentor, but he was a handsome devil, even to my inexperienced eye. My initial thoughts appalled me, for I knew the nature of this man, had witnessed the abuse he piled upon his younger brother. The latest injury was inflicted in the last week, by a grown man, a medical student, against his thirteen-year-old brother. I gave a sigh of relief as George moved on to the next stall and I returned to my position at the other end of the table with Ralph still hiding in the corner. With George out of the way Ralph's spirits rose, and soon we were laughing as he recounted a story about his school.

I wasn't so happy ten minutes later when I felt Jimmy tugging at my apron strings.

"Hi, Jimmy, do you want some lemonade?" I smiled at my little brother as I poured him a small glass and gave him some cake. Looking around I expected Maggie to be with him, but she was nowhere to be seen. Coming out from behind the table I scanned the gathering on the large lawns and there she was, a good forty feet away, chatting to George Haughton. Or being chatted to. From this distance it was hard to tell.

"Maggie." I tried to keep my voice low, for I didn't want to attract attention.

I watched as George tipped his hat to her and bowed low as if saying farewell to a young lady and not the daughter of the cook's helper. Maggie came walking towards me, her cheek flaming, and a smile on her face that spelt trouble.

"Maggie, what were you talking about to Master George?"

"Ah, Lizzie, something, and nothing really. He was really nice, asking me if I was enjoying myself..." She leaned closer to whisper in my ear. "He said I was a pretty little thing."

"What...? Be careful, Maggie. Master George is a grown man and a spiteful one at that. I don't know what he's at, you're only a child."

"I'm nearly thirteen," she said, indignance colouring her complexion further. "I couldn't be rude to Master Haughton, could I? Ma would have my guts for garters, wouldn't she?"

She had a point. Us McCarthy children had been brought up to speak when we were spoken to, and the Haughtons were our landlords. Although I knew she was right to a certain degree, niggling away at the back of my mind was his exaggerated bow in her direction and that smile on his face as Maggie turned away.

The following afternoon me, Maggie and Jimmy ventured up to the big house to meet our mother after work. We knew there were extras to bring home for our tea and we were all excited at the prospect of cake for a second day running. It was a beautiful summer's day. In no hurry, I dallied along the path, relishing the sound of the crickets in the long grass and the hum of the bees as they flitted from bloom to bloom, while Maggie chased after Jimmy who was ahead of her.

I didn't see them at first. It was the voices that pierced my senses and brought my eyes upwards to the walkway outside the formal drawing rooms. Ralph was yelling at George, which was very unusual. I was sure I had never heard Ralph raise his voice before. Still the voice of a young boy, high-pitched and angry. George laughed, a loud, deep-throated, derisory laugh that appeared to agitate Ralph even more. He made a run at his brother, his childish body dwarfed by George's manly frame. George swung his arm and batted his brother away as if he were swatting a fly. Ralph disappeared from view and all we could hear was George laughing.

"Get up, you little idiot."

Ralph ran at his brother again, only to be swatted to the side again. He whacked off the wall and landed flat on his back. George walked away, his laughter echoing after him as he went inside the house. Maggie looked at me, wide-eyed, and started to run towards Ralph but I held her back, shaking my head.

"But, Lizzie, he might be hurt," she said.

"No, Maggie, his pride will be hurt if he knows we saw what happened. Let's get out of here quick, before he sees us."

Taking Jimmy's pudgy hand, we sprinted the last few yards to get out of Ralph's line of sight. Mrs Short was waiting for us at the kitchen door and ushered us inside to the table. Tall tumblers of lemonade were waiting, chasing all thoughts of Ralph's altercation with his brother out of our minds. We drank our fill and watched as she packed three large wicker baskets. I swear our mouths were drooling as we watched her wrap a side of ham, large chunks of cheese and several loaves, as well as cakes and biscuits. It was quite a haul, enough to keep us going for a few meals. Ma laughed as she handed us a basket each and Jimmy buckled under the weight. Me and Maggie helped him, taking a handle each and we sang the whole way home to Primrose Cottage for our evening's feast.

Chapter 3

The Event

It was another glorious evening, still and warm. I had no way of knowing what went on before I arrived. All I saw was George being pushed backwards and falling. I had no idea that Maggie was there. The only thing I heard was an almighty crack as George's head hit the granite pillars that adorned either side of the steps down to the lawns. I ran towards the kitchen calling for my mother. By the time I had blurted out to my ma what had happened we could hear high-pitched shouting.

"Take your hands off my son." Lady Haughton was practically screaming. "Get away from him, get away."

Ma looked at me aghast for a split second then sprinted towards the patio. Maggie was backing away, her hands outstretched towards Lady Haughton as if begging for mercy. George was propped up against the granite pillar, his face as white as my ma's apron, with blood trickling from the back of his head. Fresh blood stained Maggie's hands and smeared her torn pinafore. She was shaking, babbling incoherently.

"Get the police. Quickly, arrest that girl." Lady Haughton's shrill voice called back towards the open doors of the drawing room.

The tall, thin figure of Lord Haughton arrived on the patio along with several servants. The servants rushed forward and grabbed Maggie by each arm, forcing her to the ground.

"Stop it, stop, that's my daughter," Ma said.

"She assaulted my son," Lady Haughton shouted.

"No, she couldn't have, she's only a child," Ma pleaded with Lady Haughton.

It was then I noticed Ralph, cowering at the far end of the path, his face grey, his whole body shaking. While Ma pleaded with Lady Haughton, I made my way over to him.

"What happened, Ralph?"

His whole body trembled and he shook his head, his eyes wild as a mad hare.

"What is it, Ralph? Did you see what happened?"

But Ralph was practically catatonic, and I wondered what he had witnessed to frighten him to such an extent. It was unbelievable that my little sister Maggie could push Master George with such force to cause that severe an injury. There had to be more to it. Ma was still pleading with Lady Haughton while Mrs Short attended to George's wounds.

"That's enough," Lord Haughton said, heralding silence.

It was as if the birds in the trees paid heed and the earth had stopped rotating just for that moment. Our entire world was ruled by this man, our fate in his hands. Despite the warmth of the evening sun, I was chilled to the bone, and I could see Ma felt the same. He gave orders to his men to lock Maggie in a storeroom and ordered Catherine to return home.

"But, sir," Ma pleaded. "She didn't do anything, she's only a slip of a girl."

Ma wrung her hands together as if she were kneading the dough for the Haughtons' bread. Maggie was shaking, still babbling, not making any sense, as the men led her away.

"Maggie, darling." Ma tried to follow her. "Sir, please."

"Enough. That girl will answer to the constable." Lord Haughton's icy tone silenced her. "Get out of here now."

A flock of birds in the nearby trees took flight, screeching their disapproval at the shrill tones emanating from the garden below.

Ma's whole body was shaking as I took her hand.

"Please, Ma, come on. Let's go."

Ma stepped back and turned to look at me as if she didn't know who I was. Tendrils of her hair had broken free of her usual topknot. She stood motionless for seconds, a wildness in her eyes that I had never seen before, then something clicked in her. She raised her hands to tidy her hair and then turned her attention to her flour-dusted apron. Untying it from around her waist she crumpled it into a ball and threw it on the lawn.

"Let's go home, Lizzie. I'll not set foot in that kitchen while they hold my daughter in such a fashion."

She tightened her grip on my hand and marched us both towards Primrose Cottage. It was all I could do to keep up with her, breaking into a trot to match her pace. Jimmy was sent to the end of the driveway to the main house with strict instructions to run back and tell Ma when the police arrived. It must have been a slow day in the village for within the hour Jimmy came running into the house. A constable on a bicycle was on his way to the manor.

Ma left me to look after Jimmy and made her way back to the main house, but she arrived back an hour later, distraught. They'd refused to let her in, refused to let her speak to Maggie. When the policeman arrived, he spoke to the Haughton family. He did not talk to Maggie, nor did he talk to my mother. The policeman put Maggie in handcuffs and walked her back to the village, to the local station where she was charged with assault and locked in a cell.

When Da arrived home that evening, Ma could barely talk,

she was so upset. Da punched the wall, his huge fist leaving a dent to the right at eye level beside the front door, a permanent, constant reminder of that day every time we left the house. They left me to look after Jimmy and went into town to the police station. The hours dragged by. Evening faded into night, and I had all but given up on their return when I heard mumbled voices in the darkness outside the cottage. I ran to the door.

"Ma, Da, where's Maggie?"

Ma's face contorted as she walked down the path, held up by Da, who looked equally distraught.

"No, pet, no. Maggie's been charged, and they won't let her home until she goes in front of the judge. It could be weeks..."

"Now, love, don't be upsetting yourself. Inside now, quick as you can and we can talk about it over a cup of tea," Da said. "Lizzie, make your ma a nice cup of tea, will you, pet."

I already had the kettle simmering over the fire, waiting on them coming home, so I busied myself mashing the tea and setting the table with cups and the last of the cake left over from the field day. It felt like an age had passed since that beautiful summer day we had all enjoyed so much. The events of the past few days didn't feel real to me. It was as if I were in the midst of a nightmare. I said as much to my ma as she took her place at the table.

"Did you get to speak to her, Ma?"

"Yes, love. The sergeant in charge was kind. Sure, he knows us, knows Maggie, for God's sake. He knows she's not capable of the type of violence the Haughtons have accused her of. She said that she was at the back of the house when she heard shouting and what she thought was the noise of a scuffle. When she peeped around the corner to see what was going on Master George was on the ground with blood seeping from his head. Maggie said she thought he was dead at first but then he started moaning so she ran over and tried to prop him up. It was then that she heard Lady Haughton screaming behind her."

"So, it's all a mistake, Ma. Surely Master George has said what happened."

"You would think so, wouldn't you? The constable says that Master George has no memory of what happened, but I don't believe that. No, that lad is hiding something."

Da stood in the corner of the room, stewing over the events of the day in silent contemplation, his huge hands buried in his pockets, as if afraid that if he set them free they would go straight up to the main house and demand the truth from Master George.

"Here, Da, tea?" I offered him a cup.

He shook his head. "Listen, I'm going to talk to Mr O'Sullivan, see if he will speak up for us. Our Maggie is but a lass. Someone else did the damage to Master George. He's a big lad, sure he must be nearly twenty. How could they possibly believe that a slip of a girl like our Maggie could do any damage to him."

Of course, it didn't do any good. Mr O'Sullivan had no sway over the Haughtons, and they were adamant that our Maggie be punished. Master George said his only memory was of Maggie trying to pull him upright and that Maggie must have attacked him for no reason. Not one person asked the question why. Why would Maggie attack George like that? How was it even possible for a slight, underweight twelve-year-old girl to do damage to a six foot tall, grown man. Even when the judge arrived in town and the police brought Maggie from the police station to the courthouse to face him, no one queried Master George's story, and no one listened to Maggie's side.

Ma cried as she came out of the courthouse. Da supported her, his arm around her shoulders, his face contorted as he struggled to control his emotions. Back at the cottage I waited with Jimmy, anxious to hear news of our sister. The judge found Maggie guilty of assault and sent her to prison. Twelve years of age and sent to prison for assault on a grown man despite claiming her innocence.

There was no dinner cooked in Primrose Cottage that night. Ma and Da sat at the table staring into space, Ma crying, Da patting her hand and wiping his eyes from time to time. Feeling totally useless, I fed Jimmy and put him to bed.

"Lizzie, when will our Maggie be home?" Jimmy whispered as I leaned over him to tuck him in.

"Two years, Jimmy. What are we going to do without our Maggie for two years?"

Just uttering those words choked me and my voice broke. Jimmy threw his arms around my neck to comfort me.

"It's not fair, our Lizzie. Not one bit."

I could feel his tears on my neck as we rocked back and forth mourning Maggie as if she were dead, for that's how it felt to us. Two years in prison might as well have been a lifetime, and for what? Master George had a lot to answer for.

Chapter 4

The Baby

A few months later Ma sat me down at the kitchen table to tell me the news.

"Maggie is carrying a baby."

Ma's voice shook and great dollops of tears streamed down her face, plopping off her chin onto the table unchecked.

"A baby... but..."

This statement completely baffled me. While I wasn't exactly knowledgeable about how babies were made, I knew enough to know that it took two people, a man and a woman. Maggie was only a child. She didn't have a boyfriend, let alone a husband.

"He attacked her... Master George," Ma said.

"What do you mean, Ma?"

"He had his way with our Maggie, my little girl, he had his way with her and now she is with child and in prison." Ma's voice was little more than a whisper, as if she was afraid someone was outside the door listening to her.

It all made sense to me now. That day, the shock on Maggie's face, her tousled hair, her pinafore ripped, her inability to speak.

"Ma, did she tell the police?"

"Yes, yes, she did. Eventually. For all the good it will do. The likes of Master George will get away with it. He's denied everything. Said she threw herself at him, enticed him to have relations with her, then afterwards attacked him for no good reason," Ma said.

She lay her head on the table and sobbed. Her shoulders shook as she wailed in despair. I didn't know what to do so I stood behind Ma rubbing her back, trying to soothe her pain but nothing helped. We must have stayed like that for hours until duty niggled Ma.

"Thank you, *mo ghrá*. Time to get on with it." Ma wiped her eyes, hugged me and put on her apron. She put aside her pain and started preparation of the evening meal. By the time Da arrived home from work everything looked normal or as normal as it could be with our Maggie in prison. Ma sent me and Jimmy out to weed the vegetable patch. I knew she wanted us out of the way so she could talk to Da. When she called us in for dinner, Da was sitting in his usual spot, his face gaunt as he picked at the meal Ma put in front of him. I could barely eat myself although Jimmy, oblivious to what was going on around him, made up for that.

Ma hadn't been back to the big house since the day Maggie was arrested.

"I can't, I just can't go up there and bake for those people. I'd spit in it I would."

Da didn't argue with her, just nodded his agreement. He left for the fields at sunrise and came back to us at dusk. No more laughter, no more dancing around the table. We plodded through each day, broken people, crushed with worry and despair.

A few short months after we heard the news that Maggie was pregnant, we had a visitor. Ma's May altar sat inside the front door. The statue of the Virgin Mary with Ma's prayer book, rosary beads and a vase of fresh wild flowers I had picked that morning. Every evening we knelt and prayed to the Virgin Mary to help our Maggie. We had finished prayers when there were several curt sharp raps on the cottage door heralding the arrival of Constable Smith. He was a pleasant man, portly, his coat straining at the buttons, with a handlebar moustache and kind eyes. He introduced himself and Da brought him inside. Ma remained sitting in her chair by the fire, the darning in her hands, frozen in place while she waited on the constable to speak.

"I'm afraid it's Maggie," he said, as he twiddled his cap in his hands. "She's lost the baby."

Ma gasped, glancing from Constable Smith to Da, who paced up and down the kitchen floor.

"Lost the baby, sure she's nearly full term. Is she okay?"

"She's quite poorly, I'm afraid." Constable Smith shook his head. "She's been taken to Our Lady's Hospital."

Ma and I made our way to the city the following morning. That first glimpse of Our Lady's Hospital made my blood run cold. Red brick, Gothic, it was an imposing building. Overlooking the River Lee, it put me in mind of a giant sprawling monster standing guard over the city. Ma took my hand as we walked towards the entrance. I didn't know if Ma's action was to support me or to help herself find the strength to enter those doors. It was daunting. The smell of carbolic soap didn't quite mask the stench of boiled cabbage. We were met by the matron, a middle-aged woman in starched navy blue, with steel-grey eyes and thin lips, without a trace of a smile. She looked us up and down as if trying to measure up the type of people we were, finding us wanting.

"Follow me."

She turned and led us down a corridor, her heels clipping on the polished linoleum. Me and Ma followed, wordlessly, overwhelmed by her attitude which struck us as more like a sergeant major than a matron. The thought brought a nervous giggle which died on my lips as we moved through another set of doors and into a corridor with wards running off each side. There was a faint whiff of stale urine. Several nurses, resplendent in starched white uniforms and hats, lined the hall and bowed as the matron passed, leading me and Ma to the ward on the right in the middle of the corridor. She stopped at the foot of a cot, containing a small frame wrapped in a sheet with only a head of matted dark hair visible.

"Miss McCarthy, your mother and sister are here to see you."

Maggie turned to look at us and her face crumpled, then she buried her face back into her pillow as her sobs shook the iron cot. She was tiny, lying there, unwashed and hurting. Maggie was drugged, bleeding and in pain. Ma just put her arms around her and lifted her out of the cot. I pulled over a hard-back chair from the corner of the ward for Ma and she sat with Maggie on her lap like the child she was. Ma was distraught. We all cried together as Ma rubbed Maggie's hair and rocked her back and forth. I didn't know what to do. My little sister, the pretty one, looked like a waif and stray, and my heart broke for her. Her skin looked almost translucent; a sickly white accentuated by the dark circles under her bloodshot eyes.

"Mrs McCarthy," the matron barked. "Put that girl back into her cot immediately. She is not permitted to leave her bed."

"*That girl*, as you call her, is my daughter and I will hold her. What kind of woman are you, to treat a young girl like that? Look at the state of her. Have you no compassion?"

"I would remind you, madam, that this is my ward. That..." and she pointed at Maggie and sniffed as if an unpleasant odour had reached her nostrils, 'is a person with no morals. Sinful in someone so young. You reap what you sow, I always say, and this one deserves everything she gets."

"How dare you. My daughter is not immoral, or sinful. She was attacked, raped. It was bad enough that she became pregnant but now... to be sent here..." Ma's voice teetered off into a sob, as she gestured around the ward.

It was a large room with at least twenty beds, all filled with women of all ages. All broken. Most of them were in their nightclothes. Some were sitting on the edge of their cots, watching the matron as she castigated my mother. Most appeared deranged somehow. Less than human, and I was horrified as I envisaged a future for Maggie amongst them.

Me and Ma were silent on the way home. My mind was reeling from what I'd seen. My poor sister. She was the bubbly one, who loved to dance and sing and play tricks. The person we left in Our Lady's Hospital bore no resemblance to her. I tried to say as much to Ma but all I could say was, "Poor Maggie."

Ma drew her lips into a tight line as if she were trying to bite back words that threatened to choke her. Two red dots of anger burned on her cheeks and remained there for the rest of the evening. After dinner I brought Jimmy to bed, letting him into my bed instead of his little alcove under the rafters. Images of Maggie's tiny frame curled up in that cot haunted me, but the murmur of voices in the kitchen shook me from my reverie. I recognised Mrs Short's melodic voice. Me and Maggie always said her voice sounded like honey tasted, golden and sweet. I slipped out of bed and crept closer to the door.

"What did they tell you about the baby?" Mrs Short said.

"Only that it was a little girl. I didn't even get to see her. They took her..." Ma's voice descended into a tearful mumble, but I could hear Mrs Short comforting her.

"Poor little mite was born with the original sin on her soul and never baptised. But I'll include her in my prayers. Stay strong, Catherine. You need to stay strong for Lizzie and Jimmy. They need you now."

"My poor Maggie."

I crept noiselessly back into bed, Ma's sobs bringing a lump to my throat that threatened to choke me. That night I wondered if I would ever see Maggie again.

When we did see her again, or at least a version of her, she wasn't the spirited young girl we all knew and loved. That Maggie had disintegrated in that place. She'd become a shadow of her former self, nervous, silent, afraid of her own shadow. I didn't recognise this person and I mourned the loss of my once feisty sister.

Chapter 5

The Homecoming

Ma was overjoyed the day we got the letter to say that Maggie was to be released. Nearly two years she had been away from us, her family, and we couldn't wait to have her home. Ma set off the next morning to fetch her. When they arrived home that evening, I had a fire burning in the grate, a good dinner ready and our bed made up with clean sheets, fresh from the clothesline, the scent of summer in every thread.

Maggie looked even thinner than she had the last time we had seen her, if that were possible. She was quiet but happy to be home, walking around the cottage touching things as if expecting them to disappear. I threw my arms around her and hugged her close before leading her to our room. As children, we had shared a bed in a room just off the kitchen. The chimney breast from the kitchen fire kept the chill from the room in winter aided by the south-facing window which caught what little sun there was. In the summer it became overly warm, saved only by the open window.

For the two years that Maggie was incarcerated in that awful place, I was alone, and I missed my sister every night as I lay in our bed. Now she was back, or was she? For the Maggie who sat on our bed staring out the window was not the same person who had left this house. I sat beside her and took her hand in mine.

"Oh, Maggie, I have missed you so much," I said.

Maggie gave a weak smile, a faint copy of her former radiance, her exuberance banished.

"I'm glad to be home," she said.

"What can I do to help you, Maggie?"

"It's okay, honest. I'm only glad to be here."

"Well, it's great to have you back. I'm working in McCoy's tomorrow, but we'll get to catch up when I get home."

"Mrs McCoy, that old bat? She'll run you ragged, Lizzie."

"She's not so bad when you get to know her."

I was a little bit put out by that. Maggie calling anyone names after the rumour and innuendo the family had had to put up with since she was put away. Then I felt a bit mean for thinking like that for none of it was Maggie's fault. The old biddies in the village talked about Maggie as if she were some sort of fallen woman who had enticed Master George, had led him astray, then tried to kill him. To hear some of them talk, you would have thought she was a grown woman capable of making decisions, not a child of fourteen. They called her wicked, possessed, and other things I couldn't, or wouldn't repeat to anyone.

My days were busy at Mrs McCoy's shop. The typical small village shop, it sold everything you could think of. Fresh eggs and milk were delivered daily. Vegetables, tinned goods, cooked ham in huge hocks that hung in the cold room, ready to be sliced thinly and sold wrapped in waxed paper. Freshly churned butter, wrapped in one pound pats, and creamy red cheddar cheese cut into chunks and weighed on the counter. Sugar arrived in the shop in huge bags that had to be weighed into smaller bags for the customers. Jars upon jars of sweets; gobstoppers, tangy sherbet lemons and my favourite, wine gums, jostled for space on the shelf behind the counter, catching the eye of every child who entered the shop with their mother. Mrs McCoy baked her own bread and cakes and displayed her wares on the counter in front of the sweets. My first job every morning was to help her load up the baskets, the bread still hot from the oven, brown loaves, currant sodas, scones, and treacle bread. They were normally sold out by lunchtime.

Mrs McCoy knew everyone's business and all of it was discussed in her shop. I swear the woman spent more time gossiping than working. On the other hand, I was run off my feet, keeping the shop stocked and cleaned. Some women revelled in the gossip, but I tried to tune it out. The only exception was when I heard Maggie's name mentioned.

I certainly never repeated a word of it at home. My parents had enough to contend with. Only the people who worked on the estate knew the truth of it, for they all knew the nature of Master George. I hadn't seen Ralph since the day Maggie was arrested. Whether he had been warned to stay away or he believed his brother's lies, I had no idea, but I didn't want to see him anyway. I didn't want to have anything to do with the Haughton family. It was bad enough that we lived on the estate and that our father still worked for them.

Maggie sat on the side of the bed while I brushed her hair. Where once it was thick with a sheen like velvet, now its brittle strands broke to the touch, leaving a halo of fuzz around her tiny face and a brush full of lank dark hair.

"Are the Haughtons at home?" Maggie asked.

"The Haughtons? Why?"

"No reason."

I thought no more of it until the next morning when I felt Maggie's absence from our bed. Dread crept through my veins as I called her name. Maggie was nowhere to be seen.

"Ma, Ma, have you seen Maggie?"

Ma was at the kitchen table, kneading dough. Wiping her hands on her apron she joined the search. We couldn't find Maggie. A knock on the open door startled us. It was Mrs Short's helper, Kathleen.

"Mrs Short says you've to come quick. Maggie is in the big house causing ructions."

Catherine McCarthy had never moved so quick. She was out the door and up the hill in an instant with me on her heels. We could hear the shouting through the open doors of the drawing room. But it was the screams that put fear in my heart. High-pitched screaming like a banshee. My overriding thought was that my sister had lost her mind. Ignoring any semblance of normal etiquette, Catherine McCarthy ran straight up to the doors and launched herself into the room with me two steps behind her.

I could see Maggie crouched in the corner, her hands over her head, as she cowered from the overbearing figure of George Haughton. His face was puce as he swung a highly polished walking stick high in the air, about to bring it down on Maggie's bent head. Catherine leapt to her daughter's defence pushing Master George with her left arm as she threw herself on top of Maggie. Master George stumbled and struck a Waterford glass on the side table, which tottered for an insane second before it hit the parquet floor and shattered into a thousand shimmering pieces. Lady Haughton stood in the far corner, an embroidered handkerchief to her open mouth and horror on her face.

The door swung open, and Lord Haughton stormed into the room.

"What on earth is going on in here?"

Torn between running to my ma who was cradling Maggie in the far corner or running back out the double doors behind me, I stood statue-like in the centre of the room. Lady Haughton sank onto the nearest chair as Lord Haughton moved to her side. Master George's demeanour changed. The demonic fury he displayed seconds before now replaced by his natural haughtiness.

"That McCarthy girl broke into our house. I was trying to protect Mother."

"That's enough, George." Lady Haughton's voice shook, whether with emotion or fear no one could say.

"Mother, you don't seriously believe her, do you? Look at her, she's obviously demented. More to be pitied I'd say."

"Ralph, call the constable," Lord Haughton said.

Up until that point, I hadn't seen Ralph, standing against the wall, as if trying to blend into it, to make himself invisible in its pattern. He stumbled out of the room, muttering as he left, flashing dagger looks at his older brother. Lord Haughton moved over to Ma.

"She needs help, Mrs McCarthy. The pitiful thing has lost her mind," he said. I was struck at the kindness in his tone, at odds with his usual demeanour. He held out his hand to my ma and she took it. As he helped her to her feet, she brought Maggie with her. Maggie was still keening, an awful sound, like a wounded animal. Ma held her close, stroking her hair, trying to soothe her.

Lord Haughton pulled up an armchair and gestured to Ma to sit Maggie there. Ma said and did nothing, well nothing discernible, just made soothing sounds as Maggie gradually quietened. She nodded to me to take my sister's hand.

"If my daughter has lost her mind, it is the fault of your son. Master George attacked my daughter. He made her pregnant..."

Lady Haughton sprang from her seat.

"I will not listen to this slanderous allegation. Mrs McCarthy, do not say another word."

"It's the truth of it, and you know it…"

"Enough." Lord Haughton's tone silenced both mothers.

I could feel Maggie's heart beating in her chest, her waif-like body trembling as she clung to me, whimpering. Lord Haughton spoke again, his tone kinder.

"Mrs McCarthy, I suggest you take your daughter to the kitchen for the time being. George, call the maid to clean up this mess."

His tone brokered no argument. Ma led me and Maggie out the double doors, across the lawns and around the corner to the backyard. Mrs Short was waiting at the kitchen door and ushered us inside. Ma didn't utter a word. She sat on the chair Mrs Short pulled out for her. I sat beside her, numb, and accepted the hot tea she placed in front of us. They exchanged looks that I couldn't read. All I could think about was the state of Maggie. My once pretty little sister now looked like a mad thing, a foundling, no interest in her appearance, no life in her expression, shaking and moaning like something demented. How long we sat there, I had no idea, the only sound the loud tock of the clock above the range as we waited for the constable to arrive.

Constable Smith was a nice enough man. Mrs Short offered him tea which he accepted and sat at the table opposite us. Ma kept her arm around Maggie, as I held her hand trying to quell her shaking. Maggie's eyes were wild as if possessed and I feared for her sanity. The constable looked at Ma with compassion as he told her in his quiet way that the Haughton family had made a formal complaint against Maggie. He knew what the McCarthy family had been through, what Maggie had been through. But the Haughtons were the landowners, the upper classes. The McCarthys were the underlings, the servants. It was as if he was apologising for what he was about to do, but he still did it. He took Maggie away. Said he had no choice but to bring her back to Our Lady's Hospital again, and I swear something inside my ma broke as he led her daughter away.

Chapter 6

Spring

As a family we tried to go on as if nothing had happened, well everyone except Ma. She stayed at home and cried and cried. Da had to go to work, Jimmy to school and I had to go into Mrs McCoy's shop. One day blended into the next as we waited for word on when we could go and see Maggie. She had been admitted to Our Lady's that night and we were told she was not permitted visitors for a while.

I was cleaning shelves and trying not to think about Maggie when the bell over the door tinkled and Mrs Carson came into the shop. She marched straight up to the counter and whispered something to Mrs McCoy.

"Sure, young Maggie is home. God be good to her."

Mrs McCoy blessed herself as she answered the customer. Mrs Carson lived in the middle of the village, a spinster who spent her time twitching her curtains and spreading rumours. She was the thinnest person I had ever come across, either before or since, with long wrinkled fingers like twigs and long skinny feet that looked too big for the rest of her body.

"No, she's gone back in, Mrs McCoy. I tell ya, I have it on

good authority. She pushed her way into the Knockrath Manor and accused Master George of all sorts. Rumour has it, she accused him of putting her in the family way."

Mrs McCoy lifted her head and scanned the shop. I dropped my head to the task as if totally engrossed in cleaning the bottom shelf and unaware of the chatter behind me.

"Lizzie," Mrs McCoy said, "be a pet and go into the cold room and do a quick inventory. I need to put in an order, and I'm not sure what we need."

I stood and dropped my dirty cloth into the pail before turning to the opening in the counter at the far end of the shop. Mrs Carson turned her back to me, busying herself with the rack of vegetables. As I pulled the door of the cold room closed behind me, I could hear the murmur of nervous excitement in Mrs Carson's voice as she started to tell her story. Why is it some people take pleasure in recounting other people's miseries? People like Mrs Carson enjoyed sharing the heartbreak of others. Of course, they wrap it up with sympathy and compassion, but they take joy in the retelling of the pain of others. I put my ear to the door but all I could hear was a low murmur. Although perhaps it is just as well. I didn't want to hear the spin that the likes of Mrs Carson put on my little sister's pain.

That evening as I was leaving, Mrs McCoy called me back and handed me a bag.

"Here, Lizzie. Bring this home with you. It's nearly out of date and needs to be used up. Tell your ma that I was asking after her and send my thoughts and prayers."

I nodded, unsure what to say for Mrs McCoy was not known for her generosity. When I got home and emptied the contents onto the scrubbed table, I got quite the surprise. There must have been a half pound of ham, and the same of corned beef, a packet of tea, a bag of sugar and a loaf of her currant soda.

"You can give her my thanks, Lizzie. She's a good woman, Mrs McCoy." Ma smiled. Not the wide, loving smile we were all used to, more of an imitation of her former self, but it was a start.

The next morning, I rose early to wash and dress for work. No matter how early I rose, Da was always up before me and out to the fields before I even got into the kitchen. I could hear Ma moving around the kitchen and the rustle of Jimmy turning over for his second sleep from the alcove outside her room. Outside, the birds were twittering to each other, not the joyous dawn chorus that roused us all in the spring, more of a low-toned chatter in preparedness for packing up their homes and flying south for the winter. They were peaceful sounds. Sounds that made up the background to our life.

Which made the harsh metallic bell on the constable's bicycle sound louder than an out of tune big brass band. The birds scattered from their various branches, squawking their disapproval. The loud knock brought both Ma and me to the half-open cottage door at the same time. Constable Smith's face told us he was the bearer of bad news before he opened his mouth. Ma sank onto the kitchen chair while I ushered the constable into the cottage, before taking my place beside my ma, my hand on her shoulder in silent support. The constable whipped off his hat and stood twisting it in his large soft hands.

"Mrs McCarthy, is your husband at home?"

"No, no he's gone to work, Constable."

"I see, I see... and is there anyone you can send to fetch him?" The constable looked at me.

"I'll get my brother." I turned to call Jimmy but there was no need. Jimmy was already there and didn't need to be told twice. He nodded and took off out the door and across the fields.

"What is it, Constable, what's wrong?"

"Is there tea in the pot, Mrs McCarthy?"

Ma glared at him, then patted my hand. "Get the constable some tea, Lizzie, that's a good girl."

I did as I was bid and took a seat beside Ma while the red-faced Constable Smith sat at the other end of the long rectangular table. The silence was ominous as the clock on the mantel rang the hour and the water bubbled in the kettle over the range. Lifting it over to the side I sat back down beside my mother, reaching over to hold her hand. Da burst in through the open door, panting, sweat running down his face, beetroot red from the exertion.

"What is it, is it our Maggie?"

The constable stood, his hat once again twisting in his hands as he cleared his throat, his discomfort showing in every pore on his sweat-stained face.

"Mr McCarthy, Mrs McCarthy, I'm sorry to have to tell you that there has been an accident in Our Lady's Hospital. Your daughter Margaret has had a fall..."

Ma stood, clutching her apron. "Is she okay?"

Da moved to her side and put his arm around her shoulders.

"What kind of fall, what do you mean?"

"I'm afraid Maggie didn't survive."

"Maggie's dead?"

Ma stared at the constable as if unable to comprehend the words he had uttered.

"But how? How can she be dead?" Da stuttered.

"Maggie fell from a fourth-floor window. There was nothing anyone could do."

Ma sat heavily, open-mouthed, staring at the constable. I started to shake, an involuntary shake I couldn't control. Jimmy wrapped his arms around my waist as he started to cry.

"This cannot be true. My Maggie. How? How did she fall?

Maria McDonald

This doesn't make sense, none of it makes any sense," Ma said as she pounded the table with her fist.

Da put his hand over hers and she looked at him, as if baffled, as if she couldn't understand what he was doing. And then she screamed Maggie's name over and over.

Chapter 7

Aunt Jean

After Maggie died, Primrose Cottage oozed sorrow. It seeped out of every unswept corner, through the whitewashed walls and outwards like a creeping poison ivy, touching the whole family with hot darts of pain that couldn't be soothed. Ma cried and screamed at the injustice of it all, for she blamed the Haughtons. Da said nothing, but hung on to her every word, unable to express his pain, but I saw him, pacing up and down the pathway at the back of the cottage, pounding one fist into the other, as if he was practising for the day that he would confront George Haughton.

Me and Jimmy were left to our own devices. I minded him as best I could. Made sure he ate his porridge in the mornings before he went to school, did his homework with him, scrubbed behind his ears before I put him to bed at night. Ma turned grey overnight. No one could reach her. Da got up every morning and went out to the fields, working for the Haughtons as he always did. One morning, Ma could take no more.

"How can you? How can you work for that family? They killed our daughter, do you hear me, they killed Maggie."

The entire estate could hear her, screaming out the half

door, like the demented soul she was. I dragged Ma back into the house and slammed the whole door shut behind her. Ma fell onto the floor and stayed there, beating it with her fists, her screams turning to sobs as she curled up, like a newborn, all sense of reason left outside echoing across the estate. Jimmy was upset, we were all upset. I got Jimmy out to school and myself into Mrs McCoy's shop. All day I fretted over my mother, visualising her lying on the floor, sobbing. I was so bothered I spilled the sugar, knocked over a display of canned goods and left the cold door open. Eventually Mrs McCoy sent me home.

"Your mind's not on your work, girl. Go home to your mother and come back tomorrow fit to do your job. You'll still be paid for today, mind. I heard about your poor mother. Go home and look after her. God bless her."

I didn't need to be told twice. Grabbing my coat from the hook in the corner of the storeroom, I ran all the way home, not pausing for breath. From the outside the cottage looked normal. The half door was open as it usually was, and a waft of fresh bread danced down the path as I opened the small, latched gate.

"Ma," I called out as I slowed my step, puzzled by the normality of the scene compared to the chaos I'd left only a few short hours earlier.

Aunt Jean appeared in the doorway, and I ran straight into her outstretched arms. A large woman, she engulfed me, and relief washed over me. Aunt Jean was my ma's older sister. She had a heart of gold and a no-nonsense approach to life that I knew would get Ma back to her old self. Losing Maggie had torn our family apart, robbed us of all joy and laughter, but I knew in my heart and soul that we had a chance of getting through the pain with Aunt Jean on our side. Aunt Jean held me for several minutes, rocking me from side to side in a heartfelt hug. Coming out for air, I spotted Jimmy standing by the table, a warm smile on his tear-stained face. Ma was nowhere to be seen.

"Your mother is lying down. This has all been a bit much for her, but nothing a little rest won't solve. I'm staying for a little while, to help look after you and Jimmy as best I can," Aunt Jean said. "Don't worry, Lizzie, everything will come right in the end."

Autumn was upon us before Ma started to live again. It's my favourite time of year. Primrose Cottage was surrounded by colour, deep russets and golds in huge mounds that glistened in the evening sun. As children we hid in the abundance of fallen leaves, dry and crisp underfoot or floating down to earth like confetti on a bride. This year we could find no joy without our sister Maggie to share it with, but I did try for Jimmy's sake. Aunt Jean was right. Eventually we all learned to live without Maggie. It took a while but gradually Ma's grief and anger subsided. She stopped shouting at her husband and started baking again. Ma was a shadow of her former self, the grief she felt over Maggie never left her eyes, but at least she learned to function again, to be a wife and mother again.

As Halloween approached Aunt Jean announced that she needed to go home to Queenstown. Ma knew the day was coming and understood, but cried a little all the same. I shared my bed with Aunt Jean for those months and dreaded her leaving but I recognised that my aunt's family needed her. Aunt Jean had five children, two sons who were married with children of their own, and I know she missed seeing them. One of her older daughters was having a baby and her youngest, Aíne was the same age as me. Queenstown was only twelve miles away. The entire McCarthy family often visited there during the summer months. On that October day as Aunt Jean took her leave, I longed for the fresh salty air that swept up from the seafront along the narrow street to the house where she lived.

"I'd love to be going back with you, Aunt Jean. Fill my lungs with that sea air. I can nearly taste the salt on my tongue."

"It won't be so nice today, Lizzie," Aunt Jean said. "Sure, the breeze coming off the water today would freeze ye."

She hugged us all, one by one, and pinched my cheek.

"Take care of your little brother. I will see you soon, Lizzie."

Da picked up her case and opened the door, ushering her out. The wind roared through the trees behind our cottage, creating a whirlwind of russet and gold as it denuded the branches in preparation for winter. Battleship-grey skies threatened rain and Aunt Jean hurried down the path and into the cart that Da had borrowed to bring her to the train station, while we all waved our goodbyes from the safety of the front step.

In truth I was sorry to see her go but my heart leapt at the thought of visiting her in Queenstown in the spring. It was a beautiful town. Steep hills running down to the sea at the entrance to Cork port. The cathedral on the hill commanding views over the town and the colourful narrow houses that jostled each other for space along the seafront. There was a bandstand where the local band played on Sunday afternoons while people milled around, enjoying the sea air and the magnificent views. It was something to look forward to on a windy and cold winter's day. In the meantime, Ma needed me, so I stayed at Primrose Cottage on the Knockrath estate.

Chapter 8

France

It was Da who broke the news to us. The entire estate was agog. George Haughton had died, killed in action somewhere in France. There was no grieving in our cottage for him.

"I'd best say nothing," Ma told Da. "It's bad luck to speak ill of the dead."

Da agreed with her. We all did. George Haughton would not be missed, not by us, and not by most of the people in the estate. He was not well liked.

Two boys, workers from the estate, had also died in the same battle. Those boys were mourned, their families supported. Ma baked bread and cakes. Da brought them vegetables from our garden. There were no bodies to wake, no corpses to bury. A telegram from the War Office the only proof of their deaths. In scenes repeated up and down the country, our friends and neighbours mourned their loss.

Our family were experts at coping with grief. In a way, helping those families through their loss helped us cope with ours. Maggie was barely more than a child when she died. Those boys were seventeen and nineteen. Not old enough to vote but old enough to fight for king and country. Although there was talk our boys should be fighting for Irish freedom instead of the British king.

There were days I felt like I was drowning in grief. Surrounded by it. Waves of sorrow coming off the fields and swallowing our cottage whole. The only thing that kept me putting one foot in front of the other during that whole winter, was thoughts of going to Queenstown in the spring. I swear there were days I could smell the sea.

The Haughton family stayed on in the manor house that winter. Their usual winter residence in England had been sequestered by the authorities for use as a hospital for the officer classes.

"It was the daughter that arranged it, Catherine," Da said.

"Lady Amelia?"

"Yep, she trained as an ambulance driver. Imagine that. A slip of a girl like that," Da said, shaking his head as he grinned, apparently amused at the idea.

"Women are doing all sorts of work these days. The men are all at war."

"Yep, anyway, the word is that she volunteered their house without consulting her parents. Lady Haughton had no say in the matter and wasn't best pleased by all accounts."

Ma clicked her tongue. "It's not as if they've nowhere to live. The whole village could move into the manor house and there would still be room for the Haughton family."

Da laughed, a reminder of the wholesome laugh he had when Maggie was alive. The sound was so rare in our cottage we were all compelled to join in. It was the first laughter around our dinner table in the years since Maggie had been taken away. Ma must have had the same thought as suddenly her laughter turned to tears.

"It's okay, *mo ghrá*," Da took Ma's hand. "We can laugh."

"How? How can I feel any joy when my Maggie lies six feet under."

"You cannot live in constant sorrow, Catherine. It's not fair on you, not fair on Jimmy and Lizzie."

Ma nodded, wiped her face with her apron and smiled at him.

"True, mo ghrá, very true."

"Who cares if the lady of the manor is put out by the war. Imagine, Catherine, winter in England, summer in Ireland. Two houses the size of that manor house up there." Da shook his head. "Sure, what good is it to them? Their son lies buried in France along with the boys that laboured his land for him. Sure, Lady Haughton is more to be pitied."

Ma stood so abruptly she nearly knocked the chair over.

"More to be pitied, you say. Pity?" she roared. "Do you really expect me to pity that woman?"

She started clearing away the dinner plates, her displeasure obvious to us all.

Da reached out to her, taking the plates out of her hands.

"She is a mother, Catherine. George Haughton may not have been a good man, but he was her son."

"He was responsible for our daughter's death. Him and that so-called mother of his. I don't care if he's dead. I will never forgive him, ever, or her."

"Catherine, for God's sake. Have some compassion, woman."

Ma stomped out of the cottage, slamming the door behind her with such force the windows rattled. Da pulled on his coat and grabbed Ma's from the hook beside the door and hurried after her.

Jimmy sat, his head bowed, his hands shaking under the table. I squeezed his hand in silent support.

"Come on, Jimmy. Let's get cleared away. Da will bring Ma back."

We moved around the kitchen, washing dishes and putting them away, sweeping the floor, moving in silent harmony, each wrapped in our thoughts. Part of me was so annoyed with Ma. I understood why she was angry. Why she couldn't forgive Master George. But... sometimes, no, all the time, it felt like she thought that she was the only person allowed to grieve. As if she were the only member of this family who'd lost Maggie, who missed Maggie. She was her daughter, but she was Da's daughter too. She was my sister. Jimmy's sister. We were all grieving. Ma's grieving was so selfish, so wrapped up in her own despair she couldn't see ours.

Chapter 9

Queenstown Spring

It was spring before Aunt Jean sent for me. It was a crisp night with a promise of frost, my breath solidifying in front of me as I walked back from Mrs McCoy's shop. Christmas had been hard without Maggie. It was our fourth Christmas without her. At first, we always had the hope that she would be home for the next one so the realisation that she would never again celebrate Christmas with us was difficult. January was a long, cold month during which I dreaded the daily walk to the village and back again. February wasn't much better but at least we knew that spring was around the corner.

When I got in from work that evening, Ma was sitting at the table reading a letter. She got up as I came in and tucked it into her apron pocket before busying herself over the stove. I thought no more of it until later that evening when we were clearing away the remnants of the evening meal.

"Are you happy in McCoy's, Lizzie?" Ma said as she handed me a plate to dry.

"Yea, I mean, it's okay, it's a job, isn't it?"

"Yes, but have you ever thought of working elsewhere?"

"I wouldn't work in the big house, Ma. There's no way I

want to work for the Haughtons. I know Da has to work for them. But that's different..."

Ma placed her hand on my arm.

"No, *mo ghrá*, I didn't mean the Haughtons. I wouldn't expect you to work for them after Maggie..." Ma blessed herself, as she always did when she mentioned Maggie's name. "No, I meant, how would you feel about moving to Queenstown, living with Aunt Jean for a bit. She knows a dressmaker who is looking for a helper. Your Aunt Jean put your name forward, she knows how good you are with a needle and thread. Now that she only has Aíne at home, she has room for you. What do you think?"

Well, my heart jumped a beat, for the thought of living in Queenstown brought me such joy for the first time in months.

"Ma, I'd love it... but what about you... what about Jimmy?"

"We'll be fine, *mo ghrá*. I am well able to look after my own son. Sure, he'll be thirteen in a few months, working by next year. And it will be good for you, love. You'll mix with people your own age."

Me and Ma sat at the kitchen table as I penned a reply to Aunt Jean, accepting her offer. The following day I gave notice to Mrs McCoy. She wasn't too happy at first, but she understood, for she ended up wishing me good luck and told me to enjoy living in a large town, for Queenstown was a huge town compared to our little village. I worked out the rest of the week, then Da dropped me to the train station two days later with all my belongings in a small case.

The Crowleys lived at the top end of a terrace of colourful houses teetering on the side of a steep hill. Aunt Jean's house was painted a cheerful buttercup yellow with a bright-red door that beckoned you into its cosy interior. The sea was a constant in the background, and I loved it. Aunt Jean's husband, Pat, was a fisherman and for weeks on end he was missing from their lives. Then like a force of nature he swept back in the door, bringing the tang of the sea into the kitchen and laughter to everyone's hearts, his pockets full of trinkets. I settled in like I had always lived there.

My new employer was a gentle widow with a talent for dressmaking and design that I seriously envied and emulated every chance I got. Mrs Buckley wasn't much older than me. She had only been married two years when the war broke out and Mr Buckley went off to fight in France. Like a lot of young men, he left promising to be home by Christmas, but he never returned. He died in some field in France two years later leaving Mrs Buckley to look after their son alone.

Mrs Buckley's shop was near the seafront and every day, no matter the weather, I walked down to the sea. It was the highlight of my day, even more so when the Americans arrived in town a few weeks later. Every evening Aíne had told us about the rumours in town of the arrival of the American navy, so when they eventually arrived, they were welcomed with open arms. That first flotilla was something to see. Queenstown residents were accustomed to seeing plenty of the British naval ships sail by into Cork harbour, but these American ships were different.

The war was going badly, and the Americans were a welcome addition. German U-boats were doing major damage to the supply chain and the American ships were welcomed as saviours. The townsfolk were out in their hundreds lining the quays and giving them a big Irish welcome. There was a party atmosphere, with bands playing and people waving flags and cheering. Mrs Buckley closed the shop that day and we walked down to the seafront to join in the excitement. There was no point in being open anyway for everyone was out welcoming the Americans.

Every week more and more American sailors arrived. They were a sight to behold in their naval uniforms, like a strange exotic breed of man never witnessed before in Cork. They were mainly handsome, extremely friendly, with white teeth and deep pockets. It was common knowledge that they had plenty of money and were happy to spend it. Most of the locals were happy to accommodate them, the publicans, the shopkeepers, and the young, single women. The few young men, who weren't away fighting the war, were of a different opinion, seeing the "yanks" as thieves stealing their women. It was an interesting time to live in Queenstown.

Chapter 10

Dance Hall Days

"Be careful, girls." Aunt Jean's words rang out after us as we shut the door.

There was a monthly dance in the local church hall. Me and Aíne had been looking forward to it for weeks. The dance attracted young people from all over, even as far away as the city of Cork. It was my first time to go even though I had been living in Queenstown for three months. I had to gather up some money first before I could consider a social life. Every week I sent a postal order home to my mother to help with Jimmy. He was the smart one of the family and Ma wanted him to stay in school for as long as she could manage. At times she dreamed of him getting to college, although in her more realistic moments she realised that really was a far-fetched dream for people like us.

Anyway, by the time I'd paid for my board and keep to Aunt Jean, and then sent the postal order, there wasn't a whole lot left of my wages to splurge on luxuries. Mrs Buckley was generous though, with her time and with whatever she could spare. She had a son to bring up alone and every penny she earned went into the upkeep of her home and shop. Her skills with the needle were discovered overnight by the Americans and within weeks of their arrival, she employed another girl, Kate, to help with the sewing, mostly lost buttons, and torn hems.

That left Mrs Buckley with time to concentrate on the dressmaking. Her skills were much in demand with the upper classes. The fabrics were magnificent; satin, silks, and lace of a quality I had never seen before. Sometimes she got me to help and those were the days I became really absorbed in my job.

The dance was the most fun I'd had in my short life. Me and Aíne practised in the confines of our small bedroom until we had the moves down to a fine art. I had never witnessed so many bodies packed into one room before. And it was a large room. There was a mineral bar at one end, although we could see clusters of men gathered outside the back door swigging out of hip flasks. Me and Aíne were asked out to dance several times by different men. Big burly farmers, wind-beaten fishermen, smart soldiers in uniform, fed up with training and ready to ship out to the killing fields in France and Mesopotamia. The pungent aroma of fresh sweat and cold tar soap mixed with the gentle teasing of gardenia and lily of the valley. The band drew crowds from as far away as Cork city, all keen to dance away the worries of an uncertain future, for a few hours at least. It became a regular event for us girls. The last Saturday night of every month, me and Aíne donned our finery and made our way to the dance hall.

In early autumn, Mrs Buckley showed me how to remake a dress, out of an old one she had in the back of the shop. It had been ordered by an older lady in the city, some years earlier, paid for but returned to her unworn as the woman had died in the meantime. When Mrs Buckley told me the story of the dress, I was reluctant to even consider looking at it.

"Just take a look, Lizzie. The dress itself might be old-fashioned but the fabric is exquisite."

I did as she asked as I trusted Mrs Buckley but when I looked at the dress, I couldn't see how it could be turned into anything that I would wear.

"You can start by taking it apart at the seams, Lizzie. I'm going to teach you how to remake this dress into your dream outfit."

Mrs Buckley taught me a valuable lesson. She recut sections, added trims and the end result was delightful. It was a pale pink, dusty like a full-blown rose ready to shed its leaves. She remade it with a dropped waist and a shorter hemline which brought it right up to date with the latest fashion. It was an amazing transformation. I tried it on and twirled around the shop, delighted with it, as Mrs Buckley laughed and Kate clapped.

"Enjoy, Lizzie. Go to the dance, have fun. There has been little enough of that lately."

Mrs Buckley tidied away bits of fabric and trimmings. I hurried to change back into my work clothes and help her. Mrs Buckley was a kind soul who hid her sorrow behind gentle smiles but sometimes her sadness overwhelmed her. You could see it settling on her face, a darkness in her eyes coupled with a downturn of her mouth. I knew what it was like to love someone and feel their loss every day, for I still missed Maggie. Yet I knew that the love for a sister and the love of a man are different things, but were they? Surely love is love. But then again, what did I know, a young woman of seventeen who had never been in love.

The night of the dance we spent an age getting ready. My faded rose dress fluttered to my shins in two layers. The bodice closed with a row of satin-covered buttons to a flattering open neckline. I felt so stylish, like a young Princess Mary, no longer the poor relation to my cousin Aíne.

"Oh my, you two are going to be the belles of the ball," Aunt

Jean said as her daughter and her niece twirled in front of her in the living room. I blushed, not a good combination with my red hair and freckles. Aíne laughed and spun me around.

"You look beautiful, cuz, come on, we'll be late if we don't get a move on."

"Be careful, girls," Aunt Jean shouted after us as we closed the front door.

"Stay away from those yankees, is what she really means," Aíne whispered.

Neither of us girls had any intention of that. Staying away from them, that is. Every single female, and some already spoken-for females, were in awe of the American sailors. None of the local lads were of interest anymore now that the Americans were in town. Me and Aíne strode through the doors to the dance hall with the confidence of the young and brave, ready to meet their destiny. And I certainly met mine that night.

Ed was the most handsome man I had ever seen. Tall, athletic, with dark eyes that shone like the conkers Jimmy played with in the autumn. He asked me out to dance and I melted when I heard his accent. The Cork accent is melodic and pleasant, even the deepest of tone sounds like a song and ends its sentence on a high note. Ed's voice was totally foreign to me, exotic, intriguing, delivered in his deep bass tones. He called me *miss*, bought me a soft drink, and treated me like I was some sort of porcelain doll. I fell in love that night, hook, line and sinker.

Luckily Aíne hit it off with his friend Scott, and when the dance ended both boys walked us girls as far as the corner of our street. Ed was gentle and polite, never once trying to kiss me, a perfect gentleman. It was a cool evening with a chilly breeze along the seafront. Ed noticed me shiver despite my shawl and took off his jacket.

"Wouldn't want you getting cold, Lizzie," he said as he

placed it gently over my shoulders. My skin sizzled to his touch, and I prayed it didn't show on my face.

"Thank you, Ed," I said, looking away to hide the raised colour on my cheeks. "You are very thoughtful."

I glanced back over my shoulder at Aíne, but she was lost in conversation with Scott. Ed's hand found mine as we dawdled along the seafront as if it were a sunny summer afternoon instead of nearly midnight in October. At the end of the street, we parted company with a promise to meet in the same place the following evening. And that's how it went for the next few days. Me and Aíne left home after dinner under the pretence of going for a walk, and the boys met us at the corner. And then they went out to sea.

It came as a surprise to me to realise how much I missed Ed, how quickly he had become a large part of my life. His ship was out on patrol for six days at a time and I worried every day. It was common knowledge that the American ships were hunting down the German U-boats and for the first time since it started, three years earlier, the war entered my thoughts and stayed there. At night, when we got under the covers and the lights were out, me and Aíne could talk to each other, worrying and wondering how our boys were, but we couldn't risk saying a word in front of Aunt Jean. She wasn't so keen on the Americans. And she wasn't alone in that. In Mass of a Sunday, the priest warned mothers to keep their daughters away from them, that the yanks were preying on the purity of young Irish women.

"Chance would be a fine thing," Aíne said, which brought a snort of laughter from me.

"Would you be tempted?" I asked.

"I don't know, to be honest. You know what they say, give a man what he wants, and he'll lose respect for ya. All men want to sleep with ya, but they all want to marry a virgin."

"Do you really think so."

"Yea, I do. But then when I'm with Scott, I forget all that. All I think about is how happy he makes me."

"I know what you mean. Sometimes, when Ed kisses me, I melt inside and I wonder what it would be like, to, you know... go all the way." I hesitated, feeling my cheeks burn with embarrassment in the darkness.

"They say that once you do it... go all the way, I mean, you always want it. Like, there's something in the brain that once you've done it, you're hooked, and you have to have it all the time."

"Really?"

We lapsed into silence, each of us considering the possibility of turning into sex-crazed monsters. I'm not too sure who started to laugh first but we both buried our heads under the blankets trying to stifle our giggles.

Chapter 11

Ed and Scott

Autumn was magical. I'd always loved that time of year but with Ed it felt extra special. Us girls were swept off our feet by our yankees. I was besotted by Ed. Every time I met him my heart sang. One look from those rich brown eyes and I melted. He remained the perfect gentleman, asking permission to hold my hand and every time he kissed me, I grew more convinced that he was the one for me. It was time to introduce him to Aunt Jean. Aíne wasn't so sure. It was late at night, and we had been out at the dance with Scott and Ed. By that stage the monthly dance had become so popular they changed it to every Saturday night. We were whispering in our room in the darkness.

"But, Lizzie, she'll have a fit. She warned us, remember."

"I know, Aíne, but I love him, and I'm sure when Aunt Jean meets him, she'll see what a gentleman he is. Don't you want your ma to meet Scott?"

"Yes, of course I do, but I'm scared about how she'll react. What if she forbids me to see him again?"

"She wouldn't do that. Would she?" Aíne had a valid point. What would I do? But common sense prevailed. We decided that night we would talk to Aunt Jean after dinner the following evening, but we never got the chance.

Aunt Jean was quiet the next morning, no chatter, no singing as she stirred the porridge. She placed the bowls on the table without a word and with a scowl on her normally smiling face.

"Are you okay, Ma?" Aíne asked.

"Yes, why wouldn't I be?" she snapped.

Aíne didn't reply. She bent her head to her bowl, and everyone finished breakfast in silence before setting off to work. That evening I got home before Aíne. My stomach grumbled at the smell emanating from the kitchen.

"Stew, my favourite," I called from the hall as I put away my coat before following the delicious aroma wafting out from the large pot on the range. My aunt was sitting at the kitchen table, a grim expression on her face.

"What is it, Aunt, is something wrong?"

"Sit down, Lizzie, I want to have a word with you."

We both heard the door opening and Aíne call out.

"In here, Aíne," Aunt Jean said.

"It's cold out there this ev..." Aíne stopped when she saw her mother's expression.

"Sit down, Aíne, I want to speak to you too."

"What is it, Ma?" Aíne's eyes crinkled then opened wide. "It's not Da, is it?"

"No... Da is fine, although yes in a way it is." Aunt Jean waved at Aíne to sit. "Your Da got back early from this trip. Last night in fact, and what do you think he saw on his way home?"

There was an ominous threat in Aunt Jean's words. I could feel the heat rising from my chest, up my neck and into my face. Aíne hadn't made the connection.

"What did he see, Ma, what is it?"

Aunt Jean looked at her daughter, her eyes flashing with

anger I never knew Aunt Jean was capable of as she stabbed the table with her index finger.

"His daughter... with an American sailor." She changed the direction of her glare to me. "His niece... also with an American sailor."

Aíne looked over at me, wide-eyed. "We were going to tell you, Ma. We talked about it and decided last night that we would tell you this evening, didn't we, Lizzie?"

I nodded in agreement with Aíne. "We did, Aunt Jean, honest. We'd planned on telling you all about them tonight. Honest we did."

"What did I tell you two about hanging around with those Americans. Too fancy for their own good they are. They're only after one thing. Use you and leave you without a second thought they will. I warned you two to stay away from them, didn't I?"

"I know you did, but honestly Ed and Scott are lovely boys, aren't they, Aíne? They are total gentlemen, treat us like princesses..."

"Like princesses, you say, royalty no less." Aunt Jean's voice went up several octaves. "Just who do you two think you are?"

"Ma, please. I really like Scott. He's lovely, mannerly, has a mother back home and a younger brother. If you met him, you'd really like him."

"Oh, would I now? After telling you to stay away from them, you think I'd like one of them? I've heard the stories, girls, you are so young, so naive. Mrs Lynch from next door was only telling me yesterday about her niece, seventeen, pregnant now and the lad has buggered off, no idea where he is. Her life is ruined. Who'll marry her now and take on another man's child."

"That's unfair, Aunt Jean. There's many an Irish lad has done the same. You're tarring us all with the same brush, but you brought us up better than that. My ma brought me up better than that. Look at what happened to our Maggie. Do you think I would put myself in that position?"

Tears blurred my vision at the thought of my sister Maggie. I lowered my head and took several deep breaths to steady myself, as I felt Aíne's small hand squeeze my shoulder in silent support.

"Ma, give us some credit. Meet Scott and Ed. Give them a chance."

Aunt Jean shook her head and crossed her arms before giving a huge sigh.

"All right, all right. Ask them for tea on Sunday, but I warn you, if your da doesn't approve, then you stop seeing them, do you hear me?"

Me and Aíne mumbled our agreement as Aunt Jean rose from the table to serve the dinner, which was eaten in silence. Uncle Pat arrived down the stairs just as we finished eating.

"Quiet in here tonight," he said. "I take it you've spoke to them, Jean?"

"That I have, Pat. The two American lads are coming here for their tea on Sunday, so be on your best behaviour. We'll reserve our judgement on them until then."

Uncle Pat nodded and when Aunt Jean's back was turned, he winked at me and Aíne with a quick grin he suppressed when she turned back from the range and placed his dinner in front of him.

The week flew by and by Sunday afternoon me and Aíne were on tenterhooks. The wind whistled up the hill, blowing the last of the leaves from the trees. When the boys knocked on the front door, Aíne answered, ushering the boys inside and into the parlour. Uncle Pat sat in his favourite armchair, smoke billowing from his pipe. Ed and Scott sat awkwardly on the small settee in front of the roaring open fire.

"Well, Aíne, are you going to introduce us?" Her mother

wiped her hands on her apron, hints of brown bread and apple tart wafting after her from the kitchen. The boys had brought gifts. Whiskey and tobacco for Uncle Pat, chocolates for Aunt Jean as well as a hamper of goodies. There was butter, flour, jam, tea, and tinned meats. Their generosity overwhelmed Uncle Pat, Aunt Jean less so. She sniffed and checked out the contents as if suspicious of its origins or authenticity. Scott exchanged anxious glances with Aíne.

"Isn't that very generous of them, Jean," Uncle Pat said. "Why thank you, boys. Tell me this, how did you come by such luxuries?"

Ed spoke up in his deep drawl. "Why, sir, we were instructed by our commanding officers that if we were lucky enough to be invited to someone's home, then we should bring gifts as a token of our appreciation."

"Ed and I are honoured to be invited into your home, sir," Scott said. "It is such a pleasure to meet Aíne's parents. I sure wish you could meet mine."

Scott took a photo out of his leather wallet and handed it to Aunt Jean who warmed to him within minutes over questions about his family and his hometown. Scott had grown up in a small town outside Baltimore in Maryland. His father was dead, but his mother and younger brother still lived in the house he had grown up in.

Ed lived with his parents and two younger sisters in Florida. Places that sounded like paradise to us. They had both joined the navy after the sinking of the *Lusitania*. Something we could understand. Uncle Pat had been on one of the boats that had brought the dead to Queenstown. It was before I came to live here but I had heard the stories before. A terrible time for the town, bodies lined up waiting to be identified; men, women, and children. Both Ed and Scott had been to the graveyard outside Queenstown where 167 of the bodies were buried.

Over tea conversation flowed. There were no awkward pauses, no strained laughter. It was as if they had always been family. Even Aunt Jean approved of their manners and by the time tea was over, they had won her over. She wished them luck and invited them to call again. As she closed the door after them, she turned to us girls and blessed herself.

"Lovely boys, I must say, girls. They're grand lads. It's just a pity they're American but beggars can't be choosers in this day and age."

"Ah, Ma, I knew you'd like them once you gave them a chance."

"That doesn't excuse you two going behind my back." Aunt Jean sniffed then folded her arms. "But... like I said, they may be foreigners, but someone's put manners on them."

Me and Aíne both threw our arms around Aunt Jean before we retreated upstairs to the relative privacy of our room. It was such a relief. We could keep seeing our yankees without worrying about Aunt Jean.

Chapter 12

Local Resentment

Every Saturday night me and Aíne donned our best dresses and Scott and Ed escorted us to the dance in the local hall. Every Sunday morning, we went to Mass with Aunt Jean and kept our heads down while the priest condemned the Americans from the pulpit. It was wearing thin, these lectures about the yanks, even Aunt Joan agreed with us girls on that. In my opinion it wasn't the Americans causing the problems, it was the locals. Me and Aíne witnessed that coming home from the dance hall on numerous occasions. The worst night was instigated by an old friend of Aíne's.

"It was awful, Ma," Aíne said, when we got in after the dance.

"Lucky for us, Ed and Scott walked us right to the door," I said.

It started in the dance hall. Liam O'Donovan had always been sweet on Aíne, ever since they were in national school, but Aíne only ever thought of Liam as a friend. Maybe he'd had too much alcohol in him or maybe someone had wound him up, but at the end of the night he tackled Scott. He waited until me and

Aíne were in the ladies' room and Ed was getting our coats, leaving Scott standing outside smoking a cigarette.

"Who do you think you are? Look at the state of ya in that stupid uniform." Liam circled around Scott and flicked the still-lit butt of his cigarette on the ground at his feet. "Fecking britches on a grown man."

A few of the local lads gathered, clapping and jeering, while the yanks watched with bated breath, waiting on Scott's reaction. Me and Aíne noticed the excited crowd as we exited the building but didn't realise at first that Scott was in the middle of it, until Aíne heard his voice.

"I don't want any trouble. I'm gonna walk my girl home. Let it go, man."

"Don't call me man," Liam shouted. "Bloody yanks, coming over here and thinking they can steal our women." He swung a punch at Scott's jaw. But Scott was too quick for him. He stepped back and Liam stumbled forward. Scott instinctively held his two hands up palms outward and pushed Liam away from him. Everyone heard the crack as Liam's head hit the pavement. There was an eerie silence, almost a pregnant pause and then all hell broke loose. Punches were flying left, right and centre while me and Aíne ran to help poor Liam. He was semi-conscious and moaning as we dragged him to safety. The military police must have been nearby for within minutes the crowd were deafened by their whistles. They broke up the warring factions, dragging combatants apart and separating the Americans from the locals. A wall of military police with batons drawn placed themselves between them with Liam being administered first aid on the American side. His injuries were minor, bruising to his buttocks and legs from being dragged along the ground but no head injury other than a headache, more hangover than trauma.

"What is wrong with you, Liam O'Donovan?" Aíne stood

over him, her hands on her hips as she tore into him. "We were never an item; do you hear me? Scott is my boyfriend now and you better get used to it."

She turned, grabbed Scott by his forearm and walked away, but not before looking behind her and shouting, "I never want to see you again, Liam O'Donovan. Stay away from us."

Liam moaned and his face flamed as he got unsteadily to his feet.

"Let her go, Liam. Look what you started here tonight. Someone could have been hurt, badly at that. This was all your doing." I pointed to the line of military police and the crowd of young men in front of them, shouting obscenities and firing stones. I could hear the local Royal Irish Constabulary arriving and the placid tones of Sergeant Walsh trying to pacify the outliers and coax them to go home.

Ed took my arm to follow Aíne and Scott. Together we formed a foursome and broke through the military cordon and walked towards the baying crowd. Their jeering petered off as we approached them, and they separated to allow us through. We walked home together, wary of our surroundings. The boys escorted us uphill to our front door. Ed kept his hand on my arm, a reassurance that I was safe in his company.

After that incident Aunt Jean worried about us girls going out in the company of the boys, but they reassured her that they would always keep us safe. Liam arrived at the house the next evening and apologised to Aíne.

"Proper order too, young Liam. What on earth were you thinking of?" Aunt Jean said. "You put my Aíne in danger, young man."

Suitably chastised, Liam swore he would never do anything like that again and promised to keep an eye out for me and Aíne when we were at the dance or anywhere in town.

"No need for that, Liam," Aíne interjected. "I am quite

capable of looking after myself and I have a boyfriend. Scott may not like the idea of another man following me around."

"Of course. Sorry, Aíne."

The thought of Aunt Jean encouraging Liam to practically stalk Aíne brought a smile to my face despite the seriousness of the situation. Liam left, with his apology accepted but with his tail between his legs, in no uncertain terms. Me and Aíne went back to our normal daily routine.

On the days that Ed was off duty he met me outside Mrs Buckley's shop at closing time and walked me home. I was grateful for his company on those chilly winter evenings when the sea gales blew us up the hill, howling so loud we could barely speak. With the advent of spring, we stretched the walk home to a leisurely stroll along the seafront, reluctantly turning uphill when darkness encroached.

Easter was fast approaching, and I was expected home. I had been practising all day how I would ask Ed but now that the time was here, I was nervous. What if he said no? Was I reading too much into our relationship? What if Ed didn't care for me as much as I cared for him? Asking him to meet my parents was a big step. Maybe it was too soon.

"Ed..." I hesitated, "how would you feel about accompanying me home for Easter Sunday? Meet my parents and my brother."

I could feel my colour rising as I stared straight ahead, afraid to look at his reaction.

Ed stopped walking, turned to look straight at me, and lifted my face with his finger. His dark, molten eyes stared directly into mine.

"I would be honoured," he said as he bent to kiss me with a tenderness that melted my insides. Ed pulled me in closer, his arms wrapped around my waist. I could feel the beat of his heart against mine. I could have stayed there forever, locked in that embrace.

Ed was away on duty for the next week but the following Saturday night he called at Aunt Jean's to pick me up for the dance.

"I'm off duty Easter weekend," Ed said. "I've requested three days' furlough so we can travel up on Saturday and back to Queenstown on Monday. Is that okay?"

I was thrilled. We could be home in a couple of hours and spend Saturday evening with my family, all day Sunday and leave early on Monday to get back to work. My letters home were full of stories about Ed, so Ma knew all about him. I couldn't wait for her to meet him. I was a bit worried about Da, with Ed being an American and all. Jimmy would be okay. He had loads of questions about America.

Chapter 13

Ed and the McCarthys

The trip home was uneventful. When we alighted from the train carriage, I could see Ma waving her scarf from the end of the smoke-filled platform. I ran to embrace her as Ed followed behind carrying our bags. I was taken aback by her appearance. My ma was stick thin, her shoulder bones protruding as I hugged her. My da looked good, a little bit older, a good bit thinner but still strong. It was Jimmy who shocked me the most. He had grown a good six inches since I saw him last. The young man who towered over me bore only a passing resemblance to the young boy I had left behind at Primrose Cottage only a year ago.

Suddenly acutely aware of Ed's presence behind me, I pulled him into the group.

"Ma, Da, this is Ed," I said, making the formal introductions. "Ed, my parents, and this... is my little brother Jimmy who suddenly is not so little anymore."

Da took Ed's proffered hand. I could practically hear Ed's bones squealing in protest. Ma tapped Da's hand.

"Honestly, would you leave the lad alone," she said. "You'll frighten him off before we get a chance to talk to him."

She smiled at Ed and offered her hand instead. "We are very pleased to finally meet you, Ed. We've heard quite a lot about you."

"From Aunt Jean, not from me," I said quickly, my face colouring at the prospect of Ed thinking I had been singing his praises to my parents.

Ed laughed, and Jimmy lifted one of the cases.

"Let's get going. We've a bit of a journey yet."

Jimmy kept us all entertained on the journey back to the Knockrath estate with tales of his adventures in school. He won a scholarship to the foundation secondary school ran by the Christian Brothers. Ma was so proud of him, well, we all were. He was clever, and Ma had visions of him becoming a professional of some sort. Although I reckoned, she would have been happy with anything he did as long as it didn't involve working on the estate. Around us, dusk was swallowing up the scenery as the low clouds hid the stars from lighting their way. The air was damp with promised rain, and I was relieved when the warm glow of the fire in Primrose Cottage came into view.

Ma had the fire roaring in no time while Jimmy showed Ed to what was my old bedroom but was now Jimmy's. The two boys were sharing while I was taking Jimmy's old bed in the alcove. Ma had prepared soup earlier and she called Ed and Jimmy for supper. When Ed walked back into the room, I thought he looked larger somehow, incongruous in my childhood home. He took a chair beside me, and we all tucked in, tired and hungry after our journey. Da kept watching Ed from the corner of his eye, his usual sunny disposition hidden behind a worried expression.

I felt awkward at first, not knowing what to say or how to act around Ed and my family but Ed soon cleared the air with his open, honest manner. He'd brought whiskey for Da, chocolates for Ma, packets of tea and sugar, tins of meat, several large oranges, and a few bars of soap for the household. My parents were amazed by the treasure trove he piled on the table.

"Very generous of you, Ed," Da said, with a look that bordered on suspicion. "But where did you lay your hands on this lot?"

"Barrack stores, sir. I've been saving up my share. It's an honour to be invited into your home, sir, and I wanted to repay your kindness."

"It is very generous of you, Ed, and we appreciate it. Thank you," Ma said as she lifted an orange to inhale its citrus smell. "Don't we, Mick."

Suitably chastised, Mick mumbled something but continued to watch Ed from under his eyebrows.

"So, anyway, Ed," Ma poured Ed another cup of tea, "tell us a bit about yourself. Where are you from?"

"Pensacola, Florida, ma'am," Ed said in his droll way. "It's a great place to live, plenty of sunshine, beautiful beaches. What's not to like?"

"Sounds lovely, doesn't it, Mick?" Ma nodded at her husband.

"It does, that it does. Do you live with your family, Ed?"

"Before I joined the navy, yes, sir. I lived with Mom, Pop and my sisters, Angela and Kate."

"No brothers?"

"No, sir."

Da rose from the table and lifted three glasses from the cabinet in the corner. He opened the bottle of whiskey that Ed had given him and poured two fingers into each glass. He handed one glass to his wife and one to Ed and held his own glass up.

"Here's hoping this awful war ends soon," Mick said. "*Slainte*."

Ed's version of *slainte* sounded more like *slanty* and everyone laughed. The ice was broken, and the conversation flowed. Ma brought me up to date on the comings and goings in the village, although she never mentioned the Haughton family. It was obvious that Da was gradually warming to Ed. He asked questions and listened intently. Before long he was addressing Ed as "son" instead of his name but obviously enjoying Ed addressing him as sir.

"It was always gonna be the navy for me, sir. We're a naval family. Pop was in the navy, retired just before the war started and none too happy when they wouldn't let him join up again."

"No farmers in your background then."

"No, sir. Military, through and through."

"You must find Ireland very different, Ed," Ma asked.

"It surely is, ma'am, sure miss the heat. At home, this time of year the temperatures are in the eighties, blue skies and bright sunshine every day. The summer months can get extremely hot and sticky but we're right by the sea so a dip in the ocean every day keeps a man cool. By June we're into hurricane season. That lasts up to Thanksgiving, then the weather stays warm and sunny right through to the summer again."

They could tell by the way he talked about his home place, how much he missed it.

"Do ye not get cold weather at all?"

"No, ma'am. Not like the cold and dampness you get here. I swear I've never felt the cold in my bones like I have since I landed in Ireland. But it sure is beautiful."

"Well, imagine that." Ma stared into the fire, mesmerised. "Imagine not needing the heat of the fire on a winter's evening."

The glow of the open fire was throwing both light and heat into the room. It was hard to imagine the cottage without, for the hearth is the heart of our home. I went to bed thinking about

Maria McDonald

how different life was on the south coast of Ireland to life on the south coast of America and I wondered if our lives could ever merge.

Chapter 14

Easter Blessings

The next morning, the McCarthy family rose early for Easter Sunday Mass. Ed had been raised a Catholic. They even had a chaplain who travelled with the American fleet so Ed was a regular Mass-goer, although we all wondered would the Irish version of Mass be different? The Latin Mass is just that, a universal Latin Mass and it doesn't vary, no matter what country you hear it in. But the Irish sermon was something he had never heard before and I couldn't help but wonder what he would make of Father Brennan.

As we walked up the pathway to the front door of St Joseph's Church, I could hear the whispers as the old women of the parish commented on the McCarthy family guest. The family parted at the front door of the church. Me and Ma donned our mantillas and sat on the left while the men removed their hats and sat on the right. The whole way through the service, I noticed the congregation sneaking glimpses at Ed. The men with looks of envy, the women with naked curiosity. He stood out from the crowd with his swarthy, exotic features, and his large build framed in that naval uniform. A little piece of my heart sang in the knowledge that he was there for me. Lizzie McCarthy had an American beau, and I could sense the local gossip mill churning.

Father Brennan was in rare form that Easter morning, shouting brimstone and redemption from the pulpit. Although I barely heard him, I was so wrapped up in my thoughts about Ed. Da got on really well with him. Ma thought he was a gentleman. Jimmy had pulled me aside before Mass and told me Ed was sound. My family really liked him. I realised that was the last test in my mind and I knew that I loved him but how did he feel about me? He seemed happy, so attentive, so receptive to my needs. But he's an American. When the war ends, and it must end sometime, he will go back to the States and what would become of us then? All these thoughts ran around my head one after the other until my ma nudged me. Mass was over.

We met up outside. Ed wasn't hard to find. A circle had formed around him, friends of the family, neighbours, all inquisitive about the clean-cut yank. There were thousands of Americans in the city and in the naval towns such as Queenstown but in this little backwater they were a rarity. Mrs McCoy, my former employer, and head town gossip was waiting for me outside the door.

"Well, Lizzie, life in the big town certainly agrees with you. You're looking right well, I have to say."

"Thank you, Mrs McCoy."

"And would those rosy cheeks and that happy smile have anything to do with that young man over there in the uniform?"

I blushed, from my collarbone right up to my hairline, all composure lost.

"A very handsome young man, I must say, Lizzie."

My ma intervened. "A lovely young lad, Mrs McCoy. We are delighted he was able to join us for Easter."

Ma signalled for Da and Ed to join them and introduced him to Mrs McCoy who was then joined by several other locals. My heart rate jumped as the grilling started but Ed was well able for them. He charmed them with his easy drawl and his warm smile. I was sure Mrs McCoy was batting her eyelashes at him by the time we dragged him away.

"What did you think of Father Brennan's sermon?" Ma asked Ed. "He's old school, I'm afraid, a fire and brimstone type of preacher, even on an Easter Sunday."

"I thought he was rather tame, to be honest." Ed flashed his warm smile at her as she linked his arm for the walk back to the cottage. "You should hear some of the American preachers, especially the ones from the Deep South. Your guy is a pushover compared to some of them."

Ma laughed out loud, and I was glad to hear it. She had a musical, tinkly laugh that was rarely heard since Maggie died. I caught my father's eye and knew that he was thinking the same thing. In that instant, father and daughter shared a conspiratorial smile and my worries from earlier swept away. I decided to enjoy the moment. Enjoy the company of this wonderful man and forget about what may lie ahead for us. After all, who knew what the future would hold for any of us in a time of war and rebellion.

"Lizzie, take Ed for a walk. Show him around. Jimmy will help me get the dinner organised. See you later, Ed."

We didn't need to be told twice. The path by the river beckoned and we strolled arm in arm in the crisp sunshine, admiring the early daffodils poking their way out of the soil and the blackthorn scrambling along the bank. The trees were starting to show signs of spring, tiny buds promising new life in the coming months. Underfoot, the new growth on the riverbank was sponge soft and that bright green that only exists for a few weeks in spring. Brand new, virginal even, eager to push its way into the sun, oblivious to the wind and rain that will batter it and the sun that will burn it until it slowly loses its lustre in the autumn.

Rounding a corner, Knockrath Manor and its formal gardens appeared in front of us. Ed gasped.

"Wow, that is some house. Did you say one family lives there?"

"Yes, the owners of the estate, the Haughtons. Usually, they only live there for half the year, the winter months they spend in their estate somewhere outside London but with the war, I think they've been here permanently."

"Have you ever been inside?"

Memories of holding a demented Maggie, her heart beating inside her chest as if it would burst, sprang to my mind and I shook my head to dispel the image. I hadn't told Ed about Maggie, only that I had a younger sister who had died in an accident. This was the opening I was waiting for, an unspoken opportunity to tell him the story but I stayed quiet, unable to put into words how I felt about Maggie, how much I missed her. How much I hated George Haughton and his family. I banished those thoughts, didn't want to think about it, didn't want the horrors of the past to spoil the happiness of the day.

"Is that the time? We'll be late for dinner if we don't hurry. Let's go."

The rest of the day went by in a blur of activity. Ma had outdone herself with the dinner, with even Ed struggling to finish his plate. There was an awkward moment when I realised that Ma still set a place at the table for Maggie, but Ed didn't comment. After dinner, I helped Ma clean up while the menfolk sat outside on the wall around the cottage, smoking American cigarettes and chatting like old friends.

Some neighbours from the estate came to the house that

evening. Music was played and copious amounts of tea was drunk, and quite a lot of whiskey, which all the men thanked Ed for. It was a lovely night full of music and chatter and I went to bed happy, content that my beau, as I liked to call him in my head, had been accepted by my family.

The next morning, Da went to work on the estate from early morning, but he managed to get back to have a quick lunch with the family before we set out for the city. Jimmy brought us to the train station for the 3.43 train to Queenstown. It had been a fun visit, leaving me with a tinge of sadness, maybe even a touch of homesickness when I hugged Ma goodbye at the station. Ed helped. He said nothing, just held my hand as the beauty of the Cork landscape rushed past us. The train was busy, full of Americans heading back to duty after the Easter break. We pulled into Queenstown train station just as dusk was falling. Ed took the bags and escorted me along the seafront to the road back to Aunt Jean's house.

On our right the sea was glistening under the lights from the naval ships as they bustled back and forth into the deep water of Cork harbour. I was over my bout of homesickness for Primrose Cottage, the allure of the sea made me feel at home in Queenstown.

"It's beautiful, isn't it," I said, stopping to stare for just a minute.

"You're beautiful," Ed said as he placed the bags on the ground and placed his hands on my face and drew me in for a soft kiss. Whistles and cheers sounded around us, causing us both to pull apart and laugh. Ed led me to a bench looking out to sea where we sat hand in hand enjoying the moment.

"Marry me, Lizzie."

I turned to look at him, totally astonished as he let go of my hand and got down on one knee in front of me.

"Marry me."

"Yes, oh yes." I threw my arms around his neck while all around us the whistles and cheers of passing sailors drowned out all other sound. I was so happy I never queried where we would live after we married.

Chapter 15

Wedding Preparations

Me and Aíne planned a double wedding, for 5th August 1918 in St Colman's Cathedral. What I didn't know at the time Ed popped the question was that he had already asked my father's permission. After dinner on Easter Sunday while I thought they were discussing the weather and American produce, Ed was asking my father for my hand in marriage. Jimmy already knew when he dropped us at the train station. I had wondered why he gave me such a huge hug and shook Ed's hand so hard I thought it was going to fall off.

When I got back to the house that night, Aíne met me at the door with her news. Scott had proposed to her. The two men had planned it together, so a double wedding was inevitable. Both sets of parents were delighted to hear the news. Ma arrived in Queenstown the following weekend and stayed overnight so she could have a chat to Aunt Jean about the arrangements. The one thing I hadn't considered fully was that when the war was over, Ed would ship back to America. As his wife, I should follow him. I wanted to spend my life with Ed. It was the thoughts of leaving Ireland that scared me.

It's not as if me and Aíne hadn't talked about it. The natural progression of any relationship was marriage. If our choices had been Irish men, both me and Aíne would have left our parents' houses to go to the church and left the church as wives to go to our husbands' homes and there we would be expected to keep house and rear any family we were blessed with. But we would be near our parents, our friends and family.

Me and Aíne both realised that if we did marry our yanks then we would end up moving to live in America. The idea both thrilled and frightened us at the same time. In our room at night, while the household slept, me and Aíne talked about Scott and Ed. We talked away each other's fears. Did Scott care for Aíne as much as she cared for him? Was this feeling I had for Ed, love, or was it a stupid infatuation? We were both in love, or so we believed. It was our insecurities that made us wonder if our men felt the same way about us. Yet, when I was with Ed, I knew he loved me without reservation. I could see it in his eyes, feel it in the touch of his hand when he held mine. When he kissed me, I melted into his arms, but I was afraid to let things go any further. What happened to Maggie was never far from my mind. Aíne had no such fears.

When I told Mrs Buckley my news, she was delighted for me and offered to make my wedding dress as a present. She showed me a lovely silk and some exquisite Carrickmacross lace along with a sketch of the style of dress she thought would suit me. I was thrilled and told her so. When I told her that Aíne was wearing her older sister's wedding dress, Mrs Buckley offered to do the necessary adjustments and add some trimmings to it to bring it up to the latest fashion. I couldn't wait to get home to tell Aíne the good news. The next week Aíne met me after work one evening with her dress. Mrs Buckley showed Aíne some sketches and trims that she thought would transform her dress. I have never seen Aíne so stuck for words. She actually cried with joy.

The Keeper of Secrets

Two weeks before the wedding the two of us had a fitting with Mrs Buckley. We were both delighted with the results, for Mrs Buckley outdid herself. I twirled in front of the mirror as I admired the creation Mrs Buckley had designed for me. A full underskirt covered by layers of lace-edged silk fell to just above my ankle. The fitted silk bodice was trimmed with lace at the modest neckline. A silver headband trimmed with pearls and lace held a short veil. I was speechless. Mrs Buckley noted the last few alterations before I carefully stepped out of it and hung it carefully in her back room.

Aíne was next. Neither of us could believe it was the same dress she had modelled for Mrs Buckley only weeks earlier. Her sister's once plain white cotton dress now fell above the ankle, had a new embroidery anglaise bodice and short sleeves. A satin sash trimmed with embroidery and a headband trimmed in the same fabric completed the look. It was the latest style and it suited Aíne to perfection. It was exquisite. Tears shone in Aíne's eyes as she admired her dress in the mirror. There was something in Aíne's face when she tried on her dress that nagged at me. I couldn't quite understand it for I had no doubt that Aíne was delighted with the makeover but there was something else there I couldn't quite put my finger on.

It was a fine summer evening as we walked home along the seafront. The town was busy as usual, and the sea breeze cooled the accumulated heat that generated up from the pavement. Seagulls circled, screeching for food, drowned out every so often by the boom of ship horns sailing into port.

"What is it, Aíne? Are you having second thoughts?"

Aíne stopped, looked at me distractedly as her eyes filled with tears. She started to tremble, so I led her to a nearby bench and sat beside her with my arm around her shoulder.

"Talk to me, Aíne. You know you can tell me anything."

"Oh, Lizzie. I think I'm pregnant," she whispered as she covered her face with her hands, crying in earnest now.

"Oh, dear Lord." I hugged her, not knowing what to say. Her mother would have a fit but there was no point in saying that to Aíne. She knew that already.

"Are you sure? How late are you?"

"I'm over two weeks."

"It could be just the stress of the wedding. Sometimes that can happen, you know..."

Aíne interrupted me. "I'm sure, Lizzie. I'm normally regular as clockwork, every four weeks. And it's not just that, I feel different, and I'm tender, here," and she touched her chest.

I took her hand and held it tight.

"Does Scott know?"

"No... you are the only one that knows." I had to strain to hear her. "But you can't tell anybody. Do you hear me, Lizzie? Not a soul, not Ed, not Ma, nobody."

"Okay, okay."

Aíne accepted the offer of my hankie gratefully. Gradually her tears subsided, and we sat together facing the sea trying to figure out what she should do. But there was nothing I could offer her.

"You're going to have to tell Scott."

Aíne gave a frustrated moan.

"It's all his fault. He said I couldn't get pregnant on my first time."

"Ah, Aíne, and you believed him?"

I was incredulous that the street-smart Aíne was so naive.

"I know, I know. I just didn't think it through. I love him so much, Lizzie."

I half-turned to face Aíne.

"Listen, Scott loves you and you love him. You're getting married in two weeks. Maybe you don't need to tell anyone."

Aíne scoffed. "They'll know when the baby comes, won't they?" Aíne's eyes filled with tears again. "I can just hear it now. Oh, that Aíne Crowley one, up the pole, that's why he married her. You can just hear it, can't you?"

"Nonsense, Aíne. With the war in Europe, and the uproar going on here over conscription and the Dublin rising, sure most people have too many other things to be worrying about than whether you were pregnant getting married or not."

"You know I like to be the centre of attention."

We both started to giggle at the return of Aíne's slightly warped sense of humour. She mopped up her tears before we headed slowly up the hill to the house. Later that evening we sat around the table making the final arrangements for the wedding. The two fathers – my da and Uncle Pat – got together and booked a local tearoom for the wedding breakfast. The McCarthy family were travelling to Queenstown the night before. Aunt Jean had the spare room ready although Jimmy would have to make do with the couch. Ma had my letter of freedom from the home parish, the banns were read, so everything was in order.

"Are you feeling okay, Aíne?" Aunt Jean looked concerned. "You're a bit peaky-looking. Dear Lord, I hope you're not coming down with something so close to the wedding." She blessed herself and didn't see Aíne's look of alarm.

"Shall I make us some tea, Auntie?" I offered.

"Yes please, and there's some apple tart left over. Sure, we may as well finish it."

"I'll get it." Aíne hurried out to the pantry to fetch it.

That night as we whispered together in our bedroom, I reassured Aíne that it would be okay but in reality, I knew that there was a very real possibility that Aunt Jean would see through us and guess the truth.

"Maybe you should just tell her."

"No... no I couldn't. She'll be so disappointed in me."

The look on Aíne's face was enough for me. If she didn't want her mother to know, then so be it. I would do everything I could to keep Aunt Jean's attention away from Aíne until after the wedding.

Chapter 16

Wedding Bells

My family arrived the day before the wedding and the house went into full celebration mode. Ma and Da managed to get their hands on fresh eggs and bacon from the estate for the wedding breakfast, a real treat with the ongoing food shortages. Ma and Aunt Jean planned to get up at daybreak to bake enough soda bread to feed the whole of Queenstown. Ma brought with her a cake, baked and decorated by Mrs Short as a wedding gift. Where she managed to source the ingredients, I had no idea, but didn't ask any questions. The cake and the bundles of wild flowers Ma brought from the estate were the focal point of the wedding table.

Ma spoke to me, briefly, the night before the wedding. We managed to snatch a few minutes alone when I volunteered to start washing the dinner dishes while the others sat over their cups of tea. Ma asked me if I had any questions, but I couldn't answer her. I kept my eyes focused on the soapy water in the basin.

"A married man has conjugal rights, Lizzie. It is your duty as his wife to make your husband happy. The first time might hurt, you might bleed a bit, but when you get used to it, it's wonderful. Making love to your husband brings its own rewards, and it also brings you children."

"Thanks, Ma."

Ma hugged me, soapy hands and all.

"You will make a beautiful bride, *mo ghrá*, and a wonderful wife."

"I've been taught by the best, Ma."

We were interrupted then by Aunt Jean and Aíne carrying dirty dishes and the conversation turned to hopes for the weather, what time to put the Child of Prague out in the garden and wondering if the men had prepared their expected speeches.

August 5th was a glorious day. From early morning the sun hung in a cloudless sea of bright blue dancing off the ocean. A slight breeze kept the heat bearable as we left the house and made our way to St Colman's Cathedral. The neighbours lined the streets and clapped as the wedding party passed. Jimmy led the parade, followed by the maids of honour, Aíne's older sisters, Patricia and Bridget. The two proud mothers were next, in summer dresses, hats adorned with flowers and handbags carried in the crook of their arms. Then came the brides. First me on my father's arm, followed by Aíne and her father. Aíne's brothers-in-law shepherded the children after that, and the women of the parish took up the rear. Mrs Buckley even closed the shop so she could be there. It made for quite a procession.

When we reached the church, everyone went inside leaving the wedding party outside. While Patricia and Bridget fussed around us brides, fixing veils in place and making sure we looked perfect, our two fathers stood to one side staring at us, their daughters, as if they had never seen either of us before. Patricia and Bridget entered the church first, followed by me and Da, then Aíne and Uncle Pat. The organist played as we walked down the aisle, but neither of us could remember the tune. I only had eyes for Ed. He never took his eyes off me the whole way and when my father handed me over to him, he shook Da's hand before leading me to the altar. The four of us stood side by side and said our vows. Me and Aíne resplendent in our beautiful gowns. Ed and Scott so very handsome in their full dress uniform. Our mothers cried and our fathers beamed with pride. It was magical and our hearts sang with happiness.

Back at the tearooms the wedding party tore into bacon, eggs, fresh soda bread and gallons of tea. The two proud fathers of the brides both made speeches, welcoming the boys into the respective families. Laughter abounded and happy memories were made but all too soon it was time for us to depart to catch the afternoon train to Cork city. Ed had booked rooms in the Metropole Hotel for two nights. After that Ed and Scott were due back on duty.

The four of us tried to relax on the short journey, hand in hand. All I could think about was consummating our vows. I was nervous, I recognised that fact. There was no point in saying otherwise. But I wasn't scared. Every time I looked into Ed's eyes, I could see love reflected there, my own love and desire for him. I couldn't wait to show him how much I loved him.

I had never been inside the Metropole, never been in a hotel before that day, so I was a little overawed. Ed put me at ease.

He is such a gentleman my Ed, I thought as he checked us in at reception. Our room was ornate, with heavy mahogany furniture, red drapes and a huge bed. Ed put our cases down and unpacked his in minutes.

"I'm gonna meet Scott for a quick drink in the bar, if that's okay. It will give you a chance to unpack and undress. I'll be back in an hour."

Ed took my hands in his and drew me close. His kiss was a

promise, and I felt my heart melt. As soon as the door closed behind him, I opened my case and took out my nightdress, a present from Mrs Buckley. A special present for a young bride, she said. It was gorgeous. A soft black fabric that shimmered and skimmed over my body to slightly below the knee. Thin straps held the low neckline and I felt practically naked. I brushed my teeth at the nightstand before I hurried over to the huge bed, anxious to be under the covers before Ed returned.

I knew that my Ed was a lovely man, so gentle and thoughtful, but he was as much of a virgin as I was. Both of us were awkward, afraid that we were somehow doing it wrong. Ed was worried about hurting me. I was worried about not satisfying him. But lust and love took over and when I eventually slept, I was content, happy and eager to start my new life as Mrs Ed Anderson.

Ed rented a small place near the seafront. It had two rooms, basic enough but affordable and I wasted no time making it a home. It was a former fisherman's cottage, vacant for some time. I scrubbed the floors while Ed whitewashed the walls. We managed to get some linoleum to cover the roughened floor. The blackened windows were scrubbed with vinegar and lemon juice and buffed until they shone. My ma gave us some yellow gingham fabric that I made into curtains and pretty cushions for the two armchairs, one each side of the fire. It was a far cry from Primrose Cottage, but it was our first home together and we absolutely loved it.

Ed spent every minute he could with me, when he wasn't on duty or out at sea. When he was away, I kept myself busy homemaking and working for Mrs Buckley. The days were long but always interesting. Mrs Buckley had built a great reputation amongst the local gentry, giving us the opportunity to work with the finest fabrics and trimmings.

The Keeper of Secrets

November brought biting winds. The sea turned angry, hurling itself against the harbour walls. On days like those I feared for Ed but not as much as I worried about my uncle Pat.

"Aunt Jean said they've postponed the latest fishing trip. The conditions at sea are just too dangerous," I confided in Ed. "I wish the navy would cancel your patrol."

"They say the war is coming to an end, Lizzie."

I nodded, unable to speak, for as much as I wanted this dreadful war to end, I knew that when it did, Ed would be going home to the States. Which meant that I would have to leave Queenstown. Leave Ireland. The thought of it excited me and frightened me in equal measure.

"I don't know yet how it will work, or when it will happen. But don't worry, sweetheart, I'll send for you as soon as I can. You won't be on your own for long."

Ed's enthusiasm made me smile. "I've plenty to keep me occupied here. Mrs Buckley is so busy. I don't know how she'll manage when I leave for America. Anyway, we're getting ahead of ourselves, *mo ghrá*. You don't know yet how much longer the navy will be posted here."

"The sooner the better, as far as I'm concerned. I won't miss the Irish weather, I can tell you that for sure. I cannot wait to feel the heat of the Florida sun," Ed said as he wrapped a scarf around my neck. "Come on, you're gonna be late."

The howling wind left no chance of conversation. Looking skyward, I reckoned I would be doing well to get into work before the laden battle-grey clouds emptied biting rain into the mix. Ed left my side at the shopfront and hurried off.

By the time his patrol ended six days later, the war was over. There was jubilation everywhere. At 11am on 11th November 1918, the people of Queenstown cheered and cried as the bells of St Colman's Cathedral rang out in celebration. Mrs Buckley closed the shop so we could join the celebrations on the seafront. The whole town showed up. People gave thanks that this awful inhuman war was over, that no more lives would be lost. They prayed for those who'd died, and for the widows and orphans left behind.

Chapter 17

Memories of Maggie

Mrs Buckley heard through the grapevine that the Americans were planning a huge New Year's Eve ball and all the gentry had been invited. The upcoming ball to be held in the city centre brought us extra work. Mrs Buckley's appointment book was fully booked for weeks on end. All the gentry from the big houses were attending, the local débutantes, their chaperones, their mothers and they all had to be dressed in their finest. There were days when I daydreamed, imagining myself wearing some of those beautiful dresses. It took my mind off my other problems. It wasn't that I was unhappy, far from it. I was incredibly happy with Ed. We had so much to look forward to. I had hoped and prayed for a baby but only the previous evening my hopes were dashed yet again. Aíne was blooming. Pregnancy suited her. I couldn't suppress the slight touch of jealousy, then felt guilty for feeling that way.

That morning I was working in the back room, engrossed in the detailed bodice on a ballgown for the daughter of the commissioner when a voice filtered through from the shop counter. The hairs on the back of my neck stood up and I paused, my needle in mid-air as Mrs Haughton's shrill voice carried through the open door.

"My favourite seamstress is based in London of course. Lady Benton has been kind enough to recommend you."

"Lady Haughton's London residence has been sequestered by the military, so they are wintering in Knockrath Manor, " Lady Benton said.

"I see." Mrs Buckley's quiet tone was barely audible, and I wondered had she recognised the name. "So how can we help you?"

"My dressmaker has shipped the fabric and has written exact instructions on the style of gown I prefer. It will need to be finished before the Christmas season."

"Of course. Just a moment and I will prepare the back room for your fitting."

Mrs Buckley closed the door gently behind her.

"Help me clear the desk, Lizzie, then go up to the market and get me some bread and cheese. Take your time, I will be busy for thirty minutes or so." She placed a pound note in my hand and patted it closed.

I hoped my grateful smile was enough for I couldn't speak. We tidied away the gown I had been working on and I slipped out the rear exit minutes later. When I got back nearly an hour later, Mrs Buckley was alone and working on drawings. I put my purchases on the table.

"Thank you."

"No, thank you. I wouldn't have had time to get those this evening. We're so busy."

"I never told you..." I wrung my hands.

"You don't have to tell me anything, Lizzie." Mrs Buckley patted my hands.

"That woman ruined my sister. It's because of her and her lies that my sister is dead."

"Oh, my Lord. Whatever do you mean?"

"Her son raped my twelve-year-old sister. He got her pregnant. She had her arrested, accused her of attacking him which is ridiculous. Master George was a grown man of twenty at the time, Maggie was only a slip of a girl."

"Oh, Lizzie, how awful for her, for all of you."

"That wasn't the worst of it. They sent her to prison which was bad enough but then the baby died at birth. My poor sister. Her poor mind snapped. They put her in the mental hospital..." A sob escaped me as I raced through the story, words tumbling out one after the other. "She fell out a window. She died."

"Oh, Lizzie." Mrs Buckley put her arms around me and hugged me so tight I could barely breathe. "My goodness, such an awful chain of events."

I couldn't contain my tears. Even after all those years, thoughts of Maggie broke my heart. I hadn't seen any of the Haughton family since, nor did I want to. As far as I was concerned, they were responsible for Maggie's death. They drove her to it. My mother felt the same way. I allowed Mrs Buckley to guide me to a chair in front of the table, accepted the handkerchief offered and tried to stop my tears. But once the floodgates were opened, I couldn't stop. Mrs Buckley made tea and sat with me, patting my hand sympathetically.

"I'm so sorry, Mrs Buckley," I said, my eyes puffy and swollen. "I didn't mean to burden you."

"Not at all, my dear. You can't keep something like that bottled up. You can talk to me anytime. Does Ed know?"

"No. I never told him. I couldn't." Fresh tears welled up as thoughts of Ed flooded me. "I never told anyone before today. I can't talk about my sister, can barely say her name."

"Well, maybe you should. The more you talk about her, the easier it will be for you. Like I said, you can talk to me anytime, but I do think you should tell Ed. What happened was so traumatic for you and your family."

Mrs Buckley was right of course. I sniffed. Ed should know about my sister. Maybe tonight I should sit down with him, tell him all about Maggie. Just making the decision to talk to Ed made me feel better already.

My Ed was so perceptive. The minute he stepped inside the door he knew I had something on my mind. I had always shied away from telling Ed about what happened to Maggie, using the excuse that I didn't know where to start. Did Maggie's story begin on the day of the fête when Master George flirted with her or was it on the day that he attacked her? Telling Mrs Buckley what happened opened up something inside me. I decided to follow her advice and tell Ed everything. He was shocked of course but so supportive. My heart swelled with love for him. I was so lucky to have met this wonderful man.

Chapter 18

Spanish Flu

The jubilation after the end of the war was chased away by the spread of the black influenza. Everywhere people met was closed. All the schools, the theatres and libraries, all closed. Businesses faltered, open one day, closed the next as people fell ill. Fear stalked the town. Mrs Buckley insisted that we all wear face masks when dealing with customers. She stitched two each for us in plain white fabric. Everyone was wearing them. Ed was his usual upbeat self.

"Ed, be careful, that's all I'm saying."

"I will, Lizzie, you worry too much." Ed smiled at me. "I've managed to survive the war. I've no intention of letting influenza carry me off at this stage, when I'm so close to going home."

"Is there any word yet on when you all are leaving?"

"Not yet. The logistics of moving all those thousands of men around the world is complicated. I can't see it happening this year, honey. Hopefully we'll get to spend Christmas with your parents."

"Do you think you can cope with another cold Irish Christmas Day?"

"I'm sure I can manage one more. After all, it will be our last one. Next year we'll celebrate Christmas on the beach. I can't wait to feel the heat of the sun again."

His enthusiasm was contagious. I smiled at my handsome husband. With him at my side I could cope with anything. Despite everything that was going on in the world, my worries about influenza, my nagging doubts about leaving family behind, my concerns that I hadn't fallen pregnant yet, I was genuinely happy.

Ed walked me to the shopfront as usual. I watched him as he sauntered down the hill, whistling as his long strides carried him out of sight in minutes. Mrs Buckley was already in the back room. We had so many orders to get through. The local gentry didn't appear to be concerned about the black flu. They still had their dresses ordered for the Christmas social season and the New Year's Eve ball. Although the threat from the black flu could be gone by then. There had been quite a few people ill earlier in the year but then it appeared to disappear during the summer. It was certainly spreading fast now. There were stories of people, fit young people just dropping dead on the streets of Cork city. I blessed myself at the thought of it.

The bell over the door jamb rang out, signalling the arrival of a customer. I turned with a friendly smile on my face, ready to greet the customer. That smile froze when I recognised Lady Haughton.

"I would like to check on the progress of my ensemble," she said, lifting her eyeglasses and peering at me.

"I'll fetch Mrs Buckley."

"Do I know you?" Lady Haughton studied me intently.

"You should do. My father works on the estate. I'm the eldest McCarthy girl."

"I see." Lady Haughton continued to study me like I was some sort of insect on a pin, a look of sheer disdain on her face.

I took a deep breath to combat the anger that was boiling up inside me. This woman had the nerve to look down on me. Without saying another word, I turned on my heel and went through to the back office. Mrs Buckley was bent over the cutting table, carefully cutting a bolt of emerald-green satin.

"Mrs Buckley, Lady Haughton is here to see you."

"Oh dear. I'm so sorry, Lizzie. Are you okay?"

I nodded, unsure if I could speak normally after saying that woman's name out loud. I could feel the heat in my cheeks. I was sure Mrs Buckley would be able to hear my heart beating in my chest. Why couldn't that woman have found a local dressmaker, or even someone in the city, instead of travelling to Queenstown of all places. I listened as Lady Haughton interrogated Mrs Buckley. My employer had excellent people skills. Lady Haughton would be mistaken to assume that her gentle manner meant she could walk roughshod over her. Under that gentle exterior lived a will of pure tempered steel. Mrs Buckley ran an extremely successful business while caring for her child. She was more than a match for the Lady Haughtons of this world.

In early December the weather turned colder. Incidences of the black flu gradually faded away. Slowly life returned to normal, just in time for Christmas. In the end we got the majority of the dresses finished the week before Christmas. Only Lady Haughton's ball gown and two others were due for collection on 30th December. Mrs Buckley let me finish work early on Christmas Eve so I could make the journey home to the Knockrath estate. Lady Haughton's ball gown was ready, but I wasn't about to help that woman in any shape or form.

"She can make the journey to Queenstown to collect it. She'll be in Cork city anyway for the ball," I said to Mrs Buckley.

"I wouldn't let you bring it to her, Lizzie. What's more, she will be paying extra for the additions she made. I will not let that woman away with as much as a farthing." Mrs Buckley handed me my wages. "Now, enjoy your break. I'll see you on the 28th."

Under time pressure, I put my wages envelope into my bag unopened. I was meeting Ed at the station. We had to catch the 2pm train to Cork where Jimmy would be waiting to bring us the short ride home. I was looking forward to seeing my family. They might travel to Queenstown to visit me before I leave for America, but I was acutely aware that this could be my last time in Primrose Cottage.

Christmas was lovely. We got early Mass in the village and walked back to Primrose Cottage on a cold, bright day. Ma put on a spread for dinner that wouldn't have gone amiss in the big house. Roast goose, vegetables from the allotment, potatoes, carrots and brussels sprouts, my ma's signature stuffing and the most delicious savoury gravy. After dinner we exchanged gifts. My parents presented us with matching travel bags, a reminder of our impending journey across the ocean. Ed enthralled them with stories of life in Florida, convincing Ma and Da that I was going to live in paradise.

All too soon, it was time for me and Ed to return to Queenstown. Ma hugged me as tears threatened to overwhelm us both. Da shook Ed's hand like he never wanted to stop. The whole family accompanied us to the train station and waved from the platform as the train took off, belching black smoke as it pulled out of the station on its journey to Queenstown.

Me and Ed sat hand in hand, each wrapped in our own thoughts about what lay ahead of us in the New Year. I had a fair idea what Ed was dreaming about. It's all he ever talked about. The sunshine and the warmth of his hometown, of seeing his younger sisters again, all grown up now since the last time he saw them. His father's droll humour, his mother fussing over him. He missed them all. I dreamed of a future with a baby and a new family. I hoped that my in-laws would like me, that my new life in America would be as wonderful as Ed painted it. I stole a sly glance at my husband. With Ed by my side, life was already wonderful.

On our return, Ed received notification that he would be shipping to America in March. With a set date in mind, me and Ed began our preparations. I needed to apply for a visa from the American government. It would be my first time to leave Ireland. I never had the opportunity, but I wasn't alone. Scott was due to return on the same ship. Aíne was heavily pregnant. We attended the American consulate in Queenstown to apply for our visas together, becoming witnesses for each other.

On 25th February 1919, I received my passport. Ed immediately booked my passage on the SS *Plattsburgh,* sailing on 3rd July. Scott booked Aíne on the same sailing. We could have sailed a month or so earlier, but Aíne was due her baby in April although they had told everyone it would be May. Auntie Jean's suspicions would have been confirmed if we had booked our passage for the month Aíne had told everyone she was due to give birth. I wrote to my mother giving her the dates, praying that my mother would travel to Queenstown to say a final goodbye.

The following day I was shocked to receive a telegram. The postboy was a neighbour's son who knew I worked in Mrs Buckley's and brought it straight to the shop to me. My hands shook as he handed it to me gingerly. I turned it over several times, my heart beating in my throat. It couldn't be Ed for he had walked me to work only a few hours ago.

"Who would send me a telegram?" I looked at Mrs Buckley, eyes wide, with the offending paper shaking in my hands.

Mrs Buckley took my hand. "Open it." Her gentle voice was soothing. I carefully ripped open the telegram and read it.

```
YOUR FATHER DEAD. FLU. WILL WRITE.
    MAM
```

My mouth fell open as a sob escaped me. With shaking hands, I gestured to Mrs Buckley to take the telegram before sinking into a chair, sobbing, my heart broken. My lovely father. His rich baritone silenced forever. Mrs Buckley fussed over me, offering tea, a gentle touch and a shoulder to cry on. Eventually I dried my tears and went home to prepare the evening meal. I liked to have Ed's dinner on the table on the days he was home. But I couldn't function. Every time I picked up a spud, I remembered my father's big farmer's hands digging furrows in his allotment. Memories of him planting vegetables, teaching us all about the best way to grow, what plants to grow together, the best fertilisers, the best time to plant and the best time to harvest. Ed arrived home to a cold house with his wife weeping into the sink. Luckily Mrs Buckley got word to him before he went home.

"My poor sweetheart. Come here."

"Oh, Ed, my lovely Da. I need to go home."

Ed's arms enveloped me like a warm blanket, soothing my pain away.

"I need to go home, Ed. I have to see him."

"Ssh, shoosh, honey. That would not be a good idea. It was the black flu that killed him. You can't see him. None of us can."

I pushed myself out of Ed's embrace.

"Whatever do you mean? Of course I have to go home."

"You can't, honey. Your mother's letter will explain, I'm sure."

Ed was right. Ma's letter arrived the next morning. She urged me to stay away, to remember my father the way he was at Christmas. He succumbed to the black flu, which was highly contagious. Ma begged me not to go home but to light a candle in St Colman's Cathedral and pray for my father's soul.

I followed Ma's wishes. I paid the priest for a Mass for my father's soul. They all attended. Aunt Jean and Uncle Pat, the girls, Patricia and Bridget and their families, Aíne and Scott, Mrs Buckley and Kate and of course, my Ed. It was a lovely Mass, dedicated to my lovely father. It eased my pain to a degree. I felt it gave me license to talk about him with people who knew him and loved him as I did.

Soon after that day I realised that Ed would be leaving in a few weeks. A few months later, me and Aíne would be leaving on the SS *Plattsburgh*. I couldn't help but worry what would happen to my mother. Catherine McCarthy was a strong-willed woman, but she'd never recovered fully from Maggie's death. Her home, Primrose Cottage, came with my father's job. Would Lord Haughton allow my mother and brother to stay?

Chapter 19

Aíne's Baby

A loud banging on our cottage door woke both of us. We leapt out of bed. Ed opened the door to a frantic Uncle Pat.

"Uncle Pat, what is it?"

"I need Lizzie, come quickly. It's Aíne. She's started labour early."

We dressed hurriedly and followed Uncle Pat up the hill to the house. Scott stood waiting on the doorstep while Aíne's cries could be heard coming from the back bedroom. I bounded up the stairs. Inside the bedroom Aunt Jean was mopping Aíne's brow while the local midwife examined her. Ed remained outside with Scott, who was puffing cigarettes and pacing up and down the street, looking anxiously towards the door.

"It's no use. I can't turn the baby," the midwife whispered to Aunt Jean. "She'll have to birth it legs first."

Aunt Jean gestured to me to come closer and handed me the cloth.

"Keep mopping her brow with cold water," she instructed before stepping outside with the midwife. I couldn't make out what they were saying but their frantic whispers made me fear the worst. I could see those fears reflected in Aíne's eyes.

"Don't worry, Aíne. It will be fine. The baby might be a little early, but Mrs Nolan here knows what she's doing." I squeezed Aíne's damp hand.

Aíne smiled gratefully until another contraction hit her. Pain contorted her pretty face as she screamed, holding my hand so tightly I thought my fingers would break. With my support and the help of Mrs Nolan, Aíne gave birth two hours later. It was a long and difficult breech birth but nothing the experienced midwife hadn't dealt with before.

"You have a son."

Aíne smiled through her sweat and tears, while Aunt Jean beamed from ear to ear. The baby screamed as Mrs Nolan carefully counted ten fingers and ten toes, then wrapped the tiny bundle in a swaddling cloth before placing the little boy in Aíne's arms.

"Oh, Lizzie, look. My little boy and he is perfect, simply perfect." Aíne held her baby in the crook of her arm and smiled. I looked on, beaming at the image of motherhood my best friend presented. My smile turned to horror as Aíne mumbled something. Her face drained of colour and a pool of blood slowly formed around her. Aghast, I lifted the crying baby out of his mother's arms while Mrs Nolan tried to stem the flow of blood, but it was no use. She could not save Aíne despite her best efforts. I retreated to the corner cuddling the crying child into my chest as if to protect it from witnessing the scene unfolding in front of him. Aunt Jean's cries brought Uncle Pat and Scott to the room in time to see Aíne draw her last breath.

The next few days went by in a blur. Scott was numb with grief. He refused to even look at his son. After the funeral he went back to the port and stayed on board, refusing to talk to anyone, even Ed. Heartbroken at the loss of her daughter, Aunt Jean looked after her grandson.

"I think we should name him Scott after his father," she told me and Ed. "I've arranged for him to be christened on Saturday. Please, Ed. Do whatever you can to get Scott to come."

Ed tried but Scott refused to leave the ship. Me and Ed accompanied Aunt Jean and Uncle Pat to St Colman's and witnessed the christening of baby Scott. Ed borrowed a camera and took a photograph of the baby in his christening gown, the same gown Aíne and her sisters wore for their christenings. He got three copies printed, one for me, one for Aunt Jean and the last one for Scott to bring with him back to the States.

The date of Ed's departure came around all too quickly. On our final night together, we cuddled under the blankets with the dying fire casting a dim glow over the room. The rain splattered off the windowpanes while the wind howled down the chimney, sending gusts that threatened to scatter the embers over the flagstone floor.

"I hope this storm settles before you set sail," I said as I snuggled into Ed's broad chest.

"Jeez, I hope so. I don't fancy going out to sea in that."

"Maybe they will put back the sailing. We could have another few days together."

"That won't happen. We've went to sea in worse weather."

"I'll miss you so much."

"I'll miss you too, honey, but it's only four months. Once we put that behind us, we'll have the rest of our lives together. Anyway, it'll give me time to organise my transfer to Pensacola. New York is fine but we don't want to live there permanently."

I woke the next morning sensing the cold spot in the bed beside me. My heart sank with the realisation that he had left without saying one last goodbye. Ed had slipped away in the early hours of the morning leaving a note for me on his pillow. I sank back into the blankets, hugging myself tightly. The tears flowed with no sign of stopping. My arms ached for Ed as I wondered how I would get through the next four months without him. I opened his note and smiled. Ed knew me so well.

> *Don't cry, honey. I am with you in spirit. You are always in my thoughts and dreams. Today, I leave to prepare a home for us. Let's treat this not as a parting, but as a beginning, the start of our new life together. Think of me every day and know that I will love you forever.*

Ed's words gave me the impetus I needed to get out of bed and on with my life. After all, I had a lot to do before I set sail to join him. My mother was arriving that day and staying for a week. The cottage had to be prepared. I had to make sure it was spick and span. Folding Ed's note carefully, I tucked it inside the back cover of my prayer book, before placing it under my pillow. Knowing it was there brought me some comfort, as if it would invite Ed to inhabit my dreams at night. Not that an invitation was needed. Ed lived in my thoughts every waking minute and populated all of my dreams.

Catherine McCarthy arrived that evening, tired from her journey. At least that's what I tried to tell myself. Ma was a shadow of her former self. Her skin hung loosely on her frame. Black shadows under her eyes told their own story of grief. I hugged her tightly, shocked at her appearance. Between her husband's death and then Aíne's shocking demise, Ma had aged ten years in as many weeks. Over the following few days I concentrated on trying to get some colour back into my mother's cheeks.

The only thing that brought a smile to her face was the

baby. Ma fed him and winded him and sang softly to him. He cried a lot, even for a newborn. Aunt Jean said it was as if he knew that his mother had gone to heaven, and blessed herself. Ma was the only one who could settle him.

"It's as if that child knows that his great-aunt Catherine is grieving too. Kindred spirits they are, the two of them. Both grieving," Aunt Jean said, nodding her head to emphasise her point.

It was a foregone conclusion. Ma stayed. Aunt Jean enrolled Jimmy in the local school. Uncle Pat and Aunt Jean travelled all the way to Primrose Cottage on a borrowed horse and cart. They packed up all the belongings of the McCarthy family and fully loaded, headed back to Queenstown. Ma stayed and looked after baby Scott while Aunt Jean packed her former life into a cart and transported it to her single room in her sister's house. I didn't even pretend to protest. In my opinion it was the best solution for everyone. Looking after baby Scott had given Ma a reason to get up in the morning. Jimmy would thrive at the larger school. And I could go to America knowing that my mother and brother had a home with people who loved them.

Chapter 20

Beth, 1976

Listening to my grandma's voice telling the story of her sister broke my heart. Her voice faltered several times, choked with emotion. How difficult it must have been for her to lose her only sister that way. It's as if she'd lost her twice. The first time when she was sent away and then again when she died. Grandma mentioned her years ago, but it was the abridged version. I never understood what really happened to her. How traumatic it must have been. Not only for Grandma, but for her whole family.

I couldn't imagine how I would feel if anything happened to Conor. My older brother was my best friend. He loved Grandma as much as I did. I need to share these tapes with him. Let him hear Grandma's voice again.

Conor would love to hear Grandma talking about her husband. We called him Pops. The sheer love and affection she felt for him is evident in her voice as she talks about him. It's odd to try to reconcile the image in my head of my pops with the young Ed who swept Grandma off her feet. How brave was she to venture into a whole new world, so many miles away from the place she was born. Although I wonder how many other Irish women did the same. Married their American doughboy and set off for a new life.

Grandma's life in Ireland had been so hard yet she never gave us a hint of what she had been through. She talked about Ireland, 'the old country' as she called it, as if it were a magical place. She had told us she had a sister who had died, but this was the first time I heard the full story of what had happened to her.

I'd heard about the Spanish flu but never fully understood it until I heard Grandma talking about her father's death. I can hear her grief, feel her pain. Maybe it's because it's so close to how I'm feeling. My father died so suddenly. The first heart attack left him hospitalised but at least I had time to get home and tell him how much I loved him before the second heart attack took him from us. We were all here for the funeral. Even our Irish relatives made it over. The last time was when Grandma died.

But they're all gone back now, it's just Mom and me. Conor has gone back to work. He's a teacher but the summer break is coming up in a few weeks, so he'll be back. I've handed in my notice. It wasn't working out anyway and maybe it's about time I came home. Coming home to my old bedroom feels right for me somehow. Breaking up with Jeremy was hard but let's face it, my grandma would turn in her grave if she knew I dated a married man, and my boss at that.

I've always admired her. She was a force of nature, full of energy and fun. Grandma had always stuck up for me, argued my case with my father, whether it was over the length of my skirts or my choice of college. I don't think she would have supported me in this battle.

Of course, it's a moot point now anyway. At least the two people I admired most in the world didn't find out how stupid I had been. My grandma and my father. Grandma was my role model. She would be so disappointed in me. I can't believe how stupid I have been. Imagine falling for your boss. What a cliché. How much of an idiot am I?

Mom is curious as to why I left a job she thought I was happy in. And to a point she is right. I was happy there. The work was fulfilling, interesting even, if accountancy can ever be termed interesting. But I enjoyed it, got on well with the clients. Jeremy was the problem.

It's not as if I didn't see the warning signs. He was a player. I knew that from the first time I met him. He had the practised lines of an expert and I fell for it. I can blame my relative naivety but, in the end, I was warned he was married, and I still fell for him. I'm glad it's over before anyone else got hurt. His wife is such a lovely person. She deserves so much better than him. I deserve so much better than him.

At least I've walked away with good references. I am so ashamed of my actions but at least my work was exemplary. The firm are opening a new branch in Pensacola, and I've been offered a position there. I'm starting in a few weeks. It's something to look forward to. In the meantime, I'm listening to my grandma's recordings telling her personal story.

I'm glad I found the tapes again. Listening to them is a distraction. Hearing my grandma's voice is soothing for my tortured soul. I admired her so much as a little girl and now, as an adult, listening to her telling her own story makes me admire her even more.

Act 2

America

Chapter 21

Meeting the Family

The voyage to the States was largely uneventful. The ship was full of women just like me, leaving their friends and family behind them to start a new life in a new country with their husbands. Men barely known to them in some cases. We were scared and excited at once and bonds were formed that lasted a lifetime.

Every minute of the journey I thought of Aine. We had planned to make that journey together, but it wasn't to be. When I closed my eyes, I could still see Aine's face. Such happiness turning to horror in seconds. We had so many plans for our future. A future in a new country. Both of us with new husbands, Aine with a new baby and me with the dream of one. On that long journey across the Atlantic I felt her loss every single day. I knew several of the other women, war brides like me, and they had known Aine. Talking about her helped me grieve for my cousin and best friend. I swore that I would make a success of my new life, for Aine, as well as for myself.

I met Nuala Kelland on that voyage. It was her accent that caught my attention. Well, her accent and her gorgeous baby boy. Nuala was my age and from Belfast. For someone like me who had never left the county of Cork, she was an enigma. Nuala married her sailor the month before us. Helping her look after little Tomás passed the time. I missed Aíne, missed my mother.

"You're lucky to have family. I'm an orphan. Before I met Ulick, I lived in a boarding house in Belfast. Don't get wrong, it was a great place to live. Mrs Best looked after us all so well in Riverdale House, but she wasn't family."

Nuala was so open and honest. Quite frankly I thought of her as brave. Ready to embrace whatever life threw at her. I admired that in her. Over the duration of the journey, we became firm friends.

We parted in the line for processing, with promises to keep in touch, which we did, remaining friends for the rest of our days. While several of the women were settling in New York, the rest of us were scattered throughout the United States. Nuala's final destination was in Virginia, where her husband's family ran a hotel. None of the women were going to Florida and I felt slightly isolated. Not for long though.

Ed was waiting for me on the docks. It took forever to go through immigrant processing, and I grew increasingly anxious as I queued up with all the other women, answering questions, having paperwork checked and rechecked. Finally, they allowed us through to the waiting men. Hundreds of them waiting patiently on their new wives, and quite a few children, joining them in America.

The noise levels raised several decibels as many of these women were scooped into the arms of their sailors. I stood transfixed at the cacophony of sound around me, the emotional reunions of lovers, the touching sight of a man holding his child in his arms for the first time in nearly a year. The noise threatened to overwhelm me until it all faded into the background when I caught sight of Ed. He was standing under a large clock, twisting his cap in his hands as his molten eyes scanned the crowd. Our eyes met and his face lit up. Before I knew it, he had wrapped his arms around me, and all felt right with the world. The tension that hounded me during the long journey, accentuated by the immigrant processing, melted away, replaced with the knowledge that I was now safe, protected and loved in the arms of my husband.

The train journey to Florida was long and fascinating. I marvelled at the varied landscapes we hurtled through until we reached our destination. Ed had warned me about the heat and humidity in Florida, but nothing could have prepared me for it. I wasn't sure what I expected. In our little cottage in Queenstown, curled up together in our bed with blankets and overcoats shielding us from the cold sea breezes, Ed enthused about the place he was born. He tempted me with visions of constant sunshine, palm trees, white sand beaches and swimming in the warm waters of the Gulf of Mexico. It sounded idyllic, like some sort of paradise.

The heat of Florida was so welcome at first. I opened my face to the sun and the luxury of that heat. Ed told me all about his family and I looked forward to meeting them. I wasn't too sure what to expect but when we turned into his street, I was pleasantly surprised. Each house appeared to have its own personality. Most had a covered veranda along the front of the house, some with swings, all with seating of some sort. Ed's parents' house was painted in a sunny yellow with a swing seat to the right of the front door. Two giggling young girls leapt off the swing seat and bounded down the path to greet us.

"Welcome, Lizzie, I can call you Lizzie?" The younger girl bounced on her toes, her dark eyes, so like Ed's. "I'm Kate and this is Angela."

Ed put a protective arm around me, laughing. "Wow, girls,

give Lizzie room to breathe. Lizzie, these two beauties are my sisters."

"No denying them." I laughed. "Even a blind man would know you three were related."

The same dark-brown eyes, the same chestnut hair, Ed's cut short, Angela and Kate with shiny tresses coiled high and held loosely in place with ribbons. Their warm welcome was heartening. A noise to my left brought my eye upwards to the open screen door and my introduction to Ed's mother. She was a stout woman, but tall enough to carry it well. Her silver hair was caught neatly in an elegant chignon which elongated her swan-like neck.

"Mom," Ed said, taking my hand and leading me up the steps, "this is Lizzie."

"I'm very pleased to finally meet you, Lizzie," she said as she shook my outstretched hand. "Ed has told us all so much about you."

Her facial expression didn't match her kind words for her face was poker straight, no hint of a smile, no warmth in those steel-grey eyes that appeared to sum me up and find me wanting in one glance. Ed's lips tightened and I felt his tension as he squeezed my hand before releasing his grip to lift my bags.

"Lead the way, Mom."

Mrs Anderson led us through the doorway and into the relevant coolness of the house. A large fan whirred above us, hanging from a dark wooden ceiling. The tiles underfoot felt cool after the dusty heat outside. Mr Anderson rose from the chair in the corner, beside a dresser overflowing with books and ornaments jostling for position. He was a giant of a man, taller and broader than my Ed but with the same rich brown eyes, although grey strands streaked through his rich chestnut hair. It struck me that at least I knew how Ed would look like as an older man and I was impressed.

"So... this is Lizzie," he said. "I must say, we are mighty pleased to meet you at last. We thought our Ed was making you up."

We all laughed, with the notable exception of Ed's mother. Ed pretended not to notice as he fussed around, getting me settled on the sofa, before bringing my bags upstairs.

"So, Lizzie," Mrs Anderson sat opposite her, her pale hands folded neatly in her lap, "Ed tells us you left your mother and a brother back in Ireland?"

"That's right, Mrs Anderson."

She sat upright and stared directly into my eyes.

"I hope you realise that Ed cannot possibly support your family as well as a wife..."

"That's enough of that now, Edna," Mr Anderson interrupted. "Lizzie has only just arrived. What impression are you giving her of American hospitality?"

"It has nothing to do with hospitality, Bart. Lizzie is our son's wife, and as such, she is very welcome in our home but..."

"But nothing, dear. Let's leave this conversation for another time."

Mr Anderson flashed a warm smile at me as Mrs Anderson rose from her seat, her lips pursed together, and swept out of the room. Ed had warned me that his mother could be rather cold at times, that she was not overly demonstrative, but he never mentioned that she could be openly hostile, leaving me seriously worried. My fears must have shown on my face for Mr Anderson tapped me on the shoulder.

"Don't worry, Lizzie. My wife has her son on a pedestal. She'll come round, once she gets to know you."

His reassuring smile eased my fears and Ed's reappearance banished them completely.

Chapter 22

Black and White

We found a house not far from Ed's childhood home. My relationship with my mother in-law improved but I knew we would never have the closeness that I craved. I missed my family. I missed Mrs Buckley although she wrote regularly, filling me in on the demands of her well-heeled clients. Aunt Jean's letters were the most poignant. Raising her grandchild was so hard, yet just what she needed to get her up every morning. Losing Aíne was so sudden, so awful for everyone, but especially for Aunt Jean.

When Ma wrote about how busy she was helping to look after baby Scott and how well Jimmy was getting on in school, I said a prayer of thanks. The two sisters were always close, but their grief bound them tighter. Part of me missed Primrose Cottage but not the bricks and mortar. It was the tight-knit family childhood I had there that I missed. Those memories will always live with me, but those memories are tainted by Maggie's death for all of us. Ma wrote that she was glad to leave it and swore never to set foot in the Knockrath estate again for as long as she lived. I agreed with my mother, and it took me an awfully long time to change my mind.

The Keeper of Secrets

Me and Ed set up home with furniture donated from family and friends. We didn't care. It was as near to perfect as I imagined life could be. At times I pinched myself I felt so lucky, so fortunate to settle in such a beautiful place with such a perfect man. Ed found a job on the docks which took him away at times and I missed him terribly. His sisters were my greatest allies. Even though they were younger than me they became firm friends. When Ed was away either Angela or Kate stayed with me. I wasn't sure if that was a request from Ed to make sure I wasn't alone or his mother so she could keep an eye on me.

The community we lived in was small and friendly. The Andersons were well known. Bart was ex-military as were a lot of our neighbours. The local shops we frequented were small and full of produce that was totally alien to me. It was a steep learning curve, but I embraced the challenge.

I remember the first day I noticed the segregation of the races. Coming from Ireland I had never seen a black person. I hadn't given any thought to race, mainly because I had absolutely no experience of it. In Ireland we were Irish or English, all white people. Some rich, mostly poor, but all Caucasian.

In America there were no blacks in our immediate neighbourhood. I'm ashamed to say I was living there for weeks before I noticed. To be fair to myself I was so busy setting up home with Ed, I didn't get the chance to explore the town, outside of our close-knit community. One day Ed brought me into town to a restaurant he liked. Walking up the main street, I noticed the sign: 'Whites only'. I was baffled at first until Ed explained, then I didn't know what to think.

"Florida was a confederate state," Ed said. "Up north, the yanks may have passed laws giving blacks equal rights, but each state makes their own laws. Here in Florida, blacks and whites are kept separate. They have their own shops, we have ours. Same with schools, barber shops, restaurants, housing."

We passed the bus station. Sure enough, there were two signs, one proudly proclaiming, 'White waiting room', the other, 'Coloured waiting room'. I didn't know what to make of it. My confusion must have shown on my face.

"It's always been that way, Lizzie."

What could I say? It was the first hint that my perceived land of opportunity didn't offer the same possibilities to everyone. Certainly not to people of colour. It altered how I felt about my adopted country. But I accepted it as there was absolutely nothing I could do about it. My priority was to be the perfect wife for this perfect man I had married.

There was just one glitch in our perfect lives, and it was a big one. Every month I waited with bated breath, hoping that this was it and every month I cursed when the familiar stomach cramps started. People stopped asking about when we were going to start a family. One small mercy. Mrs Anderson was surprisingly supportive.

"I didn't like to say anything, Lizzie, but I had wondered about it. You seem so maternal at times I thought you would have had a baby by now. I know myself from personal experience that these things can take some time."

Mrs Anderson's sudden understanding caught me by surprise, and I burst into tears. My monthly had arrived that morning, after a delay of several days when I had hoped that maybe, just maybe I was pregnant, but the stains on my underwear and the cramps in my stomach told me otherwise. My emotions were all over the place and I confided my fears in my mother-in-law.

"I have tried so hard. I eat well, don't lift anything heavy, look after Ed's every need. It's been a year now and nothing. No sign of a baby and I want to give Ed a child so badly."

"Now, Lizzie, try not to be downhearted. If it is meant to be, it will happen. It took a long time for me to fall pregnant with Ed. Why, we were married almost three years before he was born. Sometimes these things just take time."

She patted my hand as she spoke and for the first time there was a spark of something between us, a bond of some sort. Our shared experience finally broke the barrier she had erected before we had even met. Something we were both grateful for.

Chapter 23

Letters

Letters from home were like manna from heaven. Ma wrote every month like clockwork. Her letters filled with stories about Aíne's baby Scott. Already two years old, he ruled the Queenstown household. She wrote of how his first word was 'mama', which broke his grandma's heart for the poor child's mama wasn't there to hear it. She wrote of how he raced to hug his grandad the second he walked in the front door, sometimes nearly knocking Uncle Pat over as he hugged his knees, the highest part of his grandad he could reach.

His father sent money every few months. Aunt Jean put it aside for his education and wrote to Scott asking him to visit his son. Although Ma scolded her for inviting Scott back to Ireland. I could understand why. Ma wrote that Aunt Jean felt she was doing the right thing by the child inviting his father to see him but at the same time she prayed that he wouldn't accept her invitation, afraid that once he set eyes on him, he would take him back to America. Ma said Aunt Jean couldn't bear to part with him, her one link to Aíne. She also said it would break her heart too because she loved him like her own.

While I loved to hear how endearing Aíne's little boy was, I hated how conflicted I felt. I missed Aíne. She was a huge part of my life. We'd had so many plans, so many hopes and dreams wrapped around Scott and Ed. Guilt nibbled at the edges of my happiness with Ed. I was living the new life we had dreamed of, while Aíne lay buried in Ireland, in the old country. Aíne's baby was motherless while I... well, I wanted to be a mother more than anything in the world but couldn't. Life felt so unfair.

Of course, when I reasoned it all out in my head, I recognised how lucky I was. I had been given the opportunity of a new life and I intended to grab it with both hands. Ed loved me dearly. Almost as much as I loved him. He was a good husband, attentive, loving. I couldn't ask for more. Well, that's not quite true. A baby would make our lives complete.

But I was starting to think it wasn't to be. I was trying to come to terms with that fact, albeit reluctantly, but I had always been practical. There was no point in harping after something you couldn't have. If I wasn't meant to be a mother, then so be it. My ma used to say, 'what is for you won't go by you' and I believed that old saying. I just needed to find out what my role in life was meant to be. The most important role for me was my role as Ed's wife. I excelled. Our home was spotless, comfortable and welcoming. I inherited my ma's cooking skills and embellished them with Ed's favourite American foods. Ed didn't want me working but with no baby on the horizon I had time on my hands.

Word spread quite early on that I was a dab hand with a needle and thread. Ed's sisters were the first to discover my dressmaking skills and certainly made the most of them. Every day someone called by, hoping I could mend a seam, let out a dress, remake a collar. At first, I wouldn't accept payment, but people left tokens of their appreciation. Ed never knew what delicacy he would come home to. We had mangos, plantains, buckets of corn, depending on what was in season. Growing up in West Cork I had never laid eyes on a mango let alone a plantain, and it took a while for me to discover the tastiest way to serve it. My mother-in-law helped but her cooking skills were dubious at best. Even Mrs Anderson appreciated my cooking.

I wrote home about cooking these exotic fruits and vegetables. A far cry from the carrots and spuds we grew behind the cottage. There were days I missed Ireland so much I could practically taste the spuds, cooked in their skins with the freshly churned butter melting into the fluffy white flesh. I longed for a soft wet day, when the raindrops drizzled, keeping the grass damp yet springy. You could walk in your bare feet and feel the grass tickle.

Florida was unbearably hot. Constant, all year round, sunshine. When it rained it poured. Heavy downpours that danced off the baked earth. The grass was green in places, but it was hard, spiky shards that hurt your feet. Ten minutes after the downpour the ground was dry again. In the beginning I thought I would never get accustomed to it. But it's amazing how quickly you can adapt to whatever life throws at you.

When Ma wasn't writing about baby Scott, she wrote about Jimmy. It was hard to believe Ireland was still at war. The year after the end of the Great War, Ireland waged war against Great Britain. It was brewing when I left for the States. The Irish set up their own government, Dáil Éireann; the British refused to recognise it and the two sides went to war. Jimmy joined the West Cork Brigade and fought against the forces of the crown. After that he only went home occasionally. Ma was worried sick. On the nights he did arrive home he was exhausted, physically and mentally. He ate and rested, just enough to slip back out again under the cover of darkness.

Jimmy's letters were intermittent out of necessity rather than out of any reluctance to keep in touch. He was fighting with the Third Battalion of the West Cork Brigade. That didn't leave him the time nor opportunity to write to his sister. I worried about him, but I understood his reasons. When I wrote to him, I begged him to stay safe, reminding him that he carried our family name. He wrote that he believed in his general, a Cork man, Michael Collins, and would gladly follow him to the ends of the earth in the fight for Irish freedom. I hoped and prayed for their success, but I couldn't see how a few thousand Irish men could hold back the might of the British Empire.

But they did. I couldn't believe it when I heard the news. Jimmy wrote that it was a tense time in Ireland. While there was a ceasefire in place, they still had to work out a treaty with the British. It was nearly Christmas before the treaty was signed but it wasn't the deal they'd wanted or expected. I wasn't surprised. The English had never treated the Irish fairly. Why did they expect them to change now? But I didn't expect the country to fall into civil war over the treaty. I read reports in the news as well as the letters from Jimmy. I feared for my brother.

When Jimmy wrote to me about Knockrath Manor, I swear I had to read it three times to take it all in. Even then I couldn't quite fathom how such a thing had happened and said as much to Ed.

"I still can't believe it. Jimmy said the IRA set fire to Knockrath Manor."

"Was anyone at home at the time?"

"Jimmy said Ralph was there. The rest of the family were in England. He said they let Ralph leave and then set fire to the house."

"There will be serious repercussions after that. I mean, it's destruction of property."

"Jimmy said lots of the big houses were targeted. It's not just Knockrath Manor."

"Well, it's good that your mother is safe with your Aunt Jean in Queenstown. Imagine if she were still in the cottage on the estate with all that violence raging around her."

Ed was right. I had a lot to be grateful for. If Ma was still living in the cottage on the Knockrath estate, she would have been totally alone for the past few years. Jimmy joined the West Cork Brigade of the IRA at the very beginning of the war against the British. He rarely put his head down in the same place twice. I was lucky to hear from him at all.

Chapter 24
Angela

Angela started dating a naval officer. Mrs Anderson was impressed by his uniform and his yankee accent, but Mr Anderson wasn't so sure. He thought Vinnie Fisher was a poser and too full of himself. Ed agreed but everyone held their tongue, hoping it would fizzle out. At nineteen Angela was a stunner, dark shiny hair that framed rich molten eyes which continually danced with devilment. She had a zest for life that worried her mother but underneath she was so sweet. Vinnie preyed on her innocence. Of that there was no doubt. He swept her off her feet and then left her when she needed him most.

She confided in me one night in late October. Ed was away on an overnight and Mrs Anderson had arranged for Angela to stay with me. She was later than usual, but I wasn't too worried for I knew she was meeting Vinnie. The moment Angela opened the door I knew something was wrong. Her eyes were red from crying, her face mottled and patchy. I rushed to her side and led her into the kitchen. Angela laid her head on the table and sobbed, while I rubbed her back and waited on her tears to subside.

"What is it? Is it Vinnie? What has he done?"

She sobbed louder and I became increasingly worried.

"Will I get your mother, Angela?"

"No." The high-pitched squeal made me step back.

"Okay, okay."

I got her some water and raided Ed's collection of pocket handkerchiefs. Shaking open a freshly laundered one I handed it to Angela.

"What happened? What is it?"

"Oh, Lizzie," she sobbed. "What am I gonna do?"

Angela laid her head on the table and sobbed inconsolably. I sat beside her, rubbing her back gently until the sobs faded again and Angela gradually sat up straight.

"Vinnie finished with me." Her voice little more than a whisper. "He's gone... back to Boston."

"Oh dear. My darling girl. Perhaps you can keep in touch..." Angela cut her off in mid-sentence.

"No, it's over. He told me in no uncertain terms that he never wants to see me again."

"How cruel. He doesn't deserve you."

"I think I'm having his ba..." Angela's face contorted as she tried to spit the words out. "I'm late, very late, at least two months late. What am I gonna do?"

"Oh no," I said. "You must tell him. He will do the right thing by you."

"No, you don't understand. That's why he doesn't want anything to do with me. I told him and..." Angela gulped huge intakes of breath to steady herself. "He... he said he wanted nothing to do with me... said he wasn't ready for marriage and a baby, that I got myself into this mess and I could get myself out of it."

"Oh, dear me, my poor girl. How dreadful for you."

I put my arms around the distraught Angela and rocked her slowly as she wept. Eventually I put her to bed with a hot-water

The Keeper of Secrets

bottle and sat with her until she fell into a fitful sleep. My thoughts were in turmoil. I tried to analyse her feelings but couldn't as one emotion after the other tumbled through my mind. Spikes of jealousy mixed with spikes of outrage. Three years I had hoped and prayed for a baby but here I was, a husband who loved me, a comfortable home and childless. Angela, a single woman, a man who deserted her and her unborn child, and a mother who will likely never forgive her.

My feelings of jealousy sickened me. How could I even contemplate feeling the slightest bit of jealousy towards poor Angela? She was so distraught, so lost. The father of her child, the man she loved, had treated her in such an ungentlemanly and cruel fashion. What kind of man would take full advantage of Angela's loving nature and then discard her when she no longer suited him? Ed had been right not to trust him.

Which led me on to my mother-in-law. I couldn't even anticipate how she would react. Her unmarried daughter carrying a child, alone and abandoned. I remembered an incident shortly after I arrived in Florida, when we were still living with my in-laws. A neighbour's daughter, much the same age as Angela is now, fell pregnant to a naval officer, who promptly transferred to another base. Mrs Anderson slated the family: the mother hadn't adequately supervised her daughter, the daughter was too free and easy with her affections. Worse still, the girl was nothing more than a floozy with no respect for herself or her family. Mrs Anderson nodded greetings in public to the girl's mother but discreetly dropped the entire family from her social circle, ostracising them quietly but very efficiently. I pondered how my mother-in-law would react to this news. It smacked of poetic justice in one way. Maybe Mrs Anderson might gain some understanding of how badly she had treated her neighbour, or maybe she would not see the comparison. The woman was so narrow-minded, so set in her ways. Her strict Catholic upbringing had a lot to do with it.

I slept fitfully that night and woke feeling anxious. Angela was already in the kitchen when I got there.

"Coffee?"

"Yes please."

Angela took a cup from the open shelving and poured some hot coffee for me. The evidence of a sleepless night was all over Angela's face.

"It's just as well you were staying with me last night. We can't let your mother see you looking like that."

Angela's smile resembled a grimace as her eyes filled again. I let her cry.

"I can't be a mother, Lizzie. How can I bring up a child? Even if Vinnie had said he would stand by me, I don't want a baby." She raised her tear-stained face. "What am I gonna do. What will become of me?" She laid her head in her arms and bawled.

I flinched. Hearing my sister-in-law say she didn't want her baby wounded me deeply. Becoming pregnant, carrying a baby, had become my obsession. I wanted to become a mother so badly it hurt. Once again, I felt the pangs of jealousy. My faith was tested. How could God let this happen? An unmarried, deeply unhappy Angela carrying a child, while me and Ed, who wanted a child desperately, couldn't conceive. Where was the natural justice in that? I tried to dismiss all negative thoughts and concentrate instead on easing Angela's distress.

"Best to let it all out," I said. "We'll figure something out. Don't worry."

Even as I uttered the words, I started to worry. What could we do? Sweet, gentle Angela could not stand up to her mother. Once Edna Anderson found out the awful truth, she'd throw Angela out into the street. Although Ed would take her in. Of

The Keeper of Secrets

that I had no doubt. Ed would never abandon his sister. It wasn't in his nature. While that would solve the short-term problem of a roof over her head, it still wouldn't help Angela. A single woman raising a child was unheard of. Angela would be a social outcast amongst her own friends and family. Of course, it would be different if I were carrying a child.

The gem of an idea started to form in my head. Angela had stated clearly that she had no wish to raise a child. The simple solution would be for me and Ed to raise Angela's baby as our own. I just had to figure out a way to do that without anyone finding out, especially Mrs Anderson.

Chapter 25

The Plan

It was obvious that we would have to act quickly. Angela was already two months gone. In another two months she would be unable to hide her changing body from her eagle-eyed mother. When I told Ed about Angela's predicament his first reaction was to want to track down Vinnie and make him marry his sister.

"That damned jerk. How dare he. I swear, I'll make him pay."

"But, Ed. He's no good. You never liked him. Why would you want your sister to marry such a man?" I said. "He has treated her so badly. He's hardly likely to change. If anything, if you force him to marry Angela, he will be horrible to her."

"But, Lizzie, what are we to do? You know what people are like. This is totally messed up. Angela is ruined. My mother will flip when she finds out. She'll worry more about what other people will say than she will about what's best for Angela."

Ed paced the floor, running his hands through his hair, then stopped, a horrified expression on his face.

"Oh Lord, she's likely to kick Angela out of the house."

"What if we managed to keep Angela's condition a secret?" I said.

"How? It's gonna be pretty obvious fairly soon."

"It's simple really. Although it does mean Angela will have to go away for a while. Do you remember me telling you about my friend Nuala? The girl who lives in Virginia. Her in-laws help young girls like Angela. She can live with them until she's ready to give birth. After that they will help her place the child with a family. Angela returns home. No one need ever know."

"Would Nuala do that for us?"

"Yes, well I need to write to her first, but yes, I'm fairly confident she will help."

"Have you spoken to Angela about this? How does Angela feel about it?"

"She's okay with it. It means she will need to invent a position in the hotel, but Nuala should be able to help with that as well."

"You've really put some thought into this, huh?" Ed said. "It sounds like it just might work. Although I hate letting that scoundrel off the hook for treating my sister that way."

"I know, *mo ghrá*, but for Angela's sake, it's best if she just forgets she ever met him."

Ed smiled, lifted my hands to his lips and kissed them.

"You're right, honey. Dealing with all of this must be hard for you. I know how much you want a child."

I gulped. This was my opportunity to tell Ed the plan that was running around my head. It was a throwaway comment by Angela that first planted the idea, but I couldn't get it out of my head.

"Yes, Ed. I want a child, and I don't know why it hasn't happened yet. Although maybe, just maybe, this is God's plan." I inhaled, squeezed his hands and looked directly into those dark eyes I loved so much. "What if we are meant to raise this child as our own?"

Ed stared at me as if I had lost my mind.

"What on earth are you talking about?"

"It's a baby, Ed. An innocent little baby whose father doesn't want to know, being carried by a young woman who doesn't want to be a mother. Not yet anyway. We could give that child a loving home. Me and you."

Ed sat heavily on the kitchen chair. He stared at me; his eyes crinkled as he shook his head.

"I know you want a baby, Lizzie. We both do, but do you really want to bring up another man's bastard?"

"Don't say that, Ed. This will be your sister's child. It will share your blood, your heritage. It is an innocent in all of this. Besides, do you think this is the first time something like this has happened? Girls get in the family way all the time. Do you think they all end up on the street?"

"But... but how, Lizzie? How can we hide Angela... or you, for that matter? Are you intending passing this child off as your own? How?"

"I haven't figured it all out yet. I wanted to talk to you first, find out if it's something you would consider. We both have to want to do this, Ed."

Ed paced the floor again. I kept quiet, hoping that Ed would come to the same realisation that I had. This could be our only chance to become parents. I watched Ed pace, a myriad of expressions passing his face as he thought through my proposal. He stopped and stared at me.

"There are openings in the navel yard up there, immediate start. They were talking about it last week in the cafeteria. Some of the lads were saying that the money is good, but the job is only temporary. I think it's for twelve months."

I threw my arms around Ed. "That's wonderful news."

Ed kissed me softly. "Honey, are you sure about this?"

"I've never been more certain of anything in my whole life. Are you sure? Can you live with bringing up this child as our own?"

"Yeah, I'm sure," Ed said. "We'll need to work out the finer details, but I think this just might work. We could tell Mom that we're bringing Angela with us. That she's heartbroken and the change of scene would do her good."

Convincing Mrs Anderson had been easier than I thought it would be. Ed's mother believed his story about getting a promotion. When I told her that I had a friend living in the same town who had offered me a job in her hotel, she was delighted for me.

"That's wonderful, dear. I will miss you both, but it sounds like too good an opportunity to miss," Mrs Anderson said.

Mr Anderson was equally supportive. "Nice spot, Virginia. Bit different to Florida but nice scenery all the same."

"It sounds great, Lizzie," Angela said.

That was the opening we had agreed on. As if the idea had only just occurred to me, I spoke with great enthusiasm.

"Why don't you come with us, Angela? I know Nuala is looking for more staff. It would make a nice change for you. If it doesn't work out, you can always come back home."

"Oh, that sounds ideal," Angela said. "What do you think, Mom?"

"I don't know. I mean..."

"Ah, Mom, that would be great. She would be company for Lizzie. And you've no need to worry about Angela. I'll look after her," Ed said.

She didn't need much more convincing after that. We were well rehearsed beforehand, anticipating every objection she might have. By the end of the evening, it was agreed that Angela would travel with us. The next evening Ed arrived home with a work colleague who wanted to rent our house for the year we would be away. A lovely chap, with a pretty young wife who was looking for a place to rent while they were waiting on their home to be built. It was as if it were meant to be. Within a few weeks we were living in Virginia.

Nuala was as good as her word. She met us off the train and brought us to our new home. The house was small, two bedrooms off a central room. It reminded me of our first home, the cottage in Queenstown. While it was basic, it was spotlessly clean with a homely feel. With the addition of a few of our personal possessions I was confident that I could make this our home for the next twelve months.

Until then I never knew how many young women ended up in the same predicament as poor Angela. Neither did Nuala until she'd married into the Kelland family. At least twice a year a young girl stayed with them and was looked after until after the birth of her baby. Some of the young women kept their babies, passing themselves off as young widows, their imaginary husband killed in some awful accident they can't bear to talk about. Sometimes I wondered if the awful deaths they made up for these men were the deaths they wished on the fathers of their children. It would be just reward for abandoning them the way they did.

Others, usually the younger ones, enlisted the Kellands' help in placing their baby with a family, who brought that child up as their own. Mrs Kelland was a tiny dynamo of a woman. What she lacked in height she made up for in personality. She had the energy and drive of a woman half her age. Her heart-shaped face was framed by silver hair always caught loosely at the back of her neck with an ornate comb, her one extravagance.

Angela took to her straight away, pouring out her heart and soul. Mrs Kelland listened to her as if she were the only person in her universe, and the first girl she had encountered who was pregnant and single. She had a way of turning every problem into a possibility. The more I got to know Mrs Kelland, the more I liked her. The more I wanted to be like her.

Two months after we arrived, Ed wrote to his mother informing her that I was expecting a baby. He didn't lie to her. We were expecting a baby, just not in the usual way. Mrs Anderson hated to travel so we knew she wouldn't even suggest travelling to Virginia for a visit. Once a month Ed wrote his mother a letter. Her reply arrived two weeks later. They were short letters. A formal enquiry after our health, especially mine. A line on Ed's father, a line about Kate, the latest news about the neighbours and then advice on a healthy pregnancy. I admit that I did feel guilty reading her good advice and best wishes on my pregnancy. We both did.

"I know we're doing the right thing, Lizzie," Ed said. "But I can't help but feel a bit guilty for lying to my mom."

"I do too, Ed, but what choice do we have?" I pulled him to me. "This may be our only chance to have a baby. If Angela had any doubt about this, I would support her. The Kellands would support her. But she doesn't. She wants us to bring up this baby as much as we do."

Ed sat down and gestured for me to sit beside him. Facing me, he took my hands in his.

"Honey, have you thought about how we are gonna manage all that?" Ed hesitated. "I mean, when we go back to Pensacola."

He cleared his throat. "What if Angela finds it difficult to be so close to her child and unable to acknowledge that she is its mom?"

"It won't be easy, Ed, I won't pretend otherwise. It would be foolish to think this will not be difficult for all of us. But it can be done."

"Do you think Angela has thought it through properly?" Ed said.

"Yes, she has. We had this exact conversation only last week with Mrs Kelland. As she said, preparation is key. Going into this arrangement with the right frame of mind is important. But we aren't the first family to come up with this type of solution. Mrs Kelland has seen it many times over the years. Sometimes it's the parents who take on their daughter's child and raise it as their own. Sometimes it's siblings like us."

"I suppose that's true. It would be foolish to think Angela was the first girl who fell pregnant like this."

"Although I must say, Ed, I am really surprised by how frequently it happens. There are so many young girls who come through this place. How many other families like the Kellands are out there?"

"Far more than either of us thought anyway, that's for sure."

With that sobering thought we went back to work. I was helping out in the hotel. As was Angela. We worked in the background, in the laundry, washing, drying and mending sheets. It was a small commercial hotel. Busy with travelling salesmen. It was a pleasant place to work. The staff were friendly, the work not overly strenuous. I made sure that Angela got enough rest and the best nutrition. After all, she was carrying our precious, so much wanted, child. All through Angela's pregnancy I put on weight and wore loose clothing. Not that it mattered. We stayed in the background of the hotel, not seen by the patrons, aided by the Kelland family. They didn't hire outsiders. It was perfect for our needs.

Chapter 26

Michael

Michael Edward Anderson was born on 28th May 1923. A healthy, bawling baby boy with ruddy cheeks, ten fingers, ten toes and a head of dark hair. I stayed with Angela, holding her hand, coaching her through it. My only other experience of childbirth was when Aíne gave birth so I was terrified but couldn't let Angela see that. Mrs Kelland was an able midwife. She steered Angela through it all with a cool head and a firm hand. When Angela birthed the baby, Mrs Kelland checked him over, wiped the gunk off him, swaddled him and placed him in my arms. I looked over hesitantly at Angela, exhausted in the bed, but she smiled at me and blew me a kiss.

"Go on, Lizzie. He's your baby," she said.

It was as if I didn't quite believe it was true until she uttered those words. I suppose in the back of my head I had prepared myself for the possibility that Angela would change her mind and want to keep her baby once she laid eyes on him. But she appeared more determined than ever.

I sat and cuddled my baby, until his cries eased. He was perfect. Complete love for this baby overwhelmed me from the first second he was placed in my arms. The fact that I didn't give birth to him didn't change the way I felt about him. He was mine. My baby. My son. And I adored him. We christened him Michael, after my father, and gave him Edward for his middle name. We debated about asking Angela to be his godmother.

"Is it too much to ask from her?" I said.

"I think she would appreciate being asked."

In the end we asked her but specified that we would understand completely if she didn't want to be so involved in Michael's life.

"Oh my Lord, I would be delighted. Are you sure?"

"Yes, of course we're sure. Are you?"

"I am thrilled," she said. Her beaming smile was testament to how happy she was. Nearly as happy as we were that she wanted to be involved in Michael's life. Angela gave us a precious gift and I will always be grateful to her.

We dithered over what to feed him. Angela did offer to feed him herself, but Mrs Kelland advised against it. I was inclined to agree with her but at the end of the day I only wanted what was best for Michael. In the end we settled on SMA formula milk. Michael took to his bottles, and I had the pleasure of feeding him. Sitting in my chair, Michael snuggled against my chest as I fed and winded him, his contented gurgles music to my soul.

Ed adored him. He hung over his bassinet every evening, admiring his downy cheeks and his shock of dark hair. Our son was very much loved and wanted. Our lives together were complete. It felt so right.

We worried about Angela of course. It took her a while to bounce back after the birth. She threw herself into work in the hotel, taking over most of my work as well as her own, giving me time to look after the baby. Mrs Kelland helped. She kept an eye on her, made sure she was eating right, but more importantly feeling right about giving us her baby.

The Keeper of Secrets

"She is fine with her decision, Lizzie," Mrs Kelland reassured me over tea and apple pie.

"Are you sure? I'm just so worried about her. What if having the baby has resurrected all those feelings she had for Vinnie Fisher? That scoundrel who put her in this position. She did love him once."

"Don't even mention his name. An excuse for a man, that's what he is," Mrs Kelland said. "Angela may have loved him once, but she doesn't anymore. Love has to be nurtured, shared between two people, for it to survive. Her love for that guy never had a chance because it was never reciprocated. He used her, then abandoned her."

"I hope you're right. I really do."

"Look how things turned out. You and Ed have your little family. The precious little boy has a mother and a father who will cherish him. And as for Angela, she knows she has made the right decision. Not only for her but for that little baby."

Mrs Kelland was right of course. Angela bounced back. A little heavier, a little wiser but the old bubbly Angela emerged again, and we welcomed her back.

Michael was six months old when we made the journey back to Pensacola. We were all sad to leave the Kellands. Nuala was a true friend whose generosity I will always treasure. As for Mrs Kelland, we all cried when we said our goodbyes. Such a dynamo of a woman, she was an example to us all and we swore to keep in touch.

Back home we were treated to a hero's welcome. Our house had been sublet while we were away. The tenants had looked after it well and left it in good condition. That wasn't enough for Mrs Anderson. With Kate's help they got it ready for us, cleaning it and polishing the floors and windows. As a final touch they strung the veranda with bunting and a large 'welcome home' sign.

Mrs Anderson cooed over Michael. It was touching to see her usually cross features soften when she looked at him.

"Why, Lizzie. Such a gorgeous boy. The spit of his father, of course. He looks just like Ed did as a baby."

"He's a real Anderson all right, Mom." Angela grinned.

Which he was. We were not telling any lies in that regard. It helped that he looked like the Andersons. Not one person doubted his parentage. Not Ed's parents or any of the neighbours and friends. Our secret was safe.

Chapter 27

Catherine McCarthy

The fact that Ma lived on another continent made it easy to keep the secret from her. I felt guilty writing that first letter home, announcing his birth, but leaving out the fact that I didn't give birth to him. After that it became so much easier. When I wrote to her, telling her every detail of Michael's life, I wrote as a doting mother and that is what I was. I adored that child, loved every inch of his sweet little body. The facts of his birth disappeared into the inner regions of my mind. To me, he was mine. I was his mother, Ed his father. We adored him.

There were days I wished I could talk to my mother face to face. I missed her advice. At times I was at a loss to know what to do with this little life I held in my arms. Was I feeding him right? Was I holding him right? Was he teething? Was he sick? Mrs Anderson assured me I was a great mother, that I had taken to motherhood like a duck to water, but I missed my mother. Ireland was so far away and the possibility of ever seeing her again was so remote.

She wrote to me every month without fail. Sometimes her letters were only one page long, but I treasured that page. Writing back was difficult at times. Between looking after our baby and keeping the household my days were long. But I was the happiest I had ever been. I loved being a mother, took pleasure in every bottle, every spoon feed. Hanging his washing on the line gave me joy. I sang as I swept the floor. Every evening Ed arrived home to a joyful household. His joy matched mine. We both felt blessed, humbled even by how happy we were.

Then a few months later I got the letter from Aunt Jean. I opened it, smiling broadly, anticipating all the frivolous news from Queenstown. How her girls were doing, stories about her grandchildren. Aunt Jean loved to pass on the gossip. I had to read the letter twice for it to make sense to me. My mother was dead. Aunt Jean wrote to tell me my mother was dead. She said it was sudden. Mum wasn't ill, no warning signs at all. She just keeled over in the kitchen and was dead before she hit the floor. As I read her words for the second time, I felt my knees buckle under me. I slowly sank to the floor with the letter still clutched in my hand.

When Ed arrived in from work, I was still sitting in the middle of the kitchen floor staring blankly at the letter. Michael played around my feet with a saucepan lid and a wooden spoon. I was totally oblivious, totally shocked, catatonic I suppose you'd call it.

"Lizzie, what is it? What's wrong?" Ed joined me on the floor.

Wordlessly I handed him the letter. I couldn't articulate its contents. My mind was numb. The words, *your mother is dead*, circulated round and round in a never-ending loop. I couldn't get past those words.

"Oh, Lizzie." Ed pulled me into his arms. "I'm so sorry, honey."

I looked at him, but I couldn't comprehend what he was saying. It was almost as if I had lost my mind, albeit temporarily.

The Keeper of Secrets

I couldn't function. Ed pulled me to my feet and led me to a chair. He set about making me a strong cup of tea. Michael was tired and hungry at that stage. He pulled at my skirts, calling me, "Mama, Mama."

It was his voice that penetrated my brain. It felt like someone was calling me out of a deep dream. The world was quiet with only the words on the page circulating, then suddenly I heard my baby's calls, the kettle boiling on the stove, the chickens outside in the henhouse clucking in annoyance at something.

"My mother is dead," I said to no one in particular. "I am an orphan."

"You are not alone, honey," Ed said. "You have me. You have Michael."

I gasped. It felt like my life up until that point danced in front of my brain. The pain when Maggie died. My mother's anguish. My father's anger. Aunt Jean and her calming presence. Introducing Ed to my family. Aíne dying. The journey across the sea leaving everything and everyone I had ever known behind me. I looked down at my son, tugging on my skirts. Lifting him into my arms I inhaled his sweet baby breath. Tears choked me and I let them fall. Michael became upset and I couldn't bear that.

"It's okay, baby. Mama is okay. Let's get you some dinner, yes?"

My son smiled at me. A wary, uncertain smile followed by a hug. Ed squeezed my shoulder and with that touch, I felt his love and support. I couldn't wallow in my grief. Yes, I'd had a dreadful shock. It was so unexpected. But the shock had now subsided. Painful, intense grief would follow but for now I had a family to look after.

After we ate and I had settled Michael for the night, we sat on the veranda, listening to the crickets in the distance. I read

Aunt Jean's letter again. This time I cried. I couldn't stop the flow. Ed held me and let me cry until I couldn't cry anymore.

"I knew this day would come but I didn't expect it to happen like this," I said. "I knew the day I left Queenstown I would never see her again. But... I suppose a part of me hoped."

Ed listened, one arm around my shoulder, the other holding a spare handkerchief.

"These past few years have been so hard on her. We were so happy in Primrose Cottage. She was so happy. Her and Da sang and danced. Don't get me wrong, they worked hard but they were happy." Another sob escaped me as memories flooded back.

"And then Maggie. Ma was so angry. When Maggie died, she lost her mind for a while. I swear she did. Aunt Jean brought her back to us."

With the memory of those months when Aunt Jean moved into Primrose Cottage came the memory of Jimmy as a young boy.

"Poor Jimmy. We lost our sister, then our Da, now Ma. I have you and Michael, but Jimmy has no one." The thoughts of Jimmy brought a fresh onslaught of tears.

Ed turned to me, his earnest face in shadow, his eyes deep pools. "Write to Jimmy. Tell him to come to us. There's nothing to keep him in Ireland anymore."

A faint stirring of hope wound around my chest. Jimmy, here in Florida. My brother living here with me. A yearning for home threatened to overwhelm me. That familiar wave of homesickness. In Ireland at this time of year, the farm workers would be flat out baling hay. Every field would have rolls of golden bales waiting to be taken away. Another month and the leaves on the trees would slowly change from worn-out green to gold, yellow and russet. The fun we had as children playing in the fallen leaves that settled on the ground around the cottage

The Keeper of Secrets

like a blanket in the autumn. There was a crispness in the air, berries on the hedges and full pantries.

Living in subtropical Florida, my son would never experience late summer or autumn the way I did. But when I found myself thinking like that, I reminded myself that he would have other memories about his childhood. They would be just as precious as mine, only different.

Ed was right. I needed my brother here with me. With Ma and Da both gone and the war over, there was nothing to keep him in Ireland. He needed a new direction. I was sure he would find it here in America. The land of opportunity.

Chapter 28

Jimmy

When Jimmy wrote to say he had booked his passage to America my heart leapt. It had been five years since I had set eyes on him. He was sailing into New York in August and planned to visit friends there but promised to make his way to Florida within a few months.

I waited expectantly week after week, watching out for the postman, anxious for word on when he would arrive. By the week before Christmas, I had given up hope.

"I don't understand it, Ed, I haven't heard a word from him. Not one letter since he left Ireland. What if something has happened to him?"

"I'm sure he's fine. He's probably working, trying to get enough money to travel this far south."

"Do you think so?"

"I do, Lizzie. Jimmy is well able to look after himself. Don't forget, he spent a couple of years fighting the British, then another year fighting in that bloody civil war. Your brother will turn up here when he's good and ready."

Ed was right of course. On Christmas Eve morning I went out to the henhouse to look for eggs. I had gathered an even dozen, placing them in my wicker basket, when I heard raised voices coming from the house. Next thing the kitchen window flew open, and Michael shouted out to me.

"Mom, come quick." He closed the window quickly and disappeared from my line of vision. Tutting to myself, annoyed at being disturbed, I opened the back door.

"What is it? What's wrong?"

I didn't recognise him at first. He was taller than I remembered. His face looked older than it should have, with the look of my father about him.

"Hello, Lizzie."

His voice was deep, raw with emotion. I couldn't speak, couldn't move, frozen in the doorway staring at my not so little brother. Michael took the basket from me, touching my arm.

"Say something, Mom."

"Jimmy," I whispered.

I threw my arms around him, hugging him so tightly, slightly afraid that if I let go, he would disappear again.

"Where were you? I was so worried. I thought something had happened to you." The questions tumbled out of my mouth, one after the other, not giving him time to answer even one. Eventually over tea and boiled eggs he filled us in on his adventures travelling from New York to Florida. We sat around the table laughing and talking. Every so often I leaned over and touched him. A tap on his arm or rub of his cheek, to convince myself that it was true, Jimmy was here in our home, with me. My little brother sat at my kitchen table, and I was ecstatic.

Of course, being Christmas Eve, he was laden down with gifts for us. There was a set of tin soldiers for Michael, a hip flask full of Irish whiskey for Ed, and a beautiful shawl for me. Then he gave me our mother's wedding ring. For the second time that day I was struck dumb. I slipped the slim band of red gold onto the third finger of my right hand. It fitted perfectly.

Instantly I was transported to happier times when my parents danced around the kitchen floor. When our cottage was filled with light, love and laughter. Before Maggie died.

As if he could read my thoughts Jimmy placed his hand over mine.

"Remember Ma and Da dancing around the kitchen? You and Maggie clapping as Da sang. They were good times, Lizzie."

"They were," I said, "but..."

"No buts. These last ten years were hard but they're behind us. Time to look forward."

I couldn't wait to introduce my brother to my in-laws the following day. It was my year to host Christmas dinner. The Andersons planned to arrive shortly after noon. That gave us time to spend with Michael before Kate and Angela descended and showered him with presents. Ed's parents arrived first. Mrs Anderson sniffed her disapproval, of course but Bart Anderson made up for her hostility. Jimmy took it all in his stride and before long had my mother-in-law giggling like a schoolgirl. I was quite impressed myself. My shy little brother had grown into a very charming, articulate man. He was mid-story when Kate and Angela arrived.

"What's going on here?"

Much to my surprise, Mrs Anderson made the introductions.

"Perfect timing, girls. This is Lizzie's brother, Jimmy."

Jimmy was the perfect gentleman and the ideal dinner guest. We had a wonderful Christmas day, full of good food and pleasant conversation. Jimmy went out of his way to charm Mrs Anderson, an achievement that wasn't lost on her daughters.

"I'd swear my mother was batting her eyelashes at Jimmy at one stage," Angela said as we washed up after dinner.

"I know. It's hilarious," said Kate. I was elbow deep in hot soapy water, while Angela wiped the clean dishes and Kate put them away.

"I don't think I've ever seen Mother so enthralled with anyone. Not even Ed," Angela said. Which was a valid point. Mrs Anderson hung on her son's every word.

"He's very charming," Kate said. I caught Angela's eye. We both saw the faint blush on Kate's normally alabaster cheeks.

Angela winked at me. "Quite good-looking too."

Kate nodded and turned away to straighten up the stack of plates she had only finished putting in the cupboard. Jimmy arrived in the kitchen then, offering to help.

"Now there's a first, ladies. A man offering to help in the kitchen," Angela said.

"Ed does help out... sometimes."

"Not when Mother is in the house," Angela said.

We all laughed at that. Mrs Anderson had very set ideas on the roles of men and women, both in the home and out of it. Her daughters were constantly lectured that they were too independent for their own good, that they needed to find husbands and settle down. Lectures that both women largely ignored.

With the kitchen cleared, I brought a pot of freshly brewed coffee to the table. Kate had set the table with my best china cups while Angela cut thick slices of Christmas cake.

"Delicious, Lizzie," Jimmy said. "It tastes just like Ma's."

I basked in the praise, not just from Jimmy but from my in-laws as well. Looking around the room I reckoned it was the best Christmas ever. Good food, surrounded by people I loved. I still missed my ma and da. There wasn't a day that went by when I didn't think of them. And Maggie. But life moves on. I counted my blessings. Initially I was scared of Mrs Anderson. I came to realise that her bark was worse than her bite. Mr Anderson was a gentleman in every sense of the word, whose support from our very first meeting was unwavering. Angela and Kate were like sisters to me. They could never replace Maggie in my heart, but Maggie remained forever a child. Angela and Kate were adult sisters, best friends, confidantes. Lucky Lizzie felt apt once again. There was so much to be grateful for. A husband I loved and respected, who loved me with equal passion. A son we both idolised. And now my brother, my last link to the country of my birth, here, in my house, part of my family. It was the perfect Christmas.

Chapter 29

Hurricane

The next few years were the happiest in my life. I don't think I wore rose-tinted glasses. Having Michael in our lives changed everything for us. We had worries of course, but they were the normal ones everyone struggled with. Angela settled in and seemed quite content as a doting aunt. Florida boomed. There was massive construction, on the railways, buildings, hotels. Jimmy found work straight away, working his way up to foreman. At one stage Ed was tempted to quit the naval yard and take up work on the railroads. Thank God he didn't. That would have been a disaster for us. As I've learned since, a boom is usually followed by a bust. Florida's bust came earlier than the rest of the States. It started with a massive hurricane the autumn after Michael turned three.

Born in West Cork, the south-west of the island of Ireland, I was accustomed to strong winds and heavy rain, but nothing prepared me for the hurricane. It arrived in late September and nearly brought us to our knees. We had advance warning which Ed paid heed to, thankfully. Not everyone did pay attention to the weather warning and paid dearly for it. When Ed heard the warnings, he arrived home and started work securing our home.

When he told me to move the furniture from the veranda inside the house, I told him he was overreacting. He wasn't. Ed covered the windows with timber he had been saving to build a new shed. In the garden he tied down everything that moved. He instructed me to fill pots and kettles with water, cover them and leave them in the larder. When he told me to put the hens in the bathroom, I thought he was joking. He wasn't. Finally, he pushed the kitchen table into the centre of the room and put blankets underneath it.

Ed insisted his parents and sisters stay with us until after the hurricane passed. While the weather seemed overcast, it certainly didn't look any different to any other storm I had witnessed in the seven years I had lived in Florida. However, I had never seen Ed as worried. He worked continuously, prickly with nervous tension, barely stopping to eat or drink.

When the storm hit at first, I teased Ed. To me it felt like a winter storm in West Cork. Powerful gusts that could knock trees over and lift the odd roof tile. Then instead of lessening the winds got stronger. The wind howled and screamed, battering our house so hard I was sure it would pick us up by the foundations and carry us to the sea. A glimpse through the window between the planks of wood showed debris flying through the air. Several times the house shook as objects were fired against its walls by the force of the hurricane.

Rain lashed down, dancing on the roof so hard we could barely hear ourselves speak. Ed gathered us together and put us sitting underneath the kitchen table. It was frightening. There was a loud crash from the bedroom that could only have been a window coming in. At one stage it was so loud, so violent that I covered Michael's ears. His fearful brown eyes bore into mine as I sought to reassure him. His little heart was beating so hard I could feel it. I couldn't let him see that I was frightened, so I hugged him close to me and sang a lullaby to him. Eventually he fell asleep, his head nestled on my shoulder, but he still clung to me like a limpet.

After what felt like an eternity the storm abated. We crept out from our hiding place, still listening as the rain continued to fall but not in a deluge. Outside, the sounds of the earth settling back into place. There were bangs and crashes and the sound of water gushing until eventually we could hear birdsong.

"It's over," Ed said.

"Worse one I've witnessed," Mrs Anderson said.

"Let's survey the damage." Ed opened the door.

I gasped. Our picket fence had largely disappeared. The henhouse was in pieces. One portion of it ended up in our bedroom. It's lucky we didn't take shelter in there. The house itself was largely unharmed apart from the bedroom. One by one people emerged from their homes, shaken, anxious to see the extent of the destruction. Over the next few days, we ventured further afield. There was devastation as far as the eye could see. Trees were uprooted, buildings damaged beyond repair. The downtown area was filled with broken glass, debris and rubble.

Jimmy lived in the area that had suffered the worst damage. I was worried sick. But he got word to me the day after the hurricane hit that he was safe. It was a week before I saw Jimmy in person. His accommodation had been completely destroyed. He arrived with his case and stayed with us. It took a while to repair the damage, but we were lucky, Ed and Jimmy did most of the repair work to our house themselves. The downtown area and ports suffered major damage that took a lot longer to repair. The hurricane also put paid to the boom Florida had enjoyed, as the state went into recession, a few years earlier than the rest of the States.

It was hard. My family were protected to a certain extent. Ed's job in the naval yard bought us security despite the increasing cost of living. At least he had a wage. There were so many families who were left with nothing. Once the rebuilding work finished, construction work dried up completely for Jimmy.

I knew he had something he needed to tell me, but I was dreading it.

"I've been offered work up north, Lizzie."

"Don't go, Jimmy. Something will turn up," I begged him.

"I can't do that. I need to earn my own keep. It's not fair on Ed."

"But..."

"No buts, Lizzie. There's work up north. I'll be back, as soon as things pick up again. I promise."

I was inconsolable. Jimmy was my last, my only connection to my Irish family. Life had been so good with him in it. His easy way, his charm, his constant happy demeanour had lifted all of us. He even made Kate smile, something that was a rarity. We would all miss him.

To distract me from my grief, Ed suggested that I volunteer at a soup kitchen. I brought Michael with me when he wasn't in school. He was a happy child, even-tempered and thoughtful. There was a lot of Anderson in him thankfully. His grandfather doted on him. As for Mrs Anderson, I doubt that woman ever doted on anyone. She was definitely a cold fish. It's hard to believe she raised Ed and Angela. Kate was another story altogether. She was definitely her mother's daughter. There was a hardness to her, a puritanical streak that missed Ed and Angela altogether. I wasn't surprised when Kate joined the temperance movement. She was a force to be reckoned with.

Prohibition came into force the winter after I arrived in the States. The idea of a total ban on alcoholic drinks baffled me. I wasn't much of a drinker, but Ed enjoyed the odd bottle of beer on a Saturday night. So did most of our friends. I never witnessed drunken behaviour in any of them. Then again, money was tight. None of us had money to spare after paying for the roof over our heads and food on the table. I realised we were lucky that way. There were men who drank their wages and left their families hungry. So, from their perspective I could see why some people could be totally opposed to the sale of alcohol. But it was not something Kate had experienced in her own home or in the home of anyone we knew. It baffled me how she could be so vehemently anti-alcohol. The holier-than-thou attitude I could understand, she got that from her mother but even Mrs Anderson was at a loss to explain Kate's evangelical stance.

The year Kate turned twenty-one, her and her best friend Ferdia joined the local chapter of the Women's Temperance Society. We can only surmise that perhaps Ferdia had been affected by someone in her background with an alcohol problem. That's the only explanation we could come up with. Kate was always the quieter of the two sisters. The older she got, the more morose she became.

"Honestly, Ed, Kate gets more like your mother every day."

"Yes, she does." Ed looked thoughtful. "Although she wasn't like that when she was younger. Or maybe she was, and we just didn't notice."

We were painting the veranda, a final coat to protect the wood before the rainy season.

"When I met them first, I thought she was quieter than Angela, but something has changed in her. I noticed it when we got back from Virginia."

Ed stopped, his brush raised, and he stared at me open-mouthed.

"Do you think she suspects something? Oh, dear God, what if she knows?"

"How could she know? I don't think Angela would ever tell her. No, Ed, it's not that."

Even as I uttered the words my mind went into overdrive. Would Angela have told her sister? After all, they were so close growing up. They still were. But there were some secrets best left untold. And this was one of them. The less people aware of Michael's true parentage the better. I resolved to have a chat with Angela before the end of the week. To put my own mind at ease at least.

Angela was a regular visitor. Sometimes I thought we were closer than sisters. Although when that thought crossed my mind, I felt so guilty, as if I were replacing Maggie with Angela. I couldn't forget my sister but, in my mind, she was always a child. She was sent away when she was only a young girl of twelve. Maggie never grew up. Angela was the same age as Maggie. The grown-up version of my sister.

I waited until we were settled with a cup of tea and a scone. Even though I had been rehearsing what I needed to ask her, when the time came, I was stuck for words.

"What is it, Lizzie? Something on your mind?"

"It's Michael... or rather it's Kate..."

Angela raised her eyebrows. "Two vastly different people. Which is it?"

"Ed and I were chatting about Kate, about the whole Temperance Society thing. She's changed a lot, don't you think?"

"Definitely." Angela nodded. "She's like a different person these days. I can't figure her out. I've tried to talk to her about it but no joy. Maybe she would talk to you?"

Angela looked hopefully at me, her brown eyes carbon copies of Ed's, her expression the same as Michael's when he wanted something from me. I melted. How could I not? Angela

The Keeper of Secrets

gave me the most precious gift any woman could give another. My son. My reason for living. I would do anything for her.

"Okay." I nodded. "But before I do, is it possible that she knows why we all went to Virginia?"

Angela's hands flew to her mouth. "Oh no." She stood, blew out and shook her head. "No, Lizzie, no, there is no way she could possibly know."

"That's good. I'm glad to hear you say that."

Angela paced the kitchen floor.

"For a start, how would she find out unless one of us told her?" She wheeled around to face Lizzie. "I certainly didn't tell her, and I know neither you nor Ed would tell her. Plus, she would have said something. You know what she's like. If she knew something like that, she wouldn't be able to hold it in."

"Good." I smiled. "Sit, drink your tea. There's something going on in Kate's life we don't know about but at least we now know it's nothing to do with Michael. We just have to figure out what it is."

Chapter 30

Sundays

While Angela was a frequent visitor to our home, we only saw Kate every second Sunday when the family came to dinner at our house. The two sisters were so similar in appearance and yet so different. Despite everything she had been through Angela always had a warmth about her, a ready smile and relaxed manner. While Kate had always been quieter, shy even, these days she was as prickly as a hedgehog. Something had changed in her in the year we were in Virginia, and I was determined to get to the bottom of it.

Every second Sunday I cooked an Irish Sunday dinner for the Andersons. They had never tasted Irish-style cooking before I arrived on the scene. I had to adapt what was on offer. They'd never heard of turnip, but carrots were universal. Florida is a southern state, and they loved their southern food. Cajun seasonings, lots of rice, and plenty of garlic and spices. They favoured sweet potato over the traditional spuds I was accustomed to but I learnt how to blend the two traditions together. I made a special effort that Sunday to cook Kate's favourite meal; roast chicken, mashed potato and gravy. I always served sweet potato mash as an extra, highly seasoned with chilli

The Keeper of Secrets

and garlic, a favourite with Ed's dad. Mac and cheese as a side dish was the Anderson favourite.

Dessert was an easy option, apple tart and custard. Mrs Anderson's favourite. Even Kate looked relaxed as I cleared away the empty plates from the table.

"Thank you, Lizzie. That was delicious."

Kate lifted her plate and followed me out to the kitchen. We fell into our usual routine. As I stacked dirty plates on the left of the sink, Angela, elbow deep in soapy water, washed them and added them to the pile of clean plates growing on the draining board on her right. Kate wiped them dry and stacked them on the table ready for me to put away.

We chatted about the week just gone and our plans for the week ahead. Angela was starting a new job. When we returned from Virginia she'd found a job in a local hotel, working on the reception desk. Her bubbly personality was ideally suited to the front desk in a tourist hotel. She was exceptionally good at it. So good in fact that she was headhunted by the owners of The Haven Hotel, a newly built luxury hotel on the seafront.

"I'm excited but I'm also scared stiff," she said.

"Why would you be scared?" Kate said. "You're excellent at that type of work. That's why they hired you."

"I keep telling myself that. But then it was easy being efficient in Jeff's hotel. It's a small, budget hotel. The Haven is a luxury hotel. The clientele will be wealthy socialites. They will expect so much more."

"You have nothing to fear, Angela. You're good at dealing with people, putting them at ease. It will be perfect for you."

"Mm, I hope you're right. Anyway, enough about me. You would think we lived miles apart. I've barely seen you in the last few weeks. What have you been up to?"

"Nothing much. The Temperance Society keeps me very busy."

"It must do. You're never at home."

"Well, it's important that we keep up the pressure. Bootleggers are a very real problem."

"But surely that's a problem for the government, Kate," I said. "It's not something you can do anything about."

"Lives have been destroyed by alcohol. People don't realise the danger."

"But bootleggers, Kate. They're dangerous people. Criminals." Worry crept into my voice.

"Don't worry, Lizzie. I wouldn't put myself in danger. But I can't sit back and do nothing."

"Why, Kate? Why do you feel so strongly about this? I mean, it's not as if you saw your father or your brother abusing alcohol. Before prohibition Ed would barely drink a single bottle of beer."

"Not everyone is like Ed." Kate pursed her lips, her cheeks flamed. "Have you another towel? This one is sopping."

"Of course." I handed her a fresh towel noting her obvious annoyance at my question.

"That's why I'm curious, Kate. What is it that drives you? You don't know anyone personally who has suffered because of alcohol so why? Why the Temperance Society?"

Kate bit the inside of her cheek, visibly upset.

"It's just something I feel strongly about, Lizzie, okay? Now can we talk about something else?"

I held up my hands. "Okay, okay. We're just concerned for you, Kate."

"You have nothing to be concerned about. I'm fine. I'm doing something worthwhile. Something I believe in. Let's just leave it at that."

Kate threw the towel down on the counter and stomped out of the room. Angela and I looked at each other and back to Kate's retreating figure.

"What is going on with her?" Angela said.

"There's something behind all this. We just have to figure out what."

I didn't see Kate again until a week later. A trip into town to buy fabric brought me and my son into direct contact with a chapter of the Women's Temperance Society. They were staging a protest outside a building on the main street, saying it was being used as an illegal drinking den. I stood back and watched Kate march up and down. She held a large placard with the words, *'No to alcohol, yes to family'* in her handwriting. They were chanting as they marched, mainly older women. Kate stood out because of her youth. From behind me I could hear more chanting. Only this was in a manly tone. Down the main street came a counter-demonstration. There must have been at least thirty men of varying ages, carrying placards saying, *'We want beer'*. Simple but effective, I thought.

A line of police officers arrived out of nowhere. Up until that point, people in the surrounding area were going about their business, largely ignoring the women's protest or treating it with a degree of amusement. The arrival of the men and then the police changed all that. It was as if an electrical charge ran down the street, like a lightning strike during a hurricane. Kate stood as if transfixed, staring at the protesting men. Holding Michael's hand, I hurried forward, grabbed Kate by the arm and propelled her down a laneway.

"What are you doing?" She struggled against me. "Lizzie, let me be."

As she pulled away the shrill sound of police whistles echoed down the laneway, mixed with screams and shouting. We both stopped, appalled at the noise. Kate looked from me to Michael, eyes open wide with fear as she dropped her placard. I grabbed her hand.

"Come on, Kate. We need to get out of here."

With Michael between us we hurried away through the laneways, putting as much distance between us and the protest as possible. I don't think I've ever been so happy to bump into Ed.

"Ed, what are you doing here?"

"Looking for you," he said. "Some of the men in the naval yard were talking about going to a counter-protest. I knew there would be trouble."

I was so relieved to see him. So was Kate for that matter. Michael greeted him like a hero. Without pausing for breath Ed swung Michael up on his shoulders and escorted us the rest of the way to our home.

Kate's face remained alabaster white. Ed glanced at me, and I nodded. Kate was in no fit state to go home.

"Stay with us for a while, Kate," Ed said. "I'll walk you home after dinner."

"Great idea. Your nephew will be delighted," I said.

Kate gave a nod, like someone in a trance.

"Michael, will you go into the garden and get me some carrots, like a good boy," I said, signalling to Ed to take over.

"Come on, Michael. I'll give you a hand," Ed said, leaving me and Kate alone in the kitchen.

"Kate, what is it? What's wrong? You look like you've seen a ghost."

"He's back," Kate whispered.

"Who's back?" I took her hand and held it in mine, scared for Kate. She was trembling, all her usual toughness dissolved and leaving behind a soul too sensitive for this world.

"Who, Kate?"

"Vinnie."

"Angela's Vinnie?" I was puzzled why Kate could be so upset, practically catatonic at the return of her sister's former boyfriend. It didn't make sense.

Kate snatched her hand away, a sudden flair of temper flaming her cheeks.

"He's not Angela's Vinnie. She's well rid of him. He's no good. A drunken excuse for a man."

I instinctively knew I was on the brink of learning something particularly important, but I was at a loss to know what.

"Why do you say that?" I asked, keeping my voice as gentle as I could, afraid of spooking Kate. She put her head in her hands and wept, rocking back and forward like someone demented.

"Oh, Kate, *mo ghrá*." I put my arms around her. "What is it? Whatever is the matter?"

Kate stopped rocking, laid her head on my shoulder and cried solidly for what felt like an age but could only have been five minutes. As I felt her sobs subside, I offered her a handkerchief, put on the kettle for tea and sat beside her waiting on her to speak.

"I'm so ashamed," she whispered.

"What? Why do you say that? What have you to be ashamed of?"

"Him."

I was even more puzzled.

"Vinnie?"

"Yes."

I had to lean in towards her to hear her. I took her hand in mine. "Kate, talk to me. Tell me what has upset you."

Kate hung her head and mumbled something I couldn't catch.

"What was that?"

She looked up at me with such fear in her eyes I took a breath.

"It's my fault he broke up with Angela." I felt like she was begging me to understand but I was baffled. I shook my head.

"No, Kate. It had nothing to do with you."

Kate nodded her head. "It did. He came around looking for Angela. She was in your house. Dad had gone to collect Mom from choir practice. He was drunk. So... so drunk."

She paused. I listened. The silence between us grew but I couldn't break it. Somehow, I knew what she needed to say but I also knew that she needed to say it, not me.

"Vinnie told me I was the pretty one. That he should have asked me out, not Angela. I was so stupid," she sobbed. "It was obvious he was drunk but I was so flattered. Then he raped me."

"Oh, my poor girl." I wrapped my arms around her. Suddenly it all made sense. Kate was only seventeen at the time. Since then, she had believed that Vinnie broke up with Angela because of her. That Angela was hurt, that she went away to Virginia because of her, even though it was Vinnie who was at fault, she blamed herself.

"None of this is your fault, Kate." I placed my hands on either side of her head and spoke directly to her. "That man is despicable. He raped you. He took advantage of your youth in your own home. He will pay for this."

"No, no, Lizzie," Kate cried hysterically. "I don't want anyone to know."

"Okay, Kate, it's okay." I hugged her. "I won't tell anyone."

From outside the kitchen window, we could hear Ed singing with Michael. I knew it was Ed's way of letting me know he was on the way back.

"Go into my bedroom. There's fresh water in the jug. Wash your face. Rest. I'll call you when dinner's ready."

Kate left without argument. Ed looked at me with a question in his eyes, but I shook my head. "Later," I said. He nodded then turned back to Michael.

"Now, young man. Show your mother all the lovely vegetables we dug up."

For the rest of the evening, I agonised over Kate's dilemma. I couldn't tell her why Vinnie broke up with Angela or why we went to Virginia. That was Angela's decision. I couldn't tell Angela what Vinnie had done to Kate because that was Kate's secret. Kate sat through dinner, barely touching a bite while Ed attempted to lighten the atmosphere with stories for Michael. Every so often he would throw a worried glance at Kate, then glance at me as if beseeching me to tell him what was going on. It was only when Ed left to walk Kate home, I remembered everything she said and it hit me. The one thing I hadn't focused on was that Vinnie was back.

Chapter 31

Vinnie Fisher

I waited on the porch for Ed to come back. The whole time he was gone I paced up and down debating the best course of action.

"Did Kate say anything to you?"

"Not a word. I asked her what was wrong, and she just shook her head. What's going on, Lizzie?"

I told him everything. Even though I had promised Kate I wouldn't tell anyone, I didn't know what else to do. If Vinnie Fisher was back in town, we had a big problem.

"If I get my hands on him, so help me God, I'll swing for that man."

"Don't say that, Ed. It's bad enough knowing what he has done but if he is back in town, we have a bigger problem."

"Michael?"

"Michael," I said. "What if he goes looking for Angela? What if he finds out?"

Ed sat heavily on the kitchen chair. I sat beside him, both of us utterly dejected. While I knew Angela no longer had any feelings for him, how would she react if he asked her about the baby? As for poor Kate. How could we help her deal with what he did to her? I told Ed what had happened. Should I tell Angela as well?

I felt guilty then, guilty that I was thinking of how his return would affect me over everyone else. Vinnie Fisher had ruined the lives of so many. Both Angela and Kate had suffered so much at the hands of this man. I was the only one who gained something from Vinnie Fisher. My son. Our son. Fear gripped me, rippling through my veins and into my heart.

"Are you sure he's back?"

"The only place she could have seen him was at the demonstration. I was watching her before the men arrived. She was her usual self. He must have been among those men."

"But is she sure it was him?"

"She was so upset, Ed, practically catatonic. Kate was in no doubt it was him."

The next day Ed started making enquiries.

"It's true. He is back. The navy threw him out. Behaviour unbecoming an officer."

"That shouldn't come as any great surprise, considering what he did to Kate and how he treated Angela," I said. "But it is baffling. If Vinnie Fisher was dismissed in disgrace from the navy, why would he be back in Pensacola?"

"And why would he be involved in that protest?" Ed said. "Whatever it is, he's up to no good, that's for sure."

The following Sunday afternoon we made our way to the Anderson household. Michael walked between us chattering away as children do. It was hot. Michael kept removing his hat and squinting up at me. I kept putting his hat back on and fanning him with mine. My wide-brimmed hat was my first purchase when I moved to Florida. That hat kept the sun off my face and doubled as a fan when required. It was a relief to get into the shade of the veranda. We took our seats as Mr Anderson handed us glasses of cold lemonade. There is nothing as refreshing as home-made lemonade on a sweltering day.

My contentment was short-lived. Angela hovered beside me, wringing her fingers, obviously wanting to talk to me about something. I knew instinctively it had to be about Vinnie Fisher.

"Lizzie, I must show you the new handbag I got for work." She signalled to me to follow her inside the house but before I could move Mrs Anderson appeared on the veranda.

"Ed, Lizzie, you're here. Good. Dinner will be ready in about ten minutes," she said as she accepted a glass of lemonade from her husband and sat beside me.

"Angela." Mrs Anderson spoke her name as if giving a command. "Did you tell Ed about your gentleman caller?"

Angela turned puce. "Mother, Vinnie Fisher is not my gentleman caller. I want nothing more to do with that man."

"Angela, you were fond enough of him some years ago. You should give the man a chance. He may not be a naval officer these days but he's certainly a gentleman."

"Vinnie Fisher called... here?" I asked, putting my glass down on the side table.

"Yes. He called to pay his respects to Angela," Mrs Anderson said. "Although I must say, Angela was extremely rude to him. Maybe you can talk some sense into her. It's not as if she has dozens of suitors knocking at her door. If she's not careful she'll end up an old maid."

"I would rather be an old maid than step out with Vinnie Fisher, Mom," Angela said, her voice shaking. Ed put his hand on her shoulder and squeezed.

"Mom, Vinnie Fisher is not who you think he is. He didn't leave the navy. The navy threw him out. Angela is better off without him," Ed said.

Mrs Anderson tutted. "Nonsense. Angela could do a lot worse."

The Keeper of Secrets

"No, Mom, you need to listen to me. That guy is bad news. If he comes back here, don't let him into the house, and don't let him anywhere near the girls."

Mr Anderson sat forward, staring at Ed as he listened intently.

"Edna," he said. "If Ed tells us that Vinnie Fisher is a wrong 'un, we take his word for it."

"Thank you, Papa." Angela smiled.

Mrs Anderson opened her mouth to speak but must have thought better of it. Opinionated as she was, she didn't argue with her husband. Or at least not in public. She tutted, shook her head and went back indoors to the kitchen.

Through the whole exchange, Kate sat statue-like on the veranda steps. She kept her back to us so I couldn't see her reaction, but I could only guess. I moved over beside her, nudging her as I sat.

"Not out with the Women's Temperance Society today?"

She glanced sideways at me. "No, I've decided to take a step back."

"Really?" I said, somewhat surprised at this turn of events. "Although I am glad to hear it. There are so many other things you could put your energy into."

I smiled at her, patting her hand where it lay on her lap. There was an aura of sadness around her. I was surprised no one else could see it. Particularly Angela. The two of them were so close growing up. Surely Angela could sense how unhappy Kate was. As if she could read my thoughts, Angela plonked down on the step on the other side of Kate. She put her arms around her sister.

"Thank God for Ed. At least he's put Mom right about that pratt," she said. "We're gonna have to find ourselves men who think like our brother, isn't that right, Kate?"

"Definitely," said Kate. "Although to be honest, at this stage,

I think I'd prefer to be 'an old maid', as Mom put it. It would suit me fine not to promise to love, honour and obey some man. Why do they get to be obeyed all the time?"

"I agree," Angela said, with a wry smile. "I'm quite happy in my own company. Maybe we should start our own movement. The Women Only Society."

"Mom thinks we're doomed as it is, Angela. Can you imagine her face if we told her we didn't want to marry?"

The three of us laughed out loud at the prospect.

"Although, I hate to say it but someday both of you will meet the right man for you. When you do, you will want to get married, raise a family. I never thought I would leave the county of Cork, let alone Ireland. Yet here I am, married, living in America. You never know what's ahead of you. And what's meant for you won't go past you."

Angela threw her hands up in the air. "You and your sayings, Lizzie."

Kate laughed. I was glad to hear it, relieved to see a sparkle in her eyes. Kate was going to be okay. I was quietly confident that she could put that business behind her. There's no point in harbouring over the past. It's over and done with. I just needed to convince Kate of that, remind her that she has a wonderful future ahead of her, and to concentrate on that.

Chapter 32

Rum Runners

A few weeks later Ed arrived home from the naval yard, buzzing with news.

"I've finally discovered why Vinnie Fisher was back in town," he said.

He paused, waiting for my reaction, more for effect I think than anything else.

"Well, are you going to enlighten me?"

"He's a rum runner."

"A what?" I must admit I was shocked. Yet I very quickly realised it would be right up his street. That man liked to portray a gentlemanly exterior, yet underneath he was rotten.

"He works out of the Gulf, running booze from Mexico to Texas."

"So why is he here, in Pensacola?"

"Was here. I reckon he's gone again. Spent a few days' rest and recreation then back out on the Gulf. It's only a short spin from here to Texas, especially on the type of boats the rum runners use."

"Good. I hope that's the last we see of him."

"We wouldn't be that lucky."

It turned out to be a case of famous last words. The following week I had only put Michael to bed when a tearful Angela burst in through the door.

"Vinnie Fisher checked into the hotel."

"What? When?"

"This afternoon. He strolled right up to reception, greeted me like I was his girlfriend."

"Oh, Angela." I led her to a chair. "What did you do?"

"What could I do? I treated him like any other customer, checked him in, but then he leaned over and kissed me... on the cheek. I was so embarrassed. He said, 'see ya later, doll' and winked at me."

"What did you say?"

"I said, 'not if I see you first'. Honestly, the brass neck of that man."

Calling to the Andersons' home was bad enough but now checking into Angela's place of work, well, nothing good could come out of that. Luckily Ed arrived home. Angela filled him in while I served him his dinner.

"I couldn't believe the neck of that man. He was waiting on me when I finished work. He even had the nerve to ask me about the baby."

Ed froze, his eyes wide, fear etched on his handsome face. Angela gently touched his arm.

"It's okay. I told him it was all a big mistake, that I never was pregnant. He told me he knew that all along."

"Do you think he believed you?" I asked.

"Oh, he believed me all right. He even had the audacity to think we could pick up where we left off. I put him straight on that one." Angela put her hands on her hips, reminding me of her mother when she was telling someone off.

As she retold the afternoon's events, she got more and more angry.

"Just who does that man think he is?" she said. "The nerve of him, waltzing into the hotel like he owns it."

"I'll have a word, Angela. Tell him to stay away from you," Ed said.

"I've already done that, Ed. I'm not afraid of him. Besides, he's only checked in for one night. By noon tomorrow he's gone again. Good riddance I say."

I found it hard to sleep that night. Visions of Vinnie bumping into me and my son, then putting two and two together, haunted me. The next morning as I washed Michael's face and hands I studied his features, his facial expressions, his stance. I could see nothing of his biological father in him. He was pure Anderson, thankfully. Nevertheless, I worried constantly. Just knowing Vinnie Fisher could waltz in and out of our lives filled me with dread.

It was another full week before I saw Angela again.

"I'm worried about Kate," she said.

"So am I."

"There's something going on with her, but she won't talk about it. I don't understand it. We've always been so close."

"You still are close, Angela. She will talk to you when she's ready."

"Maybe I need to be more honest with her. About Vinnie Fisher. I'm tempted to tell her the truth..."

I swear my heart jumped up into my throat. "No... no you can't..."

Angela raised her hand. "It's okay, Lizzie. As I was about to say, I'm tempted to tell her the truth but that wouldn't be fair on Michael, or on you for that matter. So, I was thinking of telling her what I told Vinnie Fisher, that I thought I was pregnant, but I wasn't. But he ran out on me."

It made sense when she put it like that. I learnt over the years that the best lies are always intertwined with a bit of truth.

Having said that, she wasn't telling Kate a lie as such, she just wasn't telling her the whole truth. Vinnie Fisher had ended his relationship with Angela because she told him she was pregnant. He was a cad, a heartless, selfish man unworthy of Angela or any woman. That much was true. Kate needed to hear that to put her mind at ease in much the same way Angela needed to hear what he did to Kate. But what happened after that was between me, Ed and Angela. No one else needed to know. For Michael's sake.

"That makes sense." I figured that once Angela told Kate how much of a cad Vinnie Fisher was, then maybe, just maybe, Kate would tell Angela what he had done to her. Their hatred of that man united the sisters, with neither of them knowing the real reasons why.

The following Saturday I watched from my porch as Kate and Angela strolled up the street arm in arm. They were chatting and looked happy enough, but a knot of anxiety ate at me while I waited for them to arrive. Angela laughed at my expression.

"It's all good, Lizzie. We've talked and it's all good. But you should have told me what that pratt did to our Kate."

"She couldn't. I swore her to secrecy," Kate said.

"I never knew Lizzie was so good at keeping secrets," Angela said.

"Girls, it wasn't my place to tell."

It was a relief to see them so relaxed. In talking to each other they had banished any hold that Vinnie Fisher had over them. Especially Kate. She was a different person, back to the carefree young woman she was before that night. Part of me felt guilty that we hadn't told her the whole truth, but it was a secret that needed to be kept. For Michael's sake.

The following week a letter from Jimmy banished all thoughts of Vinnie Fisher from my mind. Jimmy had settled in

New York into a large Irish community. He wrote monthly letters telling me all about his life in the big city. Construction was still blazing ahead in the northern states. He seemed happy but I worried about him. When he wrote that he was coming for a Christmas visit I was ecstatic. My little brother back under my roof again.

He arrived on Christmas Eve driving a flatbed truck laden with extravagant gifts for us. There was perfume for me, a bottle of rum for Ed and a hamper full of foodstuffs; coffee, baking powder, flour, tea and other items I hadn't even heard of. The biggest surprise was the refrigerator. I had read about them, but I had never seen one up close. It was huge, with a white enamel exterior and lined with cork inside.

"We can't accept it, Jimmy."

"Why not? It's just what you need." Jimmy laughed at me.

"But... but it must have cost a fortune," I said.

"I've no one else to spend my money on, sis. Let me do this for you."

I hugged him then, grateful for everything he'd brought us, happy to see him again after two long years' absence.

It was our turn to host Christmas dinner. With the help of my new refrigerator and Jimmy's generous hamper I pulled out all the stops. It was a lovely day. Kate arrived with her parents, smiling broadly and obviously in great spirits. Angela was working, something Mrs Anderson was very unhappy with, but her husband reasoned with her that Angela was now assistant manager in The Haven Hotel. She had no choice about working holidays. Jimmy's charm soon lifted Mrs Anderson's spirits while Kate hung on his every word. At the end of the evening Jimmy escorted the Andersons home, although I suspect his wish was to spend more time with Kate rather than her parents.

Angela arrived the following day, delighted to see Jimmy and made a huge fuss over Michael as always. Sometimes as I watched Angela and Michael together, I felt that the whole world could see that she was his birth mother, not me. But no one did. Not even Jimmy, who was more perceptive than most men. Angela had never given any inkling of regret over giving Michael to us. If anything, she frequently joked that motherhood was not for her. That worried me. I was so happy with my husband and my son, I wanted that happiness for Angela, and for Kate.

That morning I could tell there was something on Angela's mind. After her initial flurry of greetings, she was unusually quiet. As we chatted over lunch of cold cuts and iced tea, Angela said nothing and barely listened to us.

"Something bothering you?" Jimmy asked.

Angela gulped, her eyes sparkling with unshed tears. She thumped the table with her fist, then got to her feet and paced the kitchen. Ed and I exchanged worried glances.

"What is it?" Ed asked. "You can tell us anything."

"Vinnie Fisher." Angela almost spat out his name.

"He's back?" Ed asked.

Angela nodded. "He was already checked in when I got in to work. Yesterday he had the damned nerve to greet me like a long-lost friend in front of everyone. The Boyles were there. I couldn't say anything to him. Had to speak to him like a regular guest."

Jimmy led Angela back to the table and sat beside her.

"Okay. First, who is Vinnie Fisher and secondly, who are the Boyles?"

"The Boyles own the hotel. The whole chain. Mr and Mrs Boyle stay at our hotel at least twice a year. You've heard me talk about them before, Lizzie. They have a little girl, Evelyn, pretty little thing, and so pleasant, loves the beach. She must be about fourteen now."

"And Vinnie Fisher?" Jimmy asked.

Angela flashed a look at Ed. "He's a man I dated some years back. He treated me very badly..." She hesitated, my heart skipped a beat, wondering what she would say next.

"Don't think badly of me, Jimmy."

"I could never think badly of you."

"I thought I was pregnant, told him and he abandoned me. I wasn't... pregnant, that is, but I was very hurt. At the time I believed I loved him. He was... is a scoundrel."

"Hi, Aunt Kate." Michael's voice carried in from the front yard. Kate stepped inside the door and Angela changed the subject.

Angela exhaled. "Lizzie, you got a refrigerator."

I took her cue. "Jimmy bought it for us."

"Wow."

Kate looked from me to Angela and back again.

"What is it? What are you two trying to hide?"

Angela deflated, her bravado escaping in a long sigh.

"Vinnie Fisher is back in town."

Kate's smile disappeared, replaced momentarily by a deep frown, then a flash of anger. She tossed her head as if to shake off old memories.

"Don't let that blaggard bother you. He's not worth it."

Angela hugged Kate; the sisters caught up in supporting each other. Angela pulled away, put her hands on Kate's shoulders and looked directly at her.

"I told Jimmy about how and why he dumped me that time." She turned to face Jimmy.

"I didn't get to tell you that he reappeared a few years later, knocked on our door and invited himself into the house. He thought he could just pick up where he left off. The navy got rid of him, threw him out, behaviour unbecoming or something like that."

I made more coffee as Ed told the others the rumours he had

heard about Vinnie Fisher. Jimmy knew more about rum runners and bootleggers than I did.

"Prohibition has made matters worse. In the northern states the gangsters have completely taken over. They are a law unto themselves. You need to be very careful with a guy like that."

"Careful." Kate's hand shook so much coffee spilled over onto the scrubbed table. Angela took the cup from her and put her arm around her.

"No, Angela. Jimmy should know what he did to me." Kate looked directly at Jimmy and took a deep breath before speaking. "Vinnie Fisher called to the house one night when Angela was at work. He was drunk... he raped me. I was too young, too stupid to know what was happening. He convinced me that I'd seduced him, that it was all my fault. I didn't tell anyone for a long time."

I think all of us shed tears. Kate's anguish was so raw yet her bravery at speaking about what had happened gave us all hope. Hope and the desire for revenge.

Chapter 33

Justice

Jimmy was staying with us for a week, but he was unaccustomed to having idle hands. Ed was due back in work the next day, so Jimmy decided to go into the yard with him. They never said what they got up to that week, but I knew there was something going on. Part of me hoped that Jimmy was checking out work in our area. The prospect of having my brother living near me permanently brought joy to my heart. I was glad to see him spending so much time with Kate. Every evening they went out for a walk, either on the beach or the promenade. They were definitely an item.

The day before Jimmy was due to leave, we had the Andersons over for dinner. While Ed got his parents a drink, Kate followed me into the kitchen and pulled a newspaper clipping out of her bag.

"Did you see this?" Kate's eyes sparkled.

In large print the headline puzzled me.

RUM RUNNERS RUN OUT OF ROAD

It was only when I got to the third paragraph, I understood why she was so happy.

"Well, I never." I blessed myself. "I know it's wrong to speak ill of the dead, but let's face it, he had it coming."

The newspaper article went into great detail on how two rum runners, smuggling hundreds of crates of Bacardi, were caught by the coast guard in the Gulf of Mexico. The authorities had received an anonymous tip-off about their activities. During a shoot-out one of the rum runners was shot dead, the other was arrested and would go to prison. The article named the dead criminal as Vinnie Fisher.

I can't be hypocritical. There were no prayers for that man's soul in our house, even though he would need prayers more than most. It was such a relief to know that he could never step back into our lives again. Kate still carried the trauma of what he did to her. Some people will make excuses for him that he was drunk, even Kate lets him off the hook in a way by telling us he was drunk at the time. That didn't excuse his behaviour. At least we know that is why Kate got so caught up in the temperance movement. Her mother had asked questions about why she'd quit but accepted Kate's explanation that it was pointless when we lived in a state that most people accepted as being a "wet state".

I took great pleasure in sharing the newspaper clipping with Mrs Anderson. She turned pale as she read it. As for Angela, she definitely didn't have any feelings for him. She celebrated when Kate gave her the newspaper clipping confirming his death. I had no doubt that he would have been a frequent visitor to The Haven Hotel. Seeing Angela again may have sparked something in him. She is a stunningly beautiful woman inside and out. She could have her pick of suitors. It worried me that she'd shunned most of them. I suppose I wanted for my in-laws

The Keeper of Secrets

the type of relationship I had with Ed. I counted myself so lucky in so many ways.

Jimmy and Ed didn't comment but I saw the look that passed between them. They had something to do with it. I was sure of it. When our guests left, and we retired to bed for the night, I queried Ed, but he was tight-lipped. My Ed would never lie to me. His silence spoke volumes.

After the news of Vinnie Fisher's demise, Kate slowly regained her old sparkle.

"I'm glad she told everyone. It had been haunting her," I said to Angela. "Maybe now she can get on with her life."

"I told her that. If she had confided in me at the time, I could have put her straight."

"Hindsight is great," I said. "But don't forget she thought he had broken up with you because of what happened that night. She blamed herself."

Angela nodded. "That man had so much to answer for. I know I shouldn't say it, but... I'm glad he's dead."

I must admit, I was quite shocked to hear Angela speak so vehemently but I understood. If I was totally honest with myself, I felt the same way. Since the day Michael was born, I always had the niggling fear that somehow, Vinnie would find out he had fathered a child. Our child. That fear struck me at odd times, usually in the dead of night, while the rest of my world slept. There were nights I would wake with fear clutching my chest, leaving me breathless. Ed always knew instinctively. He would hold me and whisper that everything was fine. I believed him. I had to. If Ed ever felt the same terror as I did, he never said anything. But that was my Ed. My solid, dependable, salt-of-the-earth husband.

Chapter 34

Angela and Promotion

Angela loved her job in The Haven Hotel. It was the type of place me and Ed could never afford to stay in. The Florida hotel was situated right on the seafront offering magnificent views over the Gulf of Mexico. When a position came up in the back office, Kate jumped at the opportunity. It was perfect for her.

The hotel itself struggled. Thankfully it was part of a large chain, with luxury hotels in all the major cities and their headquarters in New York, otherwise I doubt it would have survived. It's weird how the actions of a few can affect the lives of so many. Having been brought up on a country estate with landed gentry at the helm I knew all about that. But the Wall Street Crash caused so much hardship across the United States. Work dried up for Jimmy. He came to us, thank God. It was good to have him with us. Money was tight but we pulled together, and we got through it.

I volunteered in the soup kitchens. My years at my mother's apron strings taught me a few things, although we had never been short of food. Nevertheless, I could make a lot of nourishing tasty soup out of a handful of vegetables. Flour was

The Keeper of Secrets

harder to come by but when I did, I bulked out the soup with fresh soda bread. Thankfully Ed's work in the naval yard kept us fed, and a roof over our heads. Ed's parents did okay, especially with Angela and Kate living in staff quarters at the hotel.

Michael got bigger and stronger every day. And every day I thanked God for him. He was such an intelligent, sweet boy who worked hard in school and helped me around the house. I planted a vegetable garden on the first week we moved into our house. It failed miserably. Everything my father taught me about growing fruit and vegetables in Ireland was useless to me in tropical Florida. But I'm a quick learner. Each year I became a little more knowledgeable, each year the crop improved. Within a few years I was supplying my own household, the Andersons and a few of the neighbours with potatoes, carrots, courgettes and onions. I could sell my mango chutney and as for my fruit preserves, well they were better than my mother's even if I do say so myself.

We continued to host the Anderson family every second Sunday. Angela and Kate were intermittent guests, depending on their shifts. While Kate appeared to have a sweet spot for Jimmy nothing seemed to come of it. The two sisters went on the odd double date but me and Ed worried that Vinnie Fisher had put them off men for life. Their mother frequently complained that her daughters had been 'left on the shelf', as she put it. She blamed the war, which had decimated the number of young single men, the recession, which drove the few young men left after the war into poverty and occasionally her daughters for being too fussy. They largely ignored her.

One day in late summer 1933 Angela arrived to join us for our evening meal. Something she was in the habit of doing, if she had missed Sunday lunch. She greeted Jimmy warmly, made a fuss over Michael and was even chattier than usual.

Somehow, I knew intuitively that she had something on her mind.

"How are things going in the hotel?" I asked.

"Good, yes good," she said, but I noted the slight hesitation before she answered. I could see that Ed had noticed it too, although it was Jimmy's reaction that surprised me.

"So, what's up?"

Angela laughed. "What makes you think something's up?"

"There's something you're not telling us," Jimmy said, one eyebrow raised.

Angela laughed again then sighed.

"There's nothing wrong as such. Actually, it's all good."

We were all puzzled at that stage.

"Spill," Ed said.

"Yes, Angela, what's going on?" I asked.

Angela looked at each of us in turn.

"Okay. I think you should all sit down for this one."

Intrigued, I joined Ed and Jimmy at the kitchen table while Angela paced the floor wringing her hands. She stopped suddenly and faced us all.

"Okay. Do you remember I told you the owners were staying over Christmas?"

"The hotel owners?"

"Mr and Mrs Boyle. The owners of the whole group."

I caught something in her voice.

"Mr Boyle offered me a promotion. I'm moving into management."

"That's great news," I said. "And well deserved. You work so hard."

"Yeah, congratulations, sis. I'm delighted for you," Ed said.

Jimmy said nothing. He sat with his head cocked to one side studying Angela's face.

"The Haven is part of a chain, aren't they?"

Angela blushed. "Yes, the Boyle group owns twelve hotels in America..."

The penny dropped with me. "What do you mean, in America? Do they own hotels in other countries?"

"Yes, they've bought two hotels in Europe."

"Where?" Jimmy asked before I could open my mouth.

"One is in London." She hesitated, eyes down. Then took a visible breath as if to steel herself against an expected onslaught. "The other one is in Ireland."

Jimmy was quicker than I was to guess the significance. "They've offered you Ireland?"

Angela nodded and started to pace again.

"It's a great opportunity for me. Assistant manager. It's a new hotel, only opened last year."

I was gobsmacked. It made no sense. As far as I knew, people left Ireland to make a better life for themselves. Irish people came to America to find employment. The Irish left their home country. They cried and sang about it for the rest of their lives, but they never went back. It didn't make sense to me that an American would travel to Ireland for work or any other reason. Jimmy disagreed.

"America worked out for you. You have a husband, a child. It hasn't been a land of opportunity for many others. These last few years have been hard. No work, no money. Some are wondering if they should cut their losses and go back. And besides, this is different. The ones that left during the famine and made their fortunes here are willing to invest their money back in their home country."

"Are the Boyles Irish?" Ed asked.

"Mr Boyle's grandfather was Irish. Mr Boyle is very proud of his Irish roots, even though he's as American as they come. New York born and bred."

I listened to what Angela had to say but I had serious

reservations and told her so. "It's an amazing opportunity for me. Please Lizzie, please be happy for me."

"Have you told Mom?" Ed asked.

"Not yet. I was hoping to get you on board first."

Ed nodded. "Well, for what it's worth, I think it's a great opportunity for you. Come on. I'll go with you to see Mom."

We all went. Ed, me, Michael, Jimmy and Angela. Mrs Anderson opened the door and knew something was up.

"Okay, out with it. What's up?"

For the first time since I met her, me and Mrs Anderson were on the same page.

"No, Angela. I forbid it. Do you hear me?"

"Mom, we don't live in the dark ages. You can't forbid me. But I'd rather go with your blessing."

"Lizzie, talk to her please."

"Your mother's right, Angela. Look at Jimmy. He left to find a better life, here in America. Ireland is poverty-stricken. No one has any money, certainly no one who could afford to stay in hotels."

"Ireland has changed since you left. The Boyles' know what they're doing. If they believe they can run a successful hotel in Ireland, who am I to doubt them?"

"But, Angela..."

"Mom, Lizzie... this is a great opportunity for me. I want to go, but I want to go with your blessings. And anyway, if it doesn't work out, I can always come back."

Bart Anderson had sat in the corner, listening to both sides of the argument, despite several pleas from his wife to 'talk some sense into his daughter'. Eventually he moved to Angela's side.

"Edna, leave the girl alone. Angela's a grown woman and a very capable one."

Bart took his daughter's hand and kissed it. "I've every faith in our daughter's abilities. If the Boyles believe in her, then I think we should too."

I reluctantly agreed. Bart Anderson's opinion was important to me. To all of us. He was always the rock of sense in the Anderson family. The calming influence. Mrs Anderson may argue with him but in the end even she could always see the sense in his reasoning. For reasoning was what it was. Bart Anderson's approach to all of life's problems were measured and well thought out. We all trusted his judgement. So, if he was happy for Angela to go to Ireland then we all followed his lead.

Within two months we waved goodbye to Angela. She travelled by train to New York, to board a liner to bring her to Queenstown, although it was now called Cobh. The same port I had left from some fourteen years earlier.

So much had happened in those relatively short years. I kept in touch by letter with Aunt Jean, although Uncle Pat was long dead. Aunt Jean still lived in the same house on the hill, and I wrote to her asking her to keep a watchful eye on Angela if at all possible. Mrs Buckley had remarried ten years earlier and moved to the capital. We exchanged Christmas cards but had little other communication. I had never spoken in any detail about my life before I moved to Queenstown, other than to say we lived in a cottage on a large estate. Ed was the only Anderson who knew the full truth about Maggie.

I hugged Angela tightly and made her promise that if she ever got in any kind of trouble, she was to run to my Aunt Jean. Five thousand miles away from her home, it was a comfort to know that she had someone she could rely on. Someone we could trust.

Chapter 35

The First Lady

The thirties were tough. I won't pretend otherwise. Me and mine were lucky. We had work, a roof over our heads and food on the table, but the country was in tatters. I even began to think that Jimmy had a valid point, that the land of opportunity was dead and buried under the mass unemployment. I had never witnessed poverty like it.

I didn't shy away from it. Every spare moment I had, I spent helping those less fortunate and I didn't care what colour they were. A hungry child was a hungry child. My mother-in-law didn't approve but Ed did. At the end of the day, my wedding vows were to love, honour and obey Ed, not his mother. Ed had a different experience of the blacks than his mother. Before and during the war, blacks were allowed in the navy. He served with them, in the cramped environment on board naval ships. Ed could never understand why they'd banned them from joining when the war ended.

There were so many people out of work. So many hungry people with no hope. A new government was elected. The new president, Franklin D Roosevelt promised a "new deal" for the American people, and I, for one, prayed he would deliver.

By the late thirties there were signs of improvement and I thanked God for that. By then, me and Ed were in the habit of listening to the wireless on a Sunday evening. It was then I first heard the First Lady speaking. Before that I had no idea who the president was, let alone the First Lady, but Eleanor Roosevelt changed that. I thought she was truly inspirational. Looking back on it now, I'd say she was ahead of her time. She believed in equality amongst the sexes as well as the races. Every Sunday evening we'd tune in to hear what Mrs Roosevelt chose to speak about that week. She genuinely seemed to care about the people her husband represented. Of course, my mother-in-law disagreed.

"Disgraceful carry-on. The First Lady's job is to support her husband. She has no business talking in public. She even writes a newspaper column. You'd wonder who wears the pants in that relationship," Mrs Anderson said, as we sat on the veranda after Sunday lunch.

"And a very good column it is," Bart said, rustling out the broadsheet paper.

Mrs Anderson tutted her disapproval while Kate and I exchanged amused glances. Kate was a fan of Eleanor Roosevelt and a regular reader of her column, *My Day*. She often quoted extracts to me, particularly pieces she knew I would enjoy. I had a sneaking admiration for her. She spoke her mind and I liked her thinking. To my mind she treated everyone with respect. Some of her sayings reminded me of my ma back home in Ireland, although Ma would never have put herself forward the way Eleanor Roosevelt did. But then again, she was an educated woman, some say smarter than her husband. Imagine being smarter than a man. My ma believed that education was the way forward, but for the men, not the women.

Me, I was happy with my lot in life. But that didn't mean I couldn't see the advantages of having more women in positions of power. But that meant educating women to the same standard as men. These days people were struggling to keep their boys in school. There was nothing extra to send the girls as well. People barely had money for food and a roof over their head. But I did believe that President Roosevelt could make a difference to people's lives, especially with his wife Eleanor leading the way.

Chapter 36

Kate and Jimmy

On the second Sunday in May, Americans celebrate Mother's Day. Kate managed to get Sunday off. She insisted on taking over my kitchen and giving me the day off too. I didn't argue. It felt good to sit on the porch drinking cold lemonade while someone else slaved over the cooker. I noticed the uniformed soldier as he turned the corner onto our street. As he drew nearer, I recognised the familiar gait.

"Jimmy," I squealed in delight, as I raced down the path to greet him. My squeals brought the others from the kitchen and between us, we all gave Jimmy a hero's welcome. It had been five long years. Jimmy had written on birthdays and at Christmas. Long missives full of nonsense and very little concrete information. What I didn't know about at that stage was the weekly letters to Kate.

Once I got over my initial exhilaration, I noticed how attentive he was to Kate. No matter who asked him a question, he always directed his replies to Kate. Jimmy's eyes were continually drawn to her.

"When did you sign up?" Mr Anderson asked.

"January. I'm still in training but got leave to see my sister."

"The uniform suits you," Kate said.

Jimmy grinned. To me it was obvious, this spark between them. One glance in Ed's direction confirmed he saw it too.

"I must say, you look very smart," Mrs Anderson said. "Very smart indeed."

It was a joyous day. Kate cooked a beautiful meal. Jimmy and Kate volunteered to clean up afterwards and no one argued with them. Not even Mrs Anderson. Maybe she too could see the spark between them. Kate had matured into a beautiful woman but at thirty-two her mother classed her as a spinster, left on the shelf, along with her older sister. I had no doubt that Mrs Anderson would be happy to push Kate into a relationship with Jimmy. As for me, I would be delighted. After all, they were two of my favourite people.

Jimmy stayed for two days. Most of his time was spent with Kate but I wasn't complaining. It was lovely to see the relationship between them blossom. Jimmy went back to his unit with promises to write and to visit on his next leave. There were rumours of war in Europe rumbling in the background, but Ed wasn't too worried. America was neutral, he said. There was no inclination to get involved in Europe's arguments. His father agreed. So, I put my worries aside. Jimmy was safe, for now anyway.

We saw more of Jimmy over the following few months than we had in the previous nine years. Although it wasn't me he wanted to see. Jimmy and Kate only had eyes for each other. We were all over the moon when he finally proposed. They applied for their marriage licence in early June and married in the local Catholic church the day before Kate's thirty-third birthday. The ceremony was officiated over by the newly appointed priest, Father O'Sullivan, a West Cork native, who vouched for Jimmy's bachelorhood. Kate looked stunning, the epitome of the blushing bride. I swear I heard a sharp intake of breath from

Mrs Anderson when she saw her youngest daughter in her wedding dress. She had to mask the tears that had sprung unbidden, pleading hay fever. Ed and I hosted a wedding breakfast in our home attended by family and friends. By three in the afternoon the newlyweds were ready to depart for their new life together in Jacksonville.

"I'm so happy for them, but I will miss Kate so much," I confessed to Ed.

"At least they're in the same state. Jacksonville is only 350 miles away. It's not that far."

"Spoken like a true American. That's the other end of the country to an Irish person. Don't forget I'd never left the county of Cork before I came here. I've never seen Dublin or Belfast."

Ed laughed and pulled me close to him. His earthy scent enveloped me, and I sank into his embrace. Twenty years together and he could still sweep me off my feet.

"Hey, the newlyweds are ready to leave," Bart called from the front step.

Happiness oozed out of Kate. She had changed into a dusky-pink day dress, her ebony hair curling over her shoulders, held back on the left with a silver clip, a present from her mother. Jimmy could not take his eyes off his beautiful wife.

I felt Ed's arms curl around my waist and leaned into him. Gratitude for my life welled up in me. Our son had grown into a fine young man, now fifteen and a good two inches taller than his father. My little brother was happily married to a sister-in-law I adored. Our home was a happy one. Life was good.

Chapter 37

Beth, 1976

I am stunned. This woman that I admired so much from when I was a small child has kept a secret from her only son that blows my mind. Her revelations have shaken me to the core. My grandma was not the person I thought she was, neither am I. There is no Irish blood coursing through my veins. My father was so proud of his Irish heritage. Turns out he has no Irish blood in him, that we know about anyway. His closest connection to Ireland is through the woman who gave birth to him. Angela lives in Ireland but she's American born.

Did Dad's Uncle Jimmy know? Did his sister confide in him which would mean that Kate would also know. Did all these people conspire to hide my father's true identity from him? Or did he know the truth but didn't tell us? Did Grandma tell him in later years? Did Angela? I cannot reconcile the grandma I knew and loved with this woman who passed off her sister-in-law's child as her own.

Why did Pops go along with it? My father, Michael, wasn't his biological son. I couldn't believe it. I played and replayed the tape. My biological grandfather was a rum runner named

Vinnie Fisher. Grandma obviously suspected some involvement by Pops and Uncle Jimmy in his arrest and subsequent death, but she was obscure about the details, whether deliberately or not I couldn't figure out.

I couldn't help but be curious about Vinnie Fisher. If his nature was as bad as Grandma painted him, then did his bad blood run through me? Did I inherit his genes unwittingly? I had always modelled myself on my grandma. To find out that I had no genetic link to her was devastating.

The person I always knew as my great-aunt is my grandmother. Angela is my grandma. Not that she looks like anyone's grandma. She is glamorous, perfectly groomed, with painted nails and designer clothes. I doubt she has ever worn a pinny. Not that I know her very well. I've met her three times in my entire life. The woman I've met bears no resemblance to the woman my grandma talks about on these tapes.

To say I am stunned is an understatement. In a way it makes me feel better about my stupidity with Jeremy. I had always considered Angela to be clever, career-minded, a woman who knew her own mind, an independent who forged her own path. Turns out she had been duped by a man, same as I had. She had been used and abandoned when she got into trouble. It was Grandma who came to rescue her. Although I couldn't help but wonder, who rescued who. From what Grandma said, it seemed to me like they rescued each other. The idea grew in me that if Angela could learn from her mistakes, I could do the same. She gave birth to a son, then surrendered him to her brother so that her baby could have the family he needed, and she could go on to forge a successful career. If she could do that then I could get over this stupid affair and get my life back on track.

Conor is due home next week. How can I tell him about Grandma's secret? But I have to. She left these tapes because she wanted me to know, wanted us to know. Although surely she told my father the truth about his birth. She wouldn't have left that to me. The only way to find out is to continue listening to the tapes.

Act 3
Home

Chapter 38

War in Europe

When war broke out in Europe, I didn't worry too much. Jimmy was based in Camp Blanding, Jacksonville. Public opinion seemed to be against America getting involved in Europe's conflict. We automatically worried about Angela, but Ireland pronounced themselves to be neutral, so we all gave a sigh of relief.

Life plodded along at a steady pace. Me, Ed and Michael were closer than ever. Michael seemed content working at the boatyard. He worked hard, had a selection of good friends who were always welcome in our home. Ed worried at times about his parents as they advanced in years. Bart had a hacking cough that he treated with honey, refusing to see a doctor. Edna complained bitterly about her sleepless nights, blaming Bart, but the two of them rubbed along together regardless.

One day in late October I had spent the day baking and bottling. It was a fine evening. The heat of the day had given way to a cool night breeze that revived and refreshed. I wanted to bring Edna some preserves. She was partial to my mango chutney and the marmalade I made to my mother's recipe. For Bart I baked his favourite Irish-style apple tart. With our wares packed into a wicker basket, we strolled leisurely, enjoying the relative coolness. It was my favourite time of year in Florida. Yes, I missed the autumn leaves, the colours, the cold that necessitated a blazing fire; all the memories that formed my childhood. Autumn in Florida was hugely different. The searing heat and humidity of summer melted into warm, fresher weather. Warmer than a good sunny summer day in Ireland, and I felt comfortable in it.

We could hear Bart coughing from the street. Ed looked at me, anxiety written all over his face and we hurried to him. As we went down the garden path, we heard Edna shout. Ed dropped the basket and ran. There was nothing he could do. The doctor said his heart gave out; that his heart couldn't take the pressure from the persistent cough. I wondered if his fondness for Camel cigarettes had anything to do with his cough. Ed told me I was wrong. Every man we knew smoked cigarettes at that stage. We sent a telegram to Angela informing her but with the war in Europe, travel across the Atlantic was impossible. I wrote her a long letter with all the details of the funeral, who attended, who didn't and all the good things that friends and neighbours said about Bart.

Edna was heartbroken. For all their petty arguing they were a devoted couple. It was as if she had nothing to live for without caring for Bart. They were an old-fashioned couple. Her sole purpose in life was to look after his needs. Edna wasn't a motherly person. She treated rearing her children as a duty, a chore, something that needed to be done efficiently. She firmly believed that to spare the rod was to spoil the child. There was very little overt affection in that house. It wasn't her fault. She was brought up in a puritanical household.

Bart was the opposite. He showered his children with affection. Ed often told me that he watched his father treat his mother with deference and respect no matter how much she pushed him away. When Edna railed against the world, Bart shrugged his shoulders, hugged his wife and told her everything would turn out okay. Ed felt it was a valuable lesson for him and his sisters in how to always see the good in every situation and every person.

With no one to listen to her, no one to balance her negativity, Edna gradually faded away. Trying to look after her in her last few months was difficult. She was irritable, terribly unhappy and took her pain out on those around her. It was a bleak time for all of us. She died the following spring. I swear from a broken heart. Ed agreed up to a point.

God forgive me but I felt only relief at her funeral and felt guilty about it. Until Kate admitted feeling much the same.

"To be fair, once Pop died, she was so unhappy but let's be honest, she made everyone else's life a misery."

"I know. I'm just glad to hear someone else feels the same way I do. I felt so guilty."

"Tough as nails. Sometimes I wondered how Pops put up with her, but he must have loved her. He was the only one who could make her smile. Well Pops and Ed."

We both laughed. I was well aware of how she put Ed on a pedestal. She idolised her only son and had no qualms in telling me in the early years of how I wasn't the wife she planned for him. She mellowed over the years though and by the end I think we found a mutual respect for each other.

Life moved on as it does. I remember when Maggie died, I wanted to die too. I couldn't envisage a life without her. The shock of my da's death, so sudden, so devastating. Then the letter telling me that Ma was dead. Grief overwhelmed me after each of those deaths, but I recovered. We all do. Death is a part of life but such a hard thing to deal with.

We no longer alternated Sunday lunch. No one lived in the Anderson house. Ed let it out to the son of a workmate, recently married with a baby on the way. Kate and Jimmy lived over three hundred miles away. While America wasn't at war, it looked increasingly like we would eventually end up caught up in the conflict.

The following Christmas Jimmy got leave so him and Kate came to us for a few days. I knew straight away that Kate was pregnant. She had a glow about her. Jimmy handled her as if she were a piece of porcelain that would break if she as much as stepped on a pebble. It was a joy to see and the exact news we all needed. We sent a telegram to Angela to tell her the good news.

Angela wrote monthly missives, full of cheery stories and praise for her new-found home. It sounded wonderful. Some of the scenes she painted reminded me so much of the Knockrath estate. The gardens, the river, the magical forest. At times, after reading one of her letters, I found myself homesick for the place I was born. Then I remembered Maggie and shook all traces of sentimentality from my mind.

I worried about how Angela would take Kate's news. Despite Angela's insistence that she was happy in Ireland, I knew she was terribly upset when her employer died earlier that year. The Boyles spent a lot of time in their hotel in Cork and when Mrs Boyle became ill, she made it her permanent home. Their daughter, Evelyn, had been living in New York and travelled to Ireland to be with her mother. Angela became very close to her. She wrote so much about the family I felt as if I knew them all. When Evelyn returned to New York, Angela missed her and I thought at one stage that, if it wasn't for the war, Angela would have returned home. Which would have made me incredibly happy. But it wasn't to be.

Chapter 39

Second Time Around

America joined the war. It was inevitable, after the Japanese bombed Pearl Harbour. I worried for Jimmy. Baby Nora was barely a year old when he shipped out for Europe. His first port of call, Ireland. We both laughed at the good fortune of it. I wrote to Angela giving her as much information as we could find out. Jimmy promised to look her up the moment he got leave. If he got leave.

As for Kate, well I thought it was a foregone conclusion that she would move in with us until Jimmy got back. I should have known better. The Anderson house was empty, so she decided to move back home with baby Nora to be closer to us for support but with her own independence. She was right of course. It was the perfect solution.

It was eerie preparing the house for her arrival. I scrubbed every inch of that house while Ed gave everything a good whitewash so that it was fresh and clean. Still, Edna's presence seemed to follow me from room to room but in a positive way. I think she would have been happy with Kate's choices, with Jimmy and baby Nora.

Kate was barely settled when Ed debated if he should enlist.

"Why?" I demanded. "You've already served your country in the last war."

"There's plenty of men fought in the last war and enlisted in this one."

"That doesn't make it right."

I was furious with him. Part of me knew it was purely selfish. I didn't want to be without him, feared losing him.

"Your work in the naval yard is important too."

Ed sighed, shaking his head, worn down by my arguments and possibly surprised by my vehemence.

"Okay, you have a point. Let's just leave it for now."

And he did. No more was said on the matter. Jimmy wrote home that he had landed in the north of Ireland, the part that was still under British rule. Angela was living in Cork, about the same distance as his old base in Jacksonville to us in Pensacola. He wrote that when things settled, he would try to get transport to go see her.

Despite my objections to Ed joining up, I had no problem supporting the war effort in other ways. I helped raise funds, roping in Ed and Michael as well. I felt I owed a debt of gratitude to this country that had taken me in and given me such a great life. Despite the turmoil in the world around me, I felt lucky, happy in my little bubble.

Nothing prepared me for the bombshell Michael dropped on us. He gave us no warning, no advance notice of what he was thinking. When he arrived at the front door dressed in the naval uniform, my heart sank. I sat heavily, unable to speak.

"What on earth...?"

I couldn't say any more. What more was there to say? I thought he was happy in his work. Michael was good with his hands. When he was sixteen, Ed got him an apprenticeship with a boat builder. He was happy in his work and learned his trade, quickly becoming an invaluable member of the team. His carpentry work was top class. He was dating a lovely girl, Lori, a petite dark-haired beauty who we all liked. Which made what he did all the more shocking.

My son suited the uniform. He put me in mind of his father at that age, when I met him, in Queenstown, during another war. The idea of my son leaving us and going to Europe to fight in a war filled me with dread. I knew Ed would feel differently. Perhaps it is a male thing. This desire for war, to defend one's country through violence. I was convinced that if women ruled the world, there would be no wars. That the inner maternal instinct would override everything else. That women would protect and nurture, not kill.

"What about Lori?"

"Lori is okay with it, Mom," Michael said. "I don't know why you're so surprised. I come from a long line of naval officers."

"But, Michael. There's a war..."

I knew I wasn't even making sense. The shock of seeing my precious son in a naval uniform at a time of war had rendered me incoherent. Tears sprang to my eyes while somewhere inside me my heart felt crushed.

Ed arrived home at that exact moment. His face broke into the widest smile as he shook Michael's hand.

"I'm so proud of you, son."

"Thanks, Dad."

I could barely get the words out. "Whe... when do you go?"

"Straight away. I'm here to pack a bag. I've to be in Jacksonville for the morning."

I nodded, straightened my shoulders and shook off my pain.

"Right, let's get you sorted so."

I marched into Michael's bedroom and began to systemically go through his chest, removing underwear, socks and shirts, laying them out on the bed in rows.

"Thanks, Mom." I became aware of Michael standing in the doorway watching me.

"For what? I can't have you in the barracks tomorrow half packed. I might not be happy about this, Michael, but I'm sure I'm not the only mother facing this..." and I pointed at his uniform, "this situation today."

When dusk fell, Ed and I walked Michael to the corner where an army truck picked him up. He climbed into the back, joining a dozen other young men, all in naval uniforms. All upbeat and smiling. I prayed for each and every one of them.

Chapter 40

It's Over

It is so difficult to recount the war years. What could I say about it all? My life continued in much the same vein. After Pearl Harbour there were no more bombs on American soil. The war was fought in Europe, in the Pacific, in parts of the world I had barely heard of. I combed the newspapers daily and cherished every single letter from my precious son and my beloved brother. Ed and I both shared tears over families who'd lost loved ones. We pored over casualty lists. I prayed daily to the Virgin Mary and to Saint Michael to keep my son and my brother safe.

I was so relieved when the war finally ended. Grateful that my loved ones were safe, then guilty for feeling that way when so many other families carried their grief like a badge of honour. Jimmy was in Ireland at that stage which meant he was safe, but Michael was somewhere in the Pacific, and I prayed daily for his safe return to us. Lori paid a visit once a week and we compared notes.

It was the end of the war before Jimmy got the opportunity to visit Angela. He borrowed a Land Rover and made the trip along with a colleague, Charlie, himself a Cork man. I didn't know in advance that they had planned the trip, neither did Angela. When the postman handed me a hard cardboard letter the day before Christmas Eve with an Irish postmark, I didn't quite know what to expect. I struggled opening it, the cardboard was stiff and unyielding. The photos fell out of it before I even got to the letters. One landed face upwards on the kitchen table. I gasped as I scanned the image in front of me. Angela looked so glamorous in black and white, her hair bobbed, her arms linking Jimmy on one side and Charlie on the other. All three of them with radiant smiles that brought a grin to my face.

Jimmy looked thinner than I remembered but still good. Angela looked amazing. Life in Ireland certainly seemed to suit her. I took out the two letters and spent the rest of the afternoon engrossed in reading and analysing them. Before I knew it, Ed was home. Luckily, I had made soup that morning and baked fresh bread, so supper was handy enough. My Ed was by no means a demanding husband. He had always been happy with whatever I chose to put in front of him at mealtimes.

"You'll never believe it, Ed," I said as I placed a steaming bowl of vegetable soup in front of him.

Ed grinned. "When it comes to Jimmy, I'll believe anything."

"Boyles' Haven Hotel in Ireland." I paused, still shocked by Jimmy's revelation. "It's none other than Knockrath Manor."

"What...? How..."

"Do you remember the IRA set fire to it, during the war?"

"Yes, Jimmy told us about it."

"Yes, he did. But what he didn't tell us at the time was, it wasn't badly damaged. Only the kitchen area, the rest of it survived. The estate itself was sold off to the tenants. All that remained was the house."

"Were the family still living there at the time? What was their name?"

The Keeper of Secrets

"The Haughtons. Yes, they lived there during the Great War but as soon as that was over, they went back to England. The eldest lad, George, he was killed at the Somme."

"Okay, but that doesn't explain how their house is now a hotel."

"It's all in here." I waved Jimmy's letter at him. "Lord and Lady Haughton went back to England. The youngest, Ralph was the only one there the night of the fire. The IRA ordered him out of the house, but it turns out, the fire only really engulfed the kitchen area. The majority of the house remained intact. Anyway, the Haughtons claimed compensation from the new Irish government but they didn't get anywhere near what they claimed it was worth. Then a few years later, Lord and Lady Haughton died in a train crash. Ralph had to sell what was left of the house to pay the taxes. That's where the Boyle group came in."

"What happened to Ralph?"

"Now that's really interesting. Ralph is still there. He lives in a cottage on the grounds. Supposedly he has tenancy for life, part of the sale agreement. Jimmy says he's a hermit. Lives totally on his own, wanders along the riverbank talking to himself."

"How sad," Ed said.

"Sad? Or poetic justice? How the mighty have fallen, huh?"

Ed paused as the thought suddenly struck him. "How come we're only finding this out now? Angela moved there, shucks, must be twelve, no, thirteen years ago."

"I was puzzled about that too. When she described the place in her letters, it put me in mind of Knockrath Manor, but it never dawned on me that it could be the same house. I thought it had been burnt to the ground. Besides, it's not called Knockrath Manor. It's the Haven Lodge Hotel."

"I'll be damned."

"That house is damned. Or was. The Haughtons were not nice people. They treated their tenants badly. My da had more compassion in his little finger than any member of that family. I will always hold them responsible for Maggie's death, always."

Once again, my mind flashed back to the scene in the Haughton house when Maggie lost her mind. I can still see it all so clearly. I felt Ed's arms around me, and I sank into his embrace. My husband never queried me about those days. He listened to me and offered me comfort. Exactly what I needed to lift me out of the blackness that surrounded me when I thought of Maggie.

"What has Angela got to say about it all?"

I shook myself and lifted Angela's letter.

"She didn't know. When she first moved there, she heard the stories about the house and about the Haughton family. She never made the connection to me. In fairness I don't think I ever mentioned Knockrath Manor. I only ever talked about the country estate I lived in before I moved to Queenstown. And I certainly never told her about Maggie..."

Even mentioning Maggie's name brought an unbidden sob to my throat. Ed patted my hand.

"Anyway, the story she heard was that the master of the house... George... got the daughter of a servant pregnant. When he refused to marry her, she lost her mind and threw herself out of a window in the looney asylum. The local gossips claim that the family were cursed after that. George Haughton was killed in the war, then a few years later, Lord and Lady Haughton died in a train crash in England."

"But that's not what happened." Ed's voice shook. "Did Jimmy tell Angela the truth? Did he tell her it was your sister?"

I nodded, feeling quite sheepish. "Both Jimmy and Angela gave out to me. Angela said I should have told her about Maggie years ago. She's right, of course. I know I should have said something, but I couldn't, Ed. I just couldn't talk about it."

"I know, honey. And I'm sure Angela understands. It must have come as quite a shock to her though, relaying this story to Jimmy, only to hear that the story was twisted and that the girl in question was his sister, your sister."

I felt guilty then. Had I allowed my sister's memory to die along with her body when I refused to talk about her? She may live on in my head but to the Andersons she never existed. They were such a huge part of my life, yet they didn't know this crucial fact about me and my family. My younger sister died, in tragic circumstances, and through no fault of her own. By not talking about her, I had allowed others who didn't know the facts to spread their version of events. I should never have allowed that to happen. Maggie deserved so much more.

I said as much to Jimmy several months later. Kate stayed on in the Anderson house. After the war Jimmy had enough of the army. They lived happily enough. Work was plentiful. Jimmy was the type who could put his hand to anything he had a mind to. A trait inherited from his father.

"I went to see Primrose Cottage," Jimmy said.

I looked at him expectantly, suddenly tongue-tied, unable to ask if it was derelict.

"Ralph lives there now."

My mouth formed a large O. I couldn't have been more surprised if he had told me Fionn mac Cumhaill himself, the legendary Celtic warrior, was living in our old home. Jimmy laughed.

"Yes, I know. It's mad, isn't it? The last Lord Haughton, living in our cottage. But that's where he is. He keeps it well. The gardens are in great shape, lots of vegetables, well-tended."

"But... but."

"He asked after you."

I had to sit; afraid my legs would give under me. Ralph Haughton, Lord Haughton as he was at that stage, was living in our cottage. The lord of the manor, living in a two-roomed cottage, on the estate he once owned. How Ireland had changed. I blessed myself.

"What did he have to say for himself?" I asked.

"A lot, as it happens. About Maggie," Jimmy said, and by the expression on his face I knew I was facing a long and difficult conversation. I poured coffee into two large cups and sat at the kitchen table. How many secrets had been spilled around this table I thought.

Chapter 41

Ralph

"Lizzie," Ed's puzzled voice called out.

"Oh, my Lord, I didn't realise the time."

I jumped to my feet, raked the fire and got the heat going under the stew.

"Jimmy, you'll stay for dinner."

"I can't, Lizzie. Kate is expecting me, but I'll be back later. We'll both be back if we can get a sitter. You need to talk to Ed."

Jimmy kissed me on the cheek, shook Ed's hand and left. Ed looked at me with one eyebrow raised.

"Let me dish out dinner first. Then we'll talk. It's about Maggie."

Over dinner I told him everything Jimmy had said.

"Jimmy spoke to Ralph Haughton. Lord Haughton."

"Okay, go on."

"Where do I begin? You remember I told you about Ralph. He was the youngest, the whiny one that George was always picking on. I said it to Jimmy, I'd always suspected Ralph saw more than he said. He was too much of a coward to speak up.

"It seems Ralph has finally admitted that he knew George raped our Maggie. He came across them as George was buttoning his trousers. Maggie lying on the ground, dishevelled and crying. He went for George. Pushed him... and George fell against the granite pillar, split open his head. He said he was in shock, didn't realise that Maggie would get the blame."

"Are you telling me that Maggie got arrested for something that Ralph did?"

"Yes. Jimmy said he told him that he was, still is, deeply ashamed by his actions, but I find it hard to have any sympathy for him. Maggie went to prison because of him. He had the chance to say something when Maggie went up to the house and confronted George. I was there that day. Ralph clung to the wall like a limpet, said absolutely nothing. My sister lost her mind. He could have saved her. He chose not to."

"You're right. How could he allow an innocent young girl to suffer that way? What kind of a man is he?"

"I know he was afraid of George. Christ, he was afraid of his own shadow, but this... this was too much."

"So why is he telling the truth now?"

"Well..." I hesitated, for I still couldn't get my head around this new gem of information. "After everything that happened, George killed in the war, losing the estate, his parents dying, then having to sell the manor to cover the death duties, Ralph felt he had to make amends for what had happened to Maggie. He told Jimmy that at first his motives were purely selfish. He thought that the family were cursed, and it all traced back to the injustice of what happened to Maggie. He went to the police, but they weren't interested. Then he bumped into a guy he was in boarding school with. That guy became a doctor and when Jimmy mentioned Our Lady's Hospital to him the guy told him some very interesting stories. About stolen babies."

"What...?" Ed was incredulous.

I nodded. "Yep. Stolen babies. It turns out that the nuns in that hospital sold babies to America. It was all hush-hush. This doctor had been suspicious for a while, but he had only found out about it, and he was horrified."

"I take it he went to the authorities?" Ed asked.

"That's just it. He couldn't. The authorities were in cahoots with the nuns. They couldn't see any wrongdoing, told him that the nuns were saving those babies from a life of poverty."

"I suppose that does make sense. If the mother believes that her baby would be better off with another family and is willing to do that, then so be it. Look at us. Angela gave us such a precious gift."

"Yes, I think we can agree on that. The problem there was, the mothers were never asked. Their babies were stolen from them, without their permission. In some cases... they were told their babies had died."

"That's preposterous," Ed said, his colour rising as the veins in his neck expanded.

"It's dreadful. Such pain those poor women went through. My poor sister. Maggie's baby died. It was so painful. We would have reared that baby with love."

Ed put out his hand, interrupting my train of thought.

"But would you have? Think about it. That baby was the result of rape. Even Maggie might not have been able to raise that child."

I could feel my anger rising, up from my stomach, clutching my chest, then roaring out my mouth. "How could you say such a thing? Do you not know me at all? She would have loved that baby. We all would have loved it. At the end of the day the baby was Maggie's flesh and blood. I thought you of all people would understand that."

Ed's face crumpled under my anger.

"I'm sorry, Lizzie," he mumbled, reaching out to take me in his arms, "I'm so sorry. I spoke without thinking. Forgive me."

My husband's remorse was instantaneous. My anger

equally so. That he could think that way about any child shocked me to the core. It shook my belief in his goodness, his honesty, my belief in our family. For if Ed felt that way, how did he feel, deep down in his very soul about our son? Michael's biological father was Vinnie Fisher, a man we abhorred. Did Ed have his doubts about raising Michael? Did he look at Michael and see the product of a waster, a bootlegger, a criminal who left both his sisters damaged? Or did he see, our dearly loved son, Michael, the child we had raised since the day he was born?

Ed put his hands out and gripped my arms, forcing me to look at his face.

"I did not mean that the way it sounded, Lizzie. I am so sorry."

He looked totally dejected, and my heart relented. I could see in his eyes that he did not feel that way. Ed was purely voicing an opinion that I am sure most people would entertain. But most people had never been in the situation we had been in.

I sat at the table with my head in my hands. Ed sat beside me, his arm around my shoulders, while the minutes ticked away. How long we sat there I have no idea, only that our food went cold, and neither of us had any appetite left. Finally, I stood and cleared away the dishes. Ed stood beside me and wiped the dishes as I washed them. We worked in silence, each lost in our own thoughts.

Ed lit the lamp and raked the fire.

"Lizzie, come sit, talk to me."

I did as I was bid for there was so much more I needed to tell Ed before Jimmy arrived back.

"Ed, there's something else. Ralph is involved with an organisation that is trying to help these women. He gave the doctor our Maggie's name and asked him to find out anything he could. The doctor managed to get hold of some old records. Our Maggie's records."

"Oh, my Lord. But that's good news, Lizzie," Ed said, then stopped when he looked at me. "What... What is it?"

"Maggie's baby didn't die. They sold it. The nuns sold her little girl."

I couldn't stop the tears that ran down my face. I don't think I even realised I was crying. Inside, I could feel Maggie's pain. The memory of Ma's grief when the constable told us that the baby had died reignited inside me. It all felt so raw, as if it had only happened yesterday, not over thirty years ago. I didn't know what to do with this new information. How to process that Maggie's baby, my niece, that I thought had died at birth, was alive and living somewhere in this country.

There were so many questions. What was her name? Did she have a good upbringing? Did her new parents love her? Was she happy? My head melted with so many questions and no answers.

Chapter 42

Michael Christmas

Thoughts of Maggie's baby kept me occupied in between worrying about my son. It was another six months before Michael arrived home. I was shocked when I saw him. He was a ghost of his former self. The once broad shoulders seemed to have shrunk, his chest concave, the flesh on his upper arms loose and flabby. It took me about thirty seconds to get over the shock. After that I resolved to nurse my son back to good health. I cooked nourishing meals, loads of spuds and green vegetables. As much red meat as I could get my hands on. Fruity drinks and snacks, plus I baked every day. Soda bread warm from the oven. Fruit cake and queen cakes and sugary shortbread.

By the autumn, he had gained the weight he had lost but there was a spark missing from his eyes. I didn't know how to fix that. It wasn't something I could cure with good food and comfortable surroundings. That would take time. I knew that, still I railed against it. My handsome son. I couldn't bear to see him suffer.

Christmas was upon us before we knew it. I offered up my prayers for Michael. Jimmy brought Michael for walks on two evenings every week. Long walks on the beach where eventually

The Keeper of Secrets

Michael talked to Jimmy about everything they had been through. Part of me felt a twinge of jealousy, that my boy would talk to Jimmy but not to me. Stupid, I know.

Kneeling in front of the altar the day before Christmas Eve, I asked God to help him and all the other young men who had returned from war, help them put the horrors behind them and focus on their futures. I don't know if it was my prayers or Jimmy's intervention, but something changed in Michael that Christmas.

I first noticed it when Lori was in his company. He looked at her in a certain way, treated her with such tenderness, without caring who was watching. One evening they were sitting on the porch in the early evening dusk, drinking lemonade. For the first time in months, we heard him laugh out loud. A full-bellied laugh, which stretched all the way to his eyes. The sound of it brought joy to my heart. Ed and I exchanged happy smiles. Our son was back. And he was in love. They married the following summer.

Angela travelled home for the wedding. It was her first time on American soil since she'd left fifteen years earlier. We all walked Michael to the local church. I straightened his tie and kissed his cheek. In all honesty I can say that I have never felt love for another human being as I did for my son. Even Ed didn't come close, and he was the love of my life. A few weeks before the wedding my husband warned me to be careful.

"You put Michael on a pedestal. He's getting married now. Do you remember how my mother treated you when I brought you home?"

"Ed, don't be silly. I'm nothing like your mother." But I paid heed to what he said. I didn't want to turn into the interfering mother-in-law. I liked Lori. She was such a lovely girl who made my son happy. What more could a mother want for her son?

I worried about Angela too. Michael wasn't much more than

a boy when she went away. Her face said it all when she saw him. Puzzlement, astonishment, then the brightest smile.

"Michael, I can't believe it. I mean, where have the years gone?"

She hugged him, then stepped back and looked him up and down from head to toe.

"You have grown into such a handsome man. I know I might be biased; you are my nephew after all, but I hope that girl of yours appreciates you."

"She does, Aunt Angela," Michael said, his face bright red. "You'll get to meet her this evening. Although she has to leave early. Ma says it's bad luck for the groom to see the bride before the day of the wedding."

Angela groaned and then laughed. "I adore your ma's sayings. After living in Ireland for so long I know quite a few myself at this stage. Although I'm still learning the traditions. Your Mom asked me to bring her a Child of Prague statue, but it broke during the journey. I was so annoyed but then she tells me that it's lucky for the statue to lose its head."

"It's a present for Lori," I said to Michael. "The Child of Prague is put out in the garden the night before the wedding to guarantee good weather. If the head is broken, it's lucky as long as it was knocked off by accident."

"Maybe that was needed in Ireland, Mom, but I think we're safe enough here."

I suppose he had a point, but I couldn't let go of the traditions I had grown up with. I had a lucky horseshoe polished and ready to attach to Lori's bridal bouquet with a blue ribbon. The flowers for the bouquet were ready for picking in my garden.

When Lori arrived, she totally charmed Angela as I knew she would. She was such a sweet girl. Ed and I were looking forward to calling her our daughter-in-law. The morning of the wedding, I rose early as always. The homely scent of fresh bread on the griddle woke Ed and Michael and brought them to the table. It was the last meal I would cook for my bachelor son. After that day he would come for dinner often but always as part of a couple and hopefully head of a family.

It was a lovely ceremony. The blushing bride in white, her grinning groom in naval dress uniform. Little Nora was a picture in the pretty yellow flower-girl dress I had made for her. After the church we went to The Haven Hotel where the bride's parents treated us to a gorgeous dinner. After dinner the newly married couple dressed in their finery. The bride threw her bouquet over her shoulder, caught by Angela, much to everyone's surprise, including Angela. The happy couple drove off in Michael's newly acquired Ford. I say newly acquired as it was new to him but at least ten years old. They were headed to Daytona Beach for a few days honeymoon.

As I stood on the steps at the front of the hotel waving into the distance, Angela put her arm around my waist and hugged me.

"You're a brilliant mother, Lizzie. You should be so proud of him."

The lump already in my throat threatened to choke me.

"Ah, Angela. That means so much to me," I said. "Really, thank you so much. It has been an honour. He is such a good man."

"Thanks to you... and Ed of course."

I had to ask. "No regrets?"

She spun me round, put her hands on my upper arms and looked me straight in the face. "None. Not once. Not ever."

We hugged. I held on so tight, so grateful to Angela for what she did for us.

"What's this?" Ed asked. "Is this a private hug or can anyone join in?"

We laughed as Ed wrapped his muscular arms around us both. Jimmy noticed what was going on and he joined in the group hug dragging Kate with him, much to the amusement of little Nora.

"I'm so lucky," I said, more to myself than to anyone in particular, but I think they all heard me.

Chapter 43

Wedding Guests

It was great having Angela with us. Despite her monthly missives that arrived by post, it was different to speak to her face to face. We had so much catching up to do. Angela scolded me of course for not telling her about our Maggie. I talked to her at length and finally got it all out in the open.

"Ralph Haughton is a recluse. He might live on the grounds, but you never see him unless you're out at the crack of dawn."

"Well, stay away from him. I will never forgive him for not speaking up for our Maggie. Such a coward. Imagine allowing a young girl to suffer the way she did."

"I'm too busy in the hotel to worry about the likes of Ralph Haughton," Angela said.

"Which reminds me, how are the newlyweds settling in?"

Evelyn Boyle had married another hotelier, Ian Dennison, the previous year. At her father's request, or maybe her own, who knows, they had returned to Ireland to run The Haven Hotel and Country Club.

"They've brought a new energy to the place. It's amazing the difference in just a few short months. Mr Boyle's heart wasn't in it, not after Mrs Boyle died. She was such a lovely woman."

Angela sighed and I could see how much she cared about this family.

"How old is the new Mrs Dennison?"

"She's younger than me, mid-thirties I'd say. He's a good five years older. They make a great team."

"No sign of anyone you'd like to team up with?" I asked.

Angela laughed.

"I don't need the complications, thank you very much. I'm quite content in my own company, that is when I get a chance to take some time for myself. Work is so busy at the moment I don't have any downtime."

"You know what they say about all work and no play."

"You and your sayings. You never change," Angela said. "And thank God for that."

The week after the wedding, I hosted the entire family for Sunday dinner. Michael and Lori were back from their honeymoon and Angela was flying back to Ireland two days later. I thought it was the perfect opportunity to get the family together one last time. With Angela living five thousand miles away, God knows when we would all be together again.

There was a nervous tension around Jimmy and Kate from the second they arrived. I knew somehow that there was something brewing but I jumped to the wrong conclusion. I thought Kate was going to announce that she was in the family way. I couldn't have got it more wrong. Jimmy waited until dessert to tell us his news. Kate sat, her head down, holding Nora's hand while he spoke for them both.

"We have something to tell you."

I clapped my hands together, eager to hear their news.

"We're moving to Ireland."

My mouth fell open as my mind spun. I stared at Ed, who

stared back at me, equally shocked. Michael got up and approached Jimmy with his hand outstretched.

"Good for you, Jimmy," he said as he shook his uncle's hand. I couldn't speak. Ed got up from his seat and he shook Jimmy's hand and kissed Kate's cheek. All the while Kate watched me, waiting for my reaction, her eyes flicking from me to Angela who was sitting to my right.

"Say something, Lizzie," Angela said.

"Did you know about this?"

Angela's face flamed. "I'll make some coffee, shall I?"

"Lizzie," Jimmy said. "The world's a much smaller place than it used to be. Ireland is not that far away. You can come visit us. Wouldn't you like to see Cork again?"

"No. No, I wouldn't," I said. "Is it Cork you're going to? What will you do? Where will you live?" A myriad of questions tumbled out of my mouth. It was such a shock to hear Jimmy say he was going back to Ireland. To my mind, there was nothing there to pull him back.

"We're going to the Haven Manor Hotel. They need a gilly."

For a moment I felt like a cartoon character. My mouth fell open, just for a second until it struck me. "Poacher turned gamekeeper?"

"Yes, Lizzie, why not? I was brought up on the Knockrath estate, roamed every inch of it as a child. I celebrated with the tenants when they took over their farms. I was there when the manor house was set on fire. I fought the British and I fought our own. God help us all. I've earned the right to live in my home county."

Jimmy's passion for his home broke something in me. How did I not know he felt so homesick? I had never felt that way about Ireland. Once I landed in America, I made it my mission in life to fit in, to appreciate the country that took me in when I had nothing. Jimmy didn't feel the same way. That much was obvious. When Jimmy finally joined me in America, I was so happy. Now I was going to lose him again.

"When are you going?"

"The end of the month," Jimmy said. He knelt in front of me and took my hands in his.

"I know it's a shock to you but it's for the best. After the war I tried to fit back in, but I can't. I'm an Irishman born and bred. I feel like a fish out of water here amongst these yanks."

"Hey," Ed shouted, but I could see the smile on his face. Jimmy laughed.

"When I went to see Angela, at the end of the war... I don't have the words to explain it but as I rounded Murphy's Corner, that last bend before the road parallels the river, I felt this warmth in my heart. It was totally weird, this feeling that I was home."

Jimmy's eyes bore into mine, begging me to understand.

"I ignored that feeling. I came back to Kate and Nora, and I got on with life but every day that passed that yearning got stronger. In the end I talked to Kate. She's happy to give it a go. We can always come back if it doesn't work out."

"But, Jimmy. Ireland... It's so far away, so different than Florida. How will Kate and Nora cope with the cold and the damp... or the wind?"

Jimmy squeezed my hands. "It will be different, yes, but they might even like it. Angela loves it there."

I looked at Kate who smiled at me. "It'll be a new experience for us. Who knows, when I get Nora settled in school, I might even take on a part-time job. I might find a whole new career."

That was it. My last Sunday family dinner together turned out to be not just a farewell to Angela but a goodbye to Jimmy, Kate and Nora as well. I cried myself to sleep that night, with

Ed rubbing my back trying to comfort me. Nothing helped. It's all right for Jimmy to say Ireland is not that far from Florida in the days of modern travel. It took fifteen years for Angela to get back for a visit. How long would it be before I saw my brother again? What age would Nora be before I saw her pretty little face again?

Chapter 44

Ed's Retirement

Jimmy was true to his word. He wrote home every month, regular as clockwork. Kate wrote too and always sent a drawing or a doodle of some sort from Nora. I missed that little girl so much. Although becoming a grandmother more than made up for that.

Lori fell pregnant straight away. Conor was born in April 1948, a week short of ten months after the wedding. I doted on him. He was the image of his father. An Anderson to the backbone. Lori was born to be a mother. They were living in the Anderson house at that stage. Before Jimmy and Kate left for Ireland, they asked Michael if he was interested in living there for a nominal rent. Michael jumped at the opportunity. It was a family home, and it was good to see it remain in the Anderson family. There was plenty of room to expand the new generation of Andersons.

Ed adored his grandson. As soon as Conor could walk, he toddled around the garden copying everything his grandad did. They were a joy to watch together. Baby number two came along eighteen months later. A little girl this time. They named her Margaret, but we called her Beth. I cried. Ed beamed. We took a photograph of all six of us, got two copies printed. Ed got one photo framed and hung it over the fireplace. The other we sent to Cork.

Lori was amazing. Even with two small babies she managed their home with military precision. It was spotless yet homely. Within a few years she started baking. No matter when you called the smell of home baking filled the air. She set up a little home business, baking cakes and pastries for the local shops. It was remarkably successful.

The years flew by. Ed retired from the naval yard. He spent most of his time in the garden, looking after the vegetables and herbs. We had quite a large operation at that stage, even selling our surplus in the local market. It was on the morning of market day I noticed the change in Ed. To me, my husband got more handsome by the day. It was so unfair. Men matured better than women. On them, grey hair looked distinguished, on us it only looked old. Ed was better-looking than most men. He had an air about him, a twinkle in his eye, a spring in his step that caught my breath and forced me to look at him and marvel at this fine specimen of a man.

That morning I looked out and saw an old man. Ed was stooped, holding his back as he pulled himself upright. It hit me violently, like a slap or a fall. My wonderful husband, my tower of strength looked old. I laughed at myself then, for we were both nearly sixty. We were grandparents. What did I expect? For us to be forever young and looking to the future? I suppose at some stage in life you start to reflect on the way life used to be. Is it because your future is no longer assured, that the majority of your years are behind you?

I said as much to Ed when he came back into the kitchen.

"Never lose it, honey. I love your fanciful nonsense."

He leaned forward and kissed my cheek, holding his muddy hands at arm's length. I kissed him back and pushed him playfully towards the sink. He laughed as he washed his hands. I examined the basket of mangos he had pulled for the market until I heard a thump behind me. I turned expecting to scold Ed for dropping something, but it was Ed who was in a heap on the floor. His eyes open and unstaring. I ran to him, calling his name. I shook him repeatedly, slapped him, tried to revive him but it was all too late. My handsome husband was dead. They told me afterwards it was a massive heart attack. Nothing I could have done.

It's funny how the mind knows what you can cope with and what you can't. The most painful moments disappear into the furthest recesses, buried only to be resurrected in flashes that disable you. My memories of that day are blurred. Flashes of pain intertwined with support from family and friends. The finer details buried somewhere beyond my comprehension.

Michael was a tower of strength. He organised everything while Lori never left my side. I was numb, unable to focus on anything but my shock at losing my other half, the other part of myself. I'm nobody's fool. We all grow old. Death is a part of life. I know that but I didn't anticipate Ed dying like that. So suddenly. No warning. I should have been more prepared. My mother died suddenly. My father too. Why did I not anticipate that Ed could die like that? Alive one second, keeled over lifeless the next.

Michael and Lori guided me through the funeral. They made all the decisions. They had to. I was incapable of any thought process. Our friends and neighbours gathered around us. They fed us casseroles and stocked my refrigerator with more. They prayed with us, supported us and carried my husband's body to the church and then to the cemetery where Ed was buried in a plot beside his parents.

And then it was over. I was alone, in the home we had built together. My neighbours returned to their lives. Michael and

Lori returned to theirs. They wanted me to go with them, but I refused. I wanted to be alone, needed to grieve.

I moved from room to room, my arms wrapped around myself, and I felt his loss, felt his absence. In the bathroom his toothbrush stood beside mine, same as always. In the bedroom, I opened the wardrobe and buried my nose in his favourite shirt. The one I had bought him for Christmas. His scent enveloped me, bringing me comfort until the realisation dawned once again that he was gone from me forever.

Ed was everything to me. I was part of a couple, one half of a whole. I couldn't figure out how to exist without him. From the day I met Ed at age seventeen, he was the first thought in my head in the morning and my last thought at night. How could I go on without him by my side? I felt as if part of my own body were missing.

For months afterwards I behaved as a widow should. Prayed for my husband's soul although why he needed prayers to get into heaven was beyond me. The man was a saint in life. He never said a bad word about anyone and wouldn't hurt a fly. Lori and Michael called to visit me several times a week. I told them I was fine. That they shouldn't worry about me. That their children needed them. And I believed that. But eventually I fell apart.

In my head I figured no one would miss me. I had been Mrs Anderson, the wife of Ed Anderson. Now I was the widow, the woman in the background with no husband, her family reared. I couldn't find my place in life. My identity had changed, and I couldn't figure out who I was.

For months afterwards I struggled to get out of bed in the mornings. I couldn't see the point. What had I to get up for? I neglected my home, my garden and myself. It became a downward spiral. Initially I made sure that on the days I knew

Michael was calling, I was up, dressed and with a pot of soup on the range. Eventually even that became too much for me.

Lori realised what was going on and took to calling after she dropped the children to school. She'd scold me and force me to get up and eat something. Michael would call in the evenings on the pretence of checking the garden. I no longer had any interest in it. Ed had taken over from me when he retired. It was his domain. At one stage I took to walking out there at night when the world was asleep. I would talk to him, try to conjure him up but it was of no comfort for all I could hear was my own voice scolding me for letting all his hard work go to rack and ruin.

Then one evening, Michael and Lori called with the children.

"Mom, we need your help," Michael said.

I looked up, surprised. It had been so long since anyone needed me for anything I wasn't sure how to react.

"Lori's been offered a permanent space at the open market. If she is to take it up, she needs help with the children."

"It's a great opportunity for us," Lori said, a beaming smile on her pretty face.

I nodded. Something stirred inside me. The prospect of a purpose to my life was enticing.

"We were hoping you could collect the children from school and keep them here for a few hours every day."

"Yes, yes of course. I would be happy to." The prospect of spending more time with my grandchildren filled me with such pleasure. Finally, something to make me get out of bed in the mornings. A reason to put one foot in front of the other every day. It was music to my ears.

"When do I start?"

The following week I walked the short distance to the children's school. I was outside the school gates twenty minutes before the bell went. Walking back to the house, chatting about their day, I felt a lightness in my heart for the first time since Ed died, instead of the dull lump of lead I had become accustomed to. Every day my heart lifted another tiny piece until eventually I felt like I was alive again.

Michael had instructed the children that they were to help out in the garden. Every afternoon the children would weed and prune for an hour before I called them in for snacks. After a few weeks the improvement was amazing. I began to feel guilty, but not enough to go out there with them. When they were in the garden, I would bake cookies as their reward. As time went on, they asked me to join them. Whether that was their idea or their father's I don't know, but eventually I acquiesced. By the first anniversary of Ed's death, I was finally at peace with it. I could feel his gentle presence in the garden, and it comforted me.

Chapter 45

Thoughts of Family

There's no point in saying I didn't miss Jimmy. I missed all of them; Jimmy, Kate, my lovely niece Nora. Angela. Even though she had been living in Ireland thirty years at that stage. She wrote to me regularly. Monthly missives. Angela wrote in the middle of the month, Jimmy at the end. When Ed was alive, I would read them in the morning when the postman delivered them, then read them again with Ed over our evening meal. After he died, I missed those discussions so much. I valued Ed's opinion, his ability to read between the lines of what was said and what wasn't. It took me a while to become accustomed to devouring the contents of those letters alone but eventually I did, although sometimes I spoke to Ed as if he were still there with me.

I never had any desire to travel back to Ireland. Yes, I missed my family, but the idea of that journey filled me with horror. When I travelled to America, I was a young woman, full of hopes and dreams. There was a purpose to my journey. My husband was waiting for me. The promise of a long and happy life lay before me. And I had all of that. Marriage to Ed was wonderful. I adored that man, loved him with all my heart. We had our ups and downs, of course we did. What married couple can say that their path was always smooth? Show me that couple and I'll show you a liar. It's the downs that reinforce the ups. The peaks that make the troughs so hard to bear.

Overall, I felt I was lucky. My da called me Lucky Lizzie and for the vast majority of my life I've felt I've earned that name. The sister I lost in Maggie was given back to me two-fold with Kate and Angela. The babies I couldn't carry were given to me with Michael. I counted my blessings on a regular basis. And as for Ed, well, I couldn't have asked for a better husband.

That sense of optimism wasn't confined to my little world. When John F Kennedy was inaugurated in January 1961 it felt like the whole country was swept up in a wave of enthusiasm. The youngest American president ever elected, the first Catholic and the first man who proudly proclaimed his Irish heritage. It made me proud to be Irish, as if somehow his achievements had rubbed off on me.

Even Michael liked him, and he was a true-blue republican.

"When I read what that man said when they swore him in, I thought, now there's a leader," Michael said.

"What did he say?"

"Ask not what your country can do for you, ask what you can do for your country."

"That's powerful."

I never had an interest in American politics. As long as my Michael was happy, then so was I. My little family were the most important thing in my world.

They were the thoughts going through my mind as I opened Jimmy's letter. I was humming along to Patsy Cline on the wireless. All the windows were open to catch the slight breeze that carried the laughter of the children as they played in the garden with the hurleys their uncle Jimmy had sent at Christmas. I was happy, content with my lot in life and totally unprepared for the contents of Jimmy's letter. I read it. Then read it again. I sat at the table stupefied. Unable to process the information contained in those pages.

Jimmy had never given up on tracing Maggie's baby. When we first found out about the stolen babies, we had discussed the possibility that she had been sold to a wealthy family. We had hopes that we could track her down. But as the years passed those hopes faded. The nuns had covered their tracks well.

I was surprised by how tenacious Ralph was in following every lead. Jimmy kept me informed of any progress. I couldn't communicate with Ralph, could never forgive him for not speaking up for Maggie. We rowed about it. Me and Jimmy that is. I felt he should have nothing to do with Ralph. In my opinion he was as responsible for our sister's death as George or the nuns for that matter.

Jimmy disagreed. He felt Ralph had paid his dues, told me he was a changed person from the boy I knew. According to Jimmy, Ralph spent all his time tracking down these stolen babies, as if by giving them back their identity he could somehow find his own identity, one he could live with.

Anyway, it turned out, Jimmy had made progress. He had found paperwork which proved that the nuns had lied to Maggie, to my mother, to the authorities. Actual proof that Maggie's baby didn't die at birth. Evidence that the nuns stole her baby girl and sold her to an American couple. Money had changed hands. How much they didn't know but they had found a paper trail. Maggie's baby was alive. Well, hardly a baby. She was nearly forty-eight years old.

I slumped in my chair, wondering who she was, where she was. Did she know that her parents had adopted her? That she was Irish by birth? What kind of life did she have? Was she loved? Did she have a family of her own? My niece lived here in this, my adopted, country. I left Ireland to follow my dreams, to start a new life in a new country. But that was my choice. Maggie's baby was brought here. She had no hand, act or part in that decision. Had they raised her as an American? The United States is a huge country. She could be anywhere. Was she still alive? Anything could have happened to her. Did she marry? Did she marry the man of her dreams? My mind buzzed with questions. I reread the letter that raised more questions than it answered. I didn't know how to feel about this news.

Chapter 46

Television

When I saw the newsreel of John F Kennedy landing in Ireland, well you could have knocked me over with a feather. The man was the most popular president ever as far as I could tell. Yet here he was, spending time in Ireland, the country so many of us had left.

Angela's letter that month was full of the trip. She said that thousands lined the streets of Dublin city the day he arrived to see his cavalcade. The next day he visited his ancestral home in Wexford then back to Dublin. On the third day he took a helicopter to Cork city before returning to Dublin where he laid a wreath in Arbour Hill for the leaders of the 1916 rising. On his last day he travelled to Galway where thousands turned out to catch a glimpse of him, then Limerick and on to Shannon.

Michael bought me one of those new television sets. He said it would keep me occupied at night. He was right. I found a whole new world. I became totally engrossed in the lives of the people in that little box. The shows entranced me, *As the World Turns, Bonanza, I Love Lucy*, and I tuned into the news every evening.

Ireland looked different on the newsreels. Different than

the Ireland I remembered. Then again it had been forty-four years. Even Florida was not the same country as it was when I first arrived. Me and Ed were certainly changed. I arrived in Florida, a young bride, full of enthusiasm, ready to forge a new life for myself in this new country. I did just that. Me and Ed were incredibly happy. Our Michael was a constant source of joy to us. The only fly in the ointment was memories of Maggie, or rather what could have been.

Knowing that her baby was out there somewhere haunted me. I tried to reason with myself that if she had been sold to a wealthy American couple, chances were that she had a good life. They would have had money for a good standard of education for her, good health care, nice clothes, a comfortable house, maybe even a pony.

But sometimes I worried that she had fallen into the wrong hands. That somehow her life had been one of hardship, poverty or abuse. Ed tried to talk to me.

"If an American couple travelled all the way to Ireland to adopt a baby, then they had serious money. They would have given her a good life."

When I thought about it logically, then he had to be right. Who would go to those lengths if they weren't going to look after her properly? Still, I waited with bated breath for updates on the search for her in Jimmy's letters.

All thoughts of Maggie's baby were relegated to the back of my mind when I heard the news about the shooting of John F Kennedy. Like most people I saw the newsreels. His poor wife scrambling over the back of that car. Her pink suit stained with her husband's blood. I was horrified. I couldn't understand it. Such hope, so much promise, wiped out. I think the whole country mourned, regardless of their political persuasion.

Michael and Lori joined me on the couch to watch the vice president being sworn in. I didn't know anything about Lyndon

Johnson other than he was now our new president. Kennedy was a tough act to follow, particularly under the circumstances. We were glued to the television for John F Kennedy's funeral. I think the image of his three-year-old son saluting his coffin was carried in most papers nationwide, even worldwide.

At the grave-site, Irish soldiers performed the foot drill. My heart filled with pride when the television presenters talked about these thirty Irish soldiers who had travelled to Washington to pay this tribute to an American president. Their presence was requested by Jackie Kennedy, a nod to the Kennedy family Irish heritage. I wondered if Jimmy was watching it on his television. For the first time since he left, I felt a strong connection to my brother. We could both be doing the same thing at the same time. Watching Irish soldiers honour an American president.

In some twisted way, that thought gave me hope. It made the world smaller. If me and Jimmy could watch the same event separated by the might of the Atlantic, then who knows what else could be achieved. The distance between the country of my birth and the country I lived in, no longer felt so vast. More importantly, it gave me renewed hope that maybe, just maybe, we would one day find Maggie's little girl.

Chapter 47

Roots

The trail ran cold. Jimmy told me not to despair. The information was out there. It was just a matter of finding it. A few months later he wrote to tell me that Ralph was travelling to America to follow up on some information that he thought could be useful. Part of me felt grateful that Ralph was putting so much effort into tracking down Maggie's baby. But that gratitude was quickly replaced with anger. It was the least he could do. Maggie would still be alive if he had only spoken the truth at the time. Her baby would never have been taken from her. All of our lives would have been so different.

I didn't feel any hatred towards him. At least that's what I told myself. Hatred was alien to me. It was an emotion that ate away at the holder. There was no purpose to it, no end to it. I couldn't bring myself to hate him, but I couldn't like him, couldn't converse with him. That was too much to ask of me. It was easier to pretend he didn't exist. Ralph was this person who existed in Jimmy's world, not mine. I separated the Ralph I knew in my childhood from this current Ralph.

In every letter that Jimmy wrote to me, he asked me to come visit him. I can't deny it. There were times I was tempted.

Maria McDonald

When I left Ireland all those years ago, I never thought I could go back. In fairness it wasn't an option, for any of us that left her shores. Travelling was expensive, still is. But the sixties brought commercial air travel and all of a sudden, the journey that took weeks by sea, could suddenly be achieved on the same day. It was unbelievable to someone like me. I watched the television programmes. There were programmes about Ireland. Aerial shots of the Emerald Isle. The beauty of it stirred a longing in me, to see my home country one more time. Part of me was scared. I had lived in Florida longer than I had ever lived in Ireland. My roots were here, in this tropical paradise with the warm seas of the Gulf of Mexico lapping at our shore. My much-loved son, his lovely wife, my grandchildren, they were all born in America, land of the free, home of the brave. I believed in all of that.

But a little voice niggled in my ear. My roots were also in Ireland. I was born there. My parents were buried there. Maggie was buried there. Making their lives there were my brother, my beloved sisters Kate and Angela, my niece Nora. I was torn.

Then I got a letter from Nora telling me she was getting married. I was delighted for her. Pleased for Kate and Jimmy. They liked her intended, a local farmer named Fionn. Nora invited us to the wedding. It was the perfect opportunity to go back. A chance to visit my brother and Kate, to visit our parents' graves. When Michael arrived later that evening I showed him the letter.

"You should go, Mom," he said.

"We should all go."

"I don't think I could afford it. Not all of us anyway. I'll check out the cost. Maybe I could send Beth with you."

Angela's next letter solved my dilemma. She sent plane tickets for all of us. Me, Michael, Lori, Conor and Beth. We had to get ourselves to New York, from there we would fly with Aer

Lingus to Shannon Airport in County Clare. About ninety-odd miles from the place I was born. I held the tickets in my hand, stunned by her generosity. My heart pounded as the thought struck me, I was going home. That shocked me even more. The idea that somewhere deep inside me was the belief that Cork was my home. Not the home I had built with Ed, the life I had built in Florida for forty-six years.

Chapter 48

Trains and Planes

Michael drove us all to Jacksonville to catch the train. The station was busy, full of young men in uniform. I blessed myself, grateful that my son had served his time in the military. At seventeen, Conor was too young yet for the draft. Hopefully that dreadful conflict in Vietnam would be over within the next two years.

I loved every second of the train journey. Despite how much I missed Ed. This was his country and seeing the changing scenery reminded me of our early years together when he enthralled me with stories about the country that he loved. The United States was so beautiful. So many different landscapes sped past our window as the train made its way from Florida through Georgia, the Carolinas, into Virginia, Delaware and Pennsylvania before we came to halt in New York's Penn Station. I slept through North Carolina and parts of Delaware. There was nothing to see at night anyway. But during daylight hours I was glued to the window, watching the changing landscape. Michael teased me.

"You'll catch the travel bug, Ma. There's a whole big world out there."

"I've travelled enough, thank you very much. It was no easy ride getting here all those years ago."

A sudden swift image of Aíne took my breath away. I could smell the sea, taste the breeze on my cheeks, feel Aíne's arm intertwined in mine as we walked the promenade in Queenstown. We were so young, so carefree, so in love with our yankees.

"Are you okay, Gran?" Beth's touch on my arm startled me back to reality.

I patted her hand. "Did I ever tell you about Aíne?"

Beth shook her head. She had the Anderson look about her, all dark hair and smouldering eyes. Definitely a heartbreaker. At fifteen she was a bit of a rebel too. I admired that in her. She was brave in a way that I had never been. But then again, it was a brave new age. Times had changed. Women's expectations were very different. Beth had an expectation of going to college, of having a career. I envied her while at the same time feared for her. Who would look after her? Beth would say she could look after herself and I had no doubt that she was quite capable. Her father was more old-fashioned. Beth's skirts were a little too short for her father's liking, but she always managed to talk him around, with her mother's help. And my support too. I liked this brave new world.

"Aíne was my cousin and my best friend. I lived with her family in Queenstown. Her mother, my Aunt Jean, was a lovely woman. Me and Aíne met our American sailors on the same night in our local dance hall. Your grandad Ed and his friend Scott. We went everywhere together, the four of us. I'm sure I told you all this before."

"Mom, I haven't heard you mention that in years," Michael said.

"Probably not. No point in raking up the past."

"What happened to them?" Beth asked.

"Aíne died in childbirth. It was awful."

The memory of that night resurfaced. I don't think it ever left me.

"How dreadful, Gran," Beth said. "What happened to the baby?"

"My Aunt Jean brought up the baby. With your great-granny's help. When Da died, Ma moved to Queenstown to live with Aunt Jean and help with the baby. A little boy, Scott, named after his daddy."

"Are they still there?" Beth said. "Can we go see them?"

I shook my head, the sorrow of it all threatened to overwhelm me again.

"They're all gone now. My da died before I left Ireland. Spanish flu. Ma died when Michael was a baby. Aunt Jean, they're all gone. I lost touch with Scott. He would be a fair age now. Late forties."

"Maybe we could look him up, while we're there," Beth said.

"Maybe we will, pet," I said.

It had been years since I'd said Aíne's name out loud. She was often in my thoughts, but I didn't speak about her. Like Maggie, like all of my past life in Ireland. I had never shared any of that life with Michael or with my grandchildren. When I moved to America, I left Ireland behind me in every sense of the word. I embraced American culture, threw myself into living the American dream. I may have brought my Irish ways with me. My recipes, my sayings that my family always teased me over. But I left the people I loved behind me. It was too painful to talk about them so in order to get on with my new life, I tucked them away in the back of my mind. Now I was travelling back to the country of my youth, those memories were resurfacing, demanding to be heard.

It was my first time on an airplane. The first time for Beth too. I could sense her excitement was matched by my trepidation. Part of me was amazed, but the bigger part was scared stiff. This metal box was going to fly us through the clouds to another continent.

"You're gonna love it," Michael said.

He was right. I did. It was such an experience. Not quite as daring as Amelia Earhart but for an old lady it felt adventurous enough. Much as I enjoyed it, I was still happy to touch down in Ireland. It was pretty amazing flying in over the southern tip of my home country and seeing how green it was. I hadn't realised how much I missed that greenery until I saw it from that vantage point.

We stayed with Jimmy and Kate. It felt surreal to be back. The school was still in the same place at the end of the village. A small supermarket stood on the site of Mrs McCoy's shop. There was a café and a bookshop, next to a television rental shop. Two hundred yards past the last of the buildings, was a petrol station. The last stop before the road to Cork city.

Jimmy and Kate opened their home to us. They really gave us the *céad míle fáilte*. Nothing was too much trouble for them. We arrived two days before the wedding. Nora shared her room with me and Beth. Michael and Lori got the spare room, with Conor in the box room. The house was full. The sitting room was stuffed full of presents from friends and family. It was so joyful.

Nora had grown into a beautiful young woman. Her beau was a farmer. Fionn Quirke had never been outside of the county of Cork. I think he found us all a bit overwhelming. He definitely thought we were noisy. Nora had lived so long in Cork that all traces of her American accent had disappeared. It was hard to believe she hadn't been born and bred in Ireland.

"I still hold my American passport though," she said when I teased her about her accent.

"Although why I don't know," Fionn said. "She hasn't used it and is not likely to either. Sure, where would she be going with a farmhouse to run?"

Nora laughed. "I might just take a notion to go visit my American cousins."

Fionn had the grace to look worried, not seeing the wink Nora gave me.

"You may get yourself a passport, Fionn, so you can come with me. I'm not leaving the country without you."

Fionn smiled at her and in the glances they exchanged the love between them shone. My niece had chosen well, I thought.

The wedding was taking place in the local parish church with a reception afterwards in The Haven Hotel. It's been forty-five years since I'd laid eyes on Knockrath Manor. Forty-six years since I left Ireland. I had so many bad memories tied up with the estate. What happened to Maggie. My mother's grief. Ralph's cowardice. On the plane journey I had plenty of time to think about it all. It would have been better if Ed were still alive to help me, but he wasn't. So, I had to think it through alone. By the time we landed I had it all boxed away in neat little compartments. The Haughton family were long gone. Knockrath Manor was a luxury hotel owned by an American family. They offered weekend breaks for the well-heeled and luxury stays for wealthy Americans. Lavishly appointed rooms, all en suite, Michelin-starred restaurant, uniformed bellboys and top-class service. A spot of golf, complete with lessons by a pro, on its specially designed eighteen-hole course. Tennis for the ladies in their designer sportswear. The house and grounds upgraded to the best the late 1960s could offer. And all at a price I could never afford. Then again, I wouldn't want to stay there.

The day before the wedding we all sat around the breakfast table discussing the day ahead. Jimmy was quiet, listening more than talking, nodding occasionally when Kate reminded him of a task he needed to complete.

"And don't forget, you've to go up to the hotel today to pay the bill."

"I haven't forgotten, *mo ghrá*," Jimmy said. "What about it, Lizzie? Would you like to come with me?"

"Yes... actually yes I really would." I hadn't expected to see the hotel until the wedding. It made perfect sense to me to go beforehand. While I was sure I had my emotions in check, I preferred to test it out.

Kate had insisted that Jimmy clean his car inside and out before we arrived. It certainly didn't have the appearance of a car used by a gilly. I felt like quite the lady as we wound our way up the driveway of Knockrath Manor.

Chapter 49

Banishing Ghosts

Magnificent lawns, as smooth and green as a billiard table, swept down to the river, bordered by mature plants in shades of pinks and purples that attracted bees and butterflies. As we pulled into the car park, I could hear the gentle lilt of two male voices carried on the summer breeze. They were working in the flowerbeds, their voices barely audible over the gentle trickle of the water as it flowed past the west wing of the manor. As I watched I couldn't help but wonder if they were local. Would they know of my family, understand what happened to us, all those years ago? Then I laughed to myself remembering that it all happened over fifty years ago, before they were even born.

The original front entrance into the main hall was now the reception area. I had never walked through those doors. The servants' entrance by the kitchen was the only door I knew. Behind the reception desk stood a young woman, her flame-red hair tied back in a ponytail. She was perfectly groomed, in a navy uniform with silver name tag.

"Good morning, Jimmy." She flashed us a dazzling smile.

"Morning, Teresa. I'd like you to meet my sister, Mrs Lizzie Anderson."

"Welcome to The Haven Hotel, Mrs Anderson. I hope you enjoy your visit."

Something about her seemed familiar to me yet I was sure I had never met her before.

"Angela will be with you shortly. Perhaps you'd like to wait in the coffee dock?"

We had coffee on the terrace. The same terrace where the Haughton family sipped their mid-morning tea. The same terrace where they sampled gin and tonics on warm summer evenings. The same terrace where Lady Haughton had screamed at Maggie, where Lord Haughton had stood as he ordered the arrest of twelve-year-old Maggie. An obviously distraught Maggie. The whole scene replayed in my mind's eye. Maggie's clothing in disarray. Lady Haughton's screams. Ralph's chalk-white face. It was surreal.

"Strange, isn't it?" Jimmy's voice cut into my thoughts. "When I started working here, I felt like I was trespassing. I kept waiting on Lord Haughton arriving and having me locked up."

"Do you still feel that way?"

Jimmy laughed. "No. The Haughtons are long gone. Knockrath Manor is dead. This is the Haven Hotel and Country Club."

I looked at Jimmy, then looked around me. The doors into what was the family living room were open, revealing how the room was the same yet different. The same wallpaper, light fittings, the magnificent fireplace: but where the chesterfield suite sat there was now an oak counter with displays of scones and pastries. There were small round tables and deep armchairs scattered around the room. The Haughton family formal living area converted to a luxurious coffee dock in a top-class hotel.

"It's very strange. I don't think I could ever feel at ease here."

"I thought that at first too, but you will, Lizzie. The past is behind us." Jimmy gestured around him. "This is the future. Ireland is a different country to the one it used to be."

Jimmy had been working for the hotel for twenty years. He'd had time to adjust to this massive change. He was right. It would take me a while.

Angela waved from the open doors. "Lizzie, I'm so glad you came. Come on, I'll give you a tour."

That felt even more surreal. I was familiar with the kitchens in Knockrath Manor, but the kitchens I knew had been destroyed in the fire. The modern, commercial kitchen bore no resemblance to the one Mrs Short presided over in my childhood. I couldn't help feeling that she would be very impressed. I had been in the formal living room that day when Maggie tried to confront Master George. Other than that, I had no idea what the rest of the house looked like.

"The Boyles took great care when they renovated. They held to as much of the original features as possible. Like that magnificent staircase," Angela said.

And it was magnificent. Mahogany balustrades wound their way up to and around the second floor. A Waterford crystal chandelier hung from the ceiling two storeys up. Angela led us through double doors to the right of the front entrance.

"This was the original dining room. It's now the guests' dining room. They moved the original table to the ballroom. It can comfortably seat twenty dinner guests. We use it for the top table in weddings."

Angela led us back into the main reception area and through another door into a magnificent ballroom.

"The family would have used this room for parties. It's a lovely function room."

It was a huge room. Several people were working, setting up for the wedding the following day. Circular tables filled the edges of the room, covered in crisp white Irish linen. The highly polished mahogany top table shone under a white runner. Silver bud vases dotted its length while a staff member carefully set out the place settings, measuring an exact distance between each.

The original wooden floor felt warm underfoot, while the walls were adorned with tapestries and paintings. Light streamed through three sets of glass double doors on one side of the room and two on the other. Angela opened one set of doors and led us through to the outside terrace. The view was magnificent.

The formal gardens were terraced leading down to the river. A large fountain stood in the middle spewing water into a pool full of carp. Paths meandered through the formal gardens. Stone steps led from one terrace to the next. Roses scrambled over a large archway connecting the patio to the rose garden. The rose garden was in full bloom.

"The gardens always were beautiful," I said, "but I have to say, they look even nicer than I remembered. Not that I ever saw them from this angle."

"They look just as good from the riverside, Lizzie," Jimmy said.

For the first time since I left the Knockrath estate, a happy memory about it flashed into my head. It was a summer evening. Da had finished work, dinner was over, and we all went for a walk along the river.

"Do you remember, Jimmy? Da pointed out the fountain in the pond on the middle terrace. He said that Lord Haughton had arranged for it to be filled with koi without talking to his gardeners. The following evening the lord escorted Lady

Haughton to view his newly acquired fish. They found an empty pond and two very full herons."

Jimmy laughed. "I remember that. Da found it very funny."

"We did have some good times."

Jimmy put his arm around my shoulders. "We did, Lizzie."

We made our way back to the main reception area. From there Angela brought us to the library. A huge marble fireplace dominated the centre of the room while floor-to-ceiling bookcases lined the walls. Plush, emerald-green couches mirrored each other by the fire, while comfortable armchairs were dotted in front of the windows. Another set of double doors brought us into the coffee dock we were in earlier.

I ventured back out to the terrace leaving Angela and Jimmy to finalise the details for the wedding. It was a beautiful day, bright and sunny and I prayed that the weather would hold for my niece's wedding. My earlier misgivings about the venue were banished. The building no longer carried the ghosts of its previous owners. It was a well-appointed, luxury hotel that promised the possibility of happy memories to be made.

Chapter 50

The Wedding

Nora married Fionn in the local parish church, St Joseph's. The bride was radiant in white satin trimmed with lace, carrying a bouquet of orange-tinted lilies and baby's breath. She was walked down the aisle by her doting father, Jimmy, who beamed from ear to ear the whole way to the altar. He handed her over to Fionn and took his seat beside Kate, who looked amazing in a green two-piece suit reminiscent of Jackie Kennedy.

The officiating priest was the oldest man I had ever seen. He still said the Mass in Latin, even though the Catholic church had stopped that practice a few years earlier. At one stage I swear he fell asleep at the altar. Luckily, he was assisted by Father O'Hagan, a much younger priest who thankfully lightened the atmosphere.

After the ceremony we made our way to the hotel although in my head I still called it Knockrath Manor. My prayers to the Child of Prague had been answered. It was a glorious day. The wedding guests mingled on the terrace while the bridal party had photos taken in the gardens. It was picture perfect. Until I saw Ralph Haughton.

I was standing directly inside the doors leading to the gardens when he arrived from the main reception area. My blood ran cold. I clenched my glass of Babycham so tightly I thought the stem would break. That man had a brass neck coming anywhere near the hotel on the day of my niece's wedding. He marched straight towards Jimmy.

"Jimmy, I need to talk to you."

I froze, completely struck dumb. Anger bubbled in my stomach as I stared at this man I had hated for so long. Jimmy looked equally apprehensive.

"This is not the time or the place," he said.

Ralph looked around him at the wedding guests as if baffled why all these people were in the ballroom. I knew they said he was a recluse, but he had to have known Jimmy's daughter's wedding was on that day. The whole village knew. How could he not?

I tried to take a step towards them, but it was as if I were rooted to the spot. Then as suddenly as he arrived, a member of staff appeared beside him and escorted him back out the way he came.

"Gran?"

Beth was beside me, concern crinkling her eyes.

I shook my head. "It's nothing, *mo ghrá*. Now where has your father got to?"

We went out to the terrace in search of Michael and Lori. I had no wish to see Ralph Haughton today or any day for that matter. Jimmy said that the hotel staff were aware of his eccentricities and on the odd occasion that he would arrive on the premises, they were adept at keeping him away from the hotel guests.

By the time the gong rang to summon the wedding guests for dinner, we were all hungry. The food was excellent. After living in the heat of Florida for all those years, I had forgotten the taste of quality Irish food. The beef melted in my mouth, served with colcannon so creamy I could taste the butter. It was delicious. For dessert they served strawberries freshly picked from the garden with a generous helping of cream.

For their first dance together as man and wife, Nora and Fionn took to the dance floor to Petula Clark's, 'This Is My Song'. Everyone sang the final chorus.

As the dancing continued, I took my turn on the dance floor. I danced with Michael and with Jimmy. Even Conor took his old gran for a spin. It was a blessed day, a joyous occasion. I was so happy I had made the journey. So thankful to Angela for sending us the tickets. So lucky to share this day with my family.

The newlyweds went off to Kerry for their honeymoon. I was reminded of my honeymoon night in Cork city all those years ago. How innocent I was, we both were. At that stage I had never been outside of County Cork, yet nearly fifty years later, I felt like a seasoned traveller. I'd been across the whole Atlantic Ocean on a ship to another country and back again on an airplane. Although the thoughts of getting back on that airplane and flying back across that huge ocean niggled at the back of my mind. I wasn't looking forward to it.

The euphoria of the wedding still hung over us the next day. We had no plans other than to relax and enjoy the company of family. I went out for a walk with Beth and Conor. It triggered so many happy memories of when I was a girl and Da brought us for walks along the river.

As we neared Knockrath Manor I stared up at its façade, finding it hard to believe that it was still standing. The morning sunshine bathed its granite exterior in soft warm hues belying the secrets it kept. The magnificent lawns swept down to the river, bordered by mature plants in shades of pinks and purples that attracted bees and butterflies. I fell silent, remembering the original owners.

"What were they like, Gran?" Beth asked.

Her voice startled me out of my reverie. It was as if that child could read my mind.

"The Haughtons?"

"Yes, I saw him yesterday at the hotel. He looked like a tramp."

I laughed at that. She was right. Ralph Haughton looked like he bought his clothes in a jumble sale. He looked frail, undernourished, as if he had never had a proper meal.

"The Haughton family were very rich, immensely powerful people. They owned all the land around here. Yet they lived in England. They only came to the Knockrath estate during the summer months."

Beth looked puzzled. "He didn't look like he had money."

"He doesn't. The family lost all their money. They're all dead now, apart from Ralph."

"Where did you live?" Beth asked.

"Primrose Cottage."

An image of the cottage sprang into my head. Smoke rising from the chimney pot, the half door framed by clambering roses. The sound of my mother's voice singing as she baked. Memories of happy days, singing, dancing days. I had forgotten those days. The happy times before Maggie. I felt as if my life was divided into before Maggie and after Maggie. The division black and white, night and day. That huge event that changed our lives.

Beth's voice cut into my thoughts.

"Can we go see it?"

"See what?"

"Primrose Cottage," Beth said.

My feet stuck to the path. My first reaction was, no way would I go anywhere near the cottage. Ralph lives there now. In my childhood home. But slowly the thought formed that maybe I should pay the cottage a visit. Maybe that's what I needed to exorcise my ghosts. After all, I had been in the manor house. If I could visit the Haughton residence, then surely, I could visit my home.

"Okay, why not."

I led Beth and Conor back the way we came and around the back of Knockrath Manor. As I neared the cottage, I could feel my heart rate rising. My palms were sweaty. I inwardly scolded myself for being so silly. It was only bricks and mortar.

I couldn't believe my eyes. Even though Jimmy had told me that Ralph took care of Primrose Cottage, I think I expected it to be run-down but it wasn't. The exterior walls were whitewashed, the roses scrambled around the door. Although the door was closed. In my childhood the half door was always open, always welcoming. The biggest difference was the forest. It was slowly reclaiming what once was its terrain, the brambles cloaking the walls as if trying to swallow our little cottage whole. The stone wall my father built was still standing, the stones polished from generations of wind and rain.

On the light breeze I imagined I could hear the laughter of my family as they danced around the kitchen table while my father sang in his molasses-rich voice.

"Is this the family home?" Beth asked. "Looks like it brings back good memories to you."

"Some lovely memories, Beth, some not so good. Maybe someday I'll tell you about them."

"Ah, Gran. You can't make a statement like that and expect me to let it go."

She's right of course. It all happened so long ago. For years I've told myself to put it all behind me, that nothing good can come of raking up the past. With hindsight I now understand that our future is built on our past. We cannot lock it away indefinitely. Instead, we need to deal with the events that shaped us so that we could learn from it. But I wasn't ready to talk to Beth about Maggie.

"Lizzie?"

His voice was deeper than I remembered. Then again he had been little more than a boy himself at the time. I felt myself stiffen as I stared at the figure in the doorway.

"Is it really you?" he asked.

I remained silent, every nerve ending in my body on edge.

"Gran?" Beth put her hand in mine.

I felt her puzzlement at the change in me. Conor stepped in front of me as if to protect me from any advancement by this strange man. I put my hand on his shoulder.

"Let's go," I said, and I turned back to the path, moving as quickly as I could without making it obvious that I was running away.

"Lizzie, Lizzie, come back." I ignored Ralph's calls, kept my head down and my feet moving.

Beth walked beside me with Conor behind us, checking every so often to make sure we weren't being followed. I didn't say another word until we got back to the village. Kate was in the kitchen and leapt to my side when she saw my face. Despite my best efforts, my distress must have showed.

"What is it? What happened?"

"Oh, Kate, don't mind me. I'm being stupid," I said. "Nothing a good cup of coffee wouldn't fix."

Beth busied herself making coffee while Kate sat beside me, holding my hand. I took long breaths trying to get my heart rate back to normal. What had started as a lovely relaxing walk had culminated in what? Why did I run away? What was wrong with me that I couldn't confront my past?

Chapter 51

Maggie

"Lizzie, you're never going to believe this."

It was the following day. I had recovered my equilibrium and was putting two loaves of soda bread in the oven, enjoying the rare time alone. Beth and Lori had gone shopping with Kate. Michael was driving them into the city. Jimmy had gone into work early and I wasn't expecting him back until the evening. They had a group of American fishermen staying at the hotel and Jimmy's expertise was in demand. I was quite surprised to see him back so early.

"What am I not going to believe?" I asked, matching Jimmy's beaming smile with one of my own. Until I saw who stood beside him. Ralph Haughton, not ten feet away from me.

All the air deflated out of my lungs, and I sat heavily. Jimmy immediately sprang to my aid, but I waved him away.

"What is he doing here?" I said, surprising myself with the vehemence in my voice.

"I invited him. He has news for us that you are going to want to hear."

"I'm not interested in anything that man has to say."

"Lizzie, I have to talk to you," Ralph said.

I withered him with a look. "Well, I don't want to talk to you."

"Listen to me. I'm sorry, so very sorry but I was only a child myself. I paid for what I did. I saw what George did to Maggie. It was me that pushed him that day. It was all my fault."

It was so odd to hear Ralph finally admit that he was the one who had hurt George. Our Maggie was sent to prison for something he had done.

"It's too late now. Maggie's dead because of you."

"I know and I am so sorry. I will make it my life's work to make amends."

There was something in his tone that reminded me of the old whiny Ralph, the coward who allowed his brother to bully him. Who let my sister take the blame for hurting him when we all knew she wasn't physically capable of it.

"Ralph, tell her about Maggie's baby." Jimmy looked annoyed, but his excitement couldn't be contained.

"What?" This change in the conversation floored me.

"Ralph. Tell Lizzie what you told me," Jimmy said, but before Ralph could answer him, he couldn't contain himself. "Maggie's baby..."

"You do realise that the baby would be at least fifty-three at this stage," I said.

"Of course, I know that. She found us, Lizzie. Maggie's child found us. And it turns out we've known her for years."

My mouth fell open. The question was there on the top of my tongue, but I couldn't ask it.

Ralph spoke up. "We've compared the paper trail. Confirmation came through this morning. It turns out she has been looking for her birth mother for nearly as long as we were looking for her. She didn't know she was adopted until after her mother died. Her father told her the truth and gave her what little paperwork he had. She has been looking ever since."

Ralph looked at Jimmy for confirmation.

"It's true," Jimmy said. "This morning I had a long chat with her. She found us, not the other way round. It's amazing. You can see the family similarity. Her daughter is a real McCarthy. She looks like you."

I remained speechless as my mind churned over what Jimmy was saying. The young woman behind the reception desk in the hotel. That's why she looked familiar. She looked like us, like me and Jimmy, like my da. My eyes widened and my mouth formed a perfect O as the implication slowly dawned on me. The young receptionist was Teresa Dennison, daughter of Evelyn Dennison, née Boyle.

"Evelyn Dennison is Maggie's daughter?"

"Yep." Jimmy nodded so enthusiastically I thought his head would fall off.

"Evelyn Boyle Dennison. She has the paperwork to back it up. Robert and Dorothy Boyle adopted a baby girl from Our Lady's in May 1914. The nuns told them that her mother died in childbirth. They even gave the Boyles Maggie's real name."

"But... why now, after all these years? If she always had Maggie's name."

"They were told she died in May 1914, but Maggie didn't die until September 1916. They couldn't find a death certificate until they widened the search, thanks to the information that Ralph Haughton unearthed."

"But still... all these years."

I found it difficult to process this information. We knew Evelyn. Angela had worked for her for the past twenty years, so had Jimmy for that matter. I had only met her once and thought she was very likeable. A smart intelligent woman. Is that the type of woman our Maggie could have been?

The thought struck me then, that she would ask who the father was, if she didn't know already.

"Did she ask who her father was?"

Jimmy exchanged glances with Ralph. "No, not yet. I think she's still stunned to find out that her mother lived on the estate. But she will ask, as soon as she assimilates the information she has already."

"That's why I'm here, Lizzie," Ralph said. "There is no paper trail to the father... to George. We could tell Evelyn about him, but does she need to know that she was the product of rape?"

Jimmy interjected. "I don't think we should say anything about him at all. She might never ask but if she does ask us, we can say we don't know."

Another conundrum. For years we had wondered where Maggie's baby had been sent. Now we knew who she was, where she was but we now worried about how much to tell her about her conception. I remembered a letter Angela had sent when she first settled in Ireland.

"You might not have a choice on any of that. Irish people have long memories. Angela heard the rumours years ago about Maggie. Only the story Angela heard was that the master of the house got Maggie pregnant, then when he refused to marry her, she lost her mind and killed herself. And we all know that was not what happened."

"But even if she's heard that rumour, she may not connect it to Maggie."

"She will. Evelyn Dennison is one smart cookie. Once she finds out how Maggie died, she'll put two and two together."

Ralph had looked thoughtful up to that point, listening to me and Jimmy. "I think it would be best to say we don't know. She doesn't need to know."

"That is so typical of you. Don't allow anything to sully the Haughton name but it's okay for Maggie's daughter to believe that her mother somehow seduced the master of the big house, then killed herself when he refused to marry her. What type of person does that make Maggie?"

Ralph shifted his weight from foot to foot.

"What?" I asked, for I could see there was something else he knew but wasn't telling us.

"The day Maggie came to the manor, the day you were there, Lizzie. She was so brave that day. You would have been so proud of her," Ralph said.

I was so confused. The memory of that day never left me. Maggie broken and keening like the child she was.

"She confronted George. Told him off for the bully he was. Her courage made me brave, so I spoke up, told Mother what I saw, what George had done to Maggie, how he had laughed at me..." Ralph gulped, staring at a point somewhere around my feet. "I told Mother that I was the one that pushed George, that Maggie had nothing to do with it."

Silence fell, like a blanket cutting off all other sound. The Haughtons knew Maggie was innocent, yet still they persisted in having her arrested. I shook my head in disbelief.

"Maggie came to George for help that day... she said that the nuns had stolen her baby." Ralph kept talking. It was as if once he had started speaking, he couldn't stop.

"She asked George to help her and when he refused, she asked Mother, implored her as a mother to help her. My mother... she shouted at Maggie like a fishwife. She told Maggie that her baby had nothing to do with her or any of the Haughton family. That her bastard child was better off without her."

"Oh my God, I can't believe I'm listening to this."

I held my hands to my ears as if in doing so I could shut out what I was hearing. Yet I couldn't bear not to know all the details. Jimmy stood silent as a statue, listening carefully, his mouth open, his eyes wide as if he too could hardly believe what Ralph was telling us.

"Go on," he croaked.

"Maggie got really angry. She screamed at George to admit what he had done, that the baby was his, a Haughton, but George slapped her really hard." Ralph put his hand to his cheek as if he could feel that slap.

"He knocked Maggie over, then he grabbed the poker. Your mother arrived just in time to stop him. I think he would have killed her."

Jimmy took a step towards Ralph who moved back, raising his arms as if to protect himself from a physical onslaught.

"What the hell? Did you really think I was going to punch you?"

"I wouldn't blame you if you did."

Jimmy turned away, his fists clenched, and I knew he was close to breaking point. Ralph wrung his hands together, a look of sheer anguish on his face. Jimmy turned back to face him.

"So, you're telling us that your brother would have beat a young girl with a poker to shut her up rather than admit to the truth." Jimmy's tone was icy cold.

"I tried to talk to Father, told him that none of it was Maggie's fault but he wouldn't listen. Mother took to her bed. But not before she warned me not to say anything to anybody. I pleaded with her, but she said it was too late. That Maggie had already served her sentence. Mother said no good would come of us telling the police that it was me that pushed George. Father agreed. He said it would damage the family name."

"Your family name," I shouted. "Your family destroyed my sister's life."

Ralph sobbed, his hand covering his face as great dollops dropped off his chin. Jimmy and I stared, not sure what to say to him or each other. The sobbing stopped as quickly as it started. Ralph blew his nose, shook his head and took a deep breath.

"There's something else."

Jimmy moved to my side. "Spit it out, Ralph. We all know what happened last time you kept your mouth shut."

"Nothing can be proved. It's something I was told by a third party, and it hasn't been corroborated. Not yet anyway. Although I can't see how I can find out the truth of it. Like I said, it's hearsay."

"What are you talking about?" Jimmy asked, inching closer to Ralph's shaking frame, his tone seriously close to a growl. "Spit it out, Ralph."

"When I was making enquiries in the hospital... it was pointed out to me that it would have been impossible for Maggie to fall out the window."

"What do you mean?" I asked.

"Maggie was pushed."

Chapter 52

Evelyn

"Evelyn wants to talk to you, Lizzie."

Jimmy sat beside me at the dinner table. He lathered a slice of my freshly baked brown bread with butter and tucked in, hungry after a busy afternoon on the river. My appetite abandoned me despite the lovely spread Kate had put in front of me.

Even though I knew it was inevitable that Evelyn would want to talk to me, I wasn't sure how I felt about it. For years I had yearned to meet Maggie's daughter, but now that I knew who she was I didn't know how to feel. It was all I had thought about for the previous forty-eight hours. I'm sure Evelyn was as stunned as we were.

"She asked if you have a photograph."

"A photograph of Maggie?" I was incredulous. How different her upbringing was to ours. When we were children, people like us, working-class people didn't have photographs taken. That was something done by the rich and famous. Not tenant farmers in the south of Ireland.

"Who's Maggie?" Beth asked.

I looked at her, suddenly realising how much I had kept

from my family. How little they knew about me and my upbringing on the Knockrath estate.

"It's a long story," I said, reluctant to speak about the past, especially now that it had caught up with me and I didn't know how to deal with it.

"You should tell them, Lizzie." Jimmy put down his knife and fork. "Why keep it from them?"

"Keep what from us?" Michael asked.

I looked at my son. Conflicted and not for the first time. There was so much I had kept hidden from him. Is it better to know the whole truth about your parentage or should some secrets be kept to the grave. Over the past forty-two years I have agonised at times over whether Michael needed to know that I did not give birth to him. Then common sense prevailed. I was his mother. I was the one who fed him and changed him. Who walked the floor with him when he was teething, who taught him how to tie his shoelaces and fasten his britches. I was his mother.

"Tell them about Maggie," Jimmy said.

Michael looked at me expectantly. Beside him Lori looked puzzled while Conor continued to eat, oblivious to the tension around him.

I took a deep breath, wondering where to start, or just how much to say. If I told them Maggie's story, it was also the story of Evelyn Dennison. Did I have the right to share the story of her birth? I made my decision. Hopefully Jimmy would follow my lead.

"Maggie was our sister. She was the middle child. She was feisty and beautiful, and we loved her very much."

I felt Jimmy's hand on mine and smiled, grateful for his support.

"We had a very happy childhood, your uncle Jimmy and

me... and Maggie. But then something terrible happened to Maggie. She had a baby... out of wedlock."

"That's not so terrible, Mom. I know it might have seemed like a terrible scandal back then but it's not the worst thing that can happen."

"I know that now, Michael, but that's not the worst of it. Maggie was very young, although girls got wed much younger then than they do nowadays."

"That's true," Jimmy said. "They were different times."

Jimmy squeezed my hand.

"Sorry, sorry, I'm not being clear." I cleared my throat. "It's just so difficult to talk about Maggie. We were so close, and I miss her so much."

I took a deep breath then looked at Jimmy who nodded at me to continue.

"Maggie was in Our Lady's Hospital in Cork city when the baby was born. The constable came to our cottage to tell us... they said the baby died."

"What do you mean, they said?" Michael asked, his head to one side.

I glanced at Jimmy who nodded for me to continue.

"The nuns said the baby died. They told Maggie her baby had died. Me and Ma went up to the hospital. It was dreadful. Poor Maggie was lying in a cot, unwashed, her hair matted. She was unrecognisable."

"But that's awful. She was only a child herself."

"She was only a slip of a thing. And so innocent. Da said she would turn heads when she got older."

A memory sprang unbidden of Da singing to Maggie on her twelfth birthday. Ma had baked a cake and made lemonade. Maggie's dark hair was tied up with a yellow ribbon in a big bow. She was so pretty. The thought of her in that moment made me smile. Until I remembered what happened a few months later.

"But she never got the chance. To grow up, to turn heads. She died."

"How?"

"She fell... out of a window in Our Lady's Hospital in Cork."

"Oh, Mom, that's shocking."

"It was. It was a terrible time. Ma fell apart for a while, until Aunt Jean took over and nursed her back to some sort of normality. But they were never the same after Maggie died."

Beth got up and gave me a hug.

"That is so sad, Gran."

"Oh, it gets worse." Jimmy took over.

"When me and Kate moved here, I got talking to Ralph Haughton. He's the last of that family. You've all seen him. He lives in our old childhood home." Jimmy had everyone's full attention, even Conor.

"Ralph heard rumours about the nuns in Our Lady's. Rumours about the nuns selling babies to wealthy Americans. So, he started digging. Turns out that Maggie's baby didn't die the way we were told. Ralph found the evidence. They stole Maggie's baby and sold her to a wealthy American family."

"Oh my God, that's so shocking," Michael said. Lori took his hand although her eyes never left mine. I couldn't match her gaze. It was as if she could somehow see inside my soul and know that I too had stolen a child. Except I didn't steal him. I was given him. A precious gift that I have treasured all these years. That both me and Ed loved with every fibre of our being.

"Gran..." Beth touched my arm, pulling me back into the conversation. "Are you okay?"

I patted her hand. "I'm okay. It's been a lot to take in. We learned about the stolen babies years ago, but I never dreamed that Maggie's baby would be one of them."

"I did," Jimmy said. "Or at least I always hoped she was."

"Maggie's baby was a girl?" Beth asked.

"Yes, and we've found her, or rather she found us."

A stunned silence like a collective intake of breath filled the room, then erupted into a chorus of "How?" and "Where?" and "Oh my God."

"This is the oddest part of the whole story," Jimmy said, then paused for dramatic effect.

"Oh, for God's sake, Jimmy. Get on with it," I said, more than a little irritated.

"The McCarthy family have come full circle. From tenants on the estate to owners."

"What are you talking about?" Michael said.

"Maggie's baby was sold to a wealthy American couple. Hoteliers. The Boyles never told her she wasn't born to them. It was only after Dorothy died that Robert Boyle told Evelyn that they had adopted her."

"Evelyn Dennison is Maggie's daughter?" Michael asked. "This is unbelievable."

"They got their baby girl from Our Lady's Hospital. Evelyn went there looking for records. She eventually got the name, Margaret McCarthy but little else. For years they couldn't find her because they were told she'd died in childbirth. They were looking in the wrong year. It was only when they widened their search, they found the death certificate."

"And now, Evelyn wants to meet Mom," Michael said. "Presumably she wants to find out more about her mother."

"I reckon she does." Jimmy looked at me. "You need to meet with her."

"I know."

Later that evening Jimmy and I took a walk by the river. It

was the first chance we'd had to talk without someone else being within earshot.

"I talked to Ralph again," Jimmy said.

"Did you find out anymore?"

"He showed me the information he has. Ralph is correct in saying nothing can be proved but it is looking very likely that our Maggie was pushed. He found it when he was researching another case. There's a note on this woman's file. The note said that she saw Maggie arguing with a 'toff' as she put it. She said that he manhandled Maggie into a room, that she heard a scream, then the man came out and hurried down the corridor. She called him but he moved faster."

"That's crazy. Why weren't we told about this? We were told that Maggie fell, the insinuation was that she jumped."

"It was never investigated."

"Why not?" I was stunned. It seemed inconceivable to me that there was a witness to our Maggie's final moments, and no one thought to look into it.

"Her story was dismissed at the time. They had her classified as a lunatic, a person of unsound mind. They didn't believe her."

We walked on in silence as I tried to analyse this latest piece of information. Since I landed in Ireland it felt like we had gone from hearing nothing for years to suddenly being bombarded with information.

"Could her story be true?"

"I believe so. So does Ralph. She died two months later. Her death certificate says cardiac arrest, but it seems unlikely. She was twenty-two."

"Why was she in there?"

"Her husband had her committed. Ralph's still trying to find out how or why. He's working with her daughter on it. She was only a baby at the time."

"That is so tragic. What went on in that place?"

"It truly was an awful institution. I have a copy of her statement."

I stopped walking and turned to look directly at Jimmy. He took a sheet of paper from his pocket and read out the details of Maggie's last minutes. It finished with a description. Older man in his sixties, tall, painfully thin, wispy hair and a monogram. Neither of us had any doubt. The description fitted Lord Haughton.

We reached the edge of the Knockrath Manor gardens. I looked up, past the designer lawns and the fountain to the imposing manor house. Such a beautiful building, I thought, with its hidden secrets. Still owned by a member of the Haughton family even though she didn't know that. I hoped and prayed she had none of her paternal characteristics. From what I knew about her, I didn't believe so. Evelyn was a good friend to Angela. She was a good employer. Her daughter was a lovely, friendly girl. I glanced to my right at Jimmy.

"I can't begin to understand how Evelyn must feel about all of this. First of all, to only find out when you're in your thirties that your mother didn't give birth to you, that your parents adopted you. Such a shock to your sense of who you are. Then all these years trying to find out who her mother was only to find out that she owns the estate her mother lived on."

Jimmy's words sent a spasm of guilt through me, but I dismissed it as I always did. I didn't adopt my son. He is mine. Ours. Me and Ed. We didn't steal him, and we didn't buy him. He was ours from the second he was born.

I nodded. "She'll ask me about her father. What should I do?"

"I don't know." Jimmy shook his head. He was as torn as I was. "She's been through so much already. Does she really need to know the rest?"

Chapter 53

Secrets

It felt so odd to sit in the living room of Knockrath Manor across from Maggie's daughter. I searched her face, but I couldn't see any family resemblance. Not to the McCarthys anyway. I didn't want to look for the Haughton in her.

After long debates with Jimmy, we finally agreed that no good could come from telling Evelyn about her conception. George and Maggie were both dead. That was firmly in the past. Evelyn knows that Maggie McCarthy was her biological mother and that was the important fact.

"I was thirty-seven when I found out that Dorothy and Robert were not my biological parents," she said. "Imagine. I'm still amazed by that. How did I not suspect something?"

"There was no reason to. They loved you, gave you a wonderful life."

"They were great parents. I never wanted for anything but... they could have told me. Mother never said a word. Papa waited until he was dying. The day before he passed, he told me that they'd adopted me, that I was born in Ireland. I was so angry with him, with Mother. It took a long time and a lot of therapy to get rid of that anger."

"Your parents did what they thought was best for you at the time."

"Was it, though? I suffered such a crisis when I found out. My whole sense of who I was, brought into question. I stared at myself in the mirror wondering who I looked like. Do you know, when I was a girl, I asked my mother that question. Who did I look like? She told me I looked like her. I had her hair and her colouring. That was her opportunity to tell me, but she chose not to."

I remained silent. My secret churning inside me. There were no such conversations with Michael. He was an Anderson to the backbone. It was a different scenario I told myself. No comparison whatsoever.

Evelyn sat twisting her rings as she talked.

"Can I ask you something?"

I straightened up. "Of course you can."

"My biological mother, Margaret. What was she like?"

After not talking about Maggie for most of my life, I suddenly wanted to talk about nothing else.

"She was a beautiful girl. Dark wavy hair that reached past her shoulders. Flawless skin like porcelain. Da said she was going to be a heartbreaker. I was slightly jealous of her when he said things like that. She was the beauty."

I became lost in the past, remembering Maggie's laugh, her infectious zest for life. That was her downfall in the end. If she hadn't been so outgoing, maybe Master George would never have noticed her that day at the fête. If she didn't stand out from the other village girls, then he might never have paid any attention to her. Yet I felt guilty thinking that way. My sister was a beauty with a larger than life personality. She had so much potential. A young woman on the cusp of life. All that possibility was smashed by the Haughton family. But I couldn't say that here, now, to this lovely woman.

"You must have loved her very much," Evelyn said.

"I did. We all did. When Maggie died, our family fell apart. Ma never recovered."

Evelyn nodded. A companionable silence fell between us. Evelyn lifted her empty coffee cup and signalled to the barista to bring more coffee. With fresh coffees in front of us she leaned forward.

"Can I ask you a very personal question?"

"Yes, I suppose."

"Why didn't she keep me? I mean, I know it was impossible in those days, well, it still is really for a single woman to bring up a child. But did she want to keep me?"

My horror must have shown on my face. I presumed when Ralph had told her the identity of her biological mother, he would have told her the circumstances. I tried to lift my cup, but my hand shook so much I couldn't. Evelyn watched, puzzlement creasing her eyes.

"She didn't have a choice," I said.

"I see. It would have been impossible I suppose," Evelyn said, staring into her coffee cup as if it held the answers. "A single girl having a baby, unmarried, well, it would have been a major scandal."

"It was. The local gossips had a field day."

"But... I don't mean to be critical, and it's immaterial anyway, your parents did what they did... did they even consider raising me?"

Unsure how to reply, my mouth opened several times, but no words came out. Evelyn paused, waiting for my answer then shook her head.

"I'm sorry, Lizzie, I shouldn't have asked you that. It really was outside your control. It's just that since I began my search to find my birth mother, I've come across many cases where a child, like me, was brought up by their grandmother as their own."

I put my cup on the table with more force than necessary, stood and walked over to the window. My mind was in turmoil. Should I tell this woman the truth about her birth? That her biological father raped her birth mother, that he denied the fact, that his family had her imprisoned for assault. It was too much.

"Lizzie, I'm sorry. I didn't mean to upset you."

Evelyn appeared at my side, a lacy handkerchief in her hand. She put her arm around my shoulders and led me back to my chair. Her compassion covered me like a blanket. I couldn't tell this woman the truth. Not yet anyway, maybe not ever. What happened to Maggie haunted me my whole life. I couldn't inflict that pain on anyone else, especially this lovely woman. Decision made, I took a deep breath and gave her the version of the truth me and Jimmy had agreed on.

"My parents were never given the opportunity to raise you. The nuns told Maggie that you died. They never let her see you. We were told you'd died."

"Oh, my word." Evelyn clutched her chest. "That is so... cruel."

"That's one word for it. We never suspected a thing. Even when Maggie came home, it was as if she had lost her mind. We thought it was because her baby died. Now we know that she suspected the nuns had stolen her baby, but she probably thought no one would believe her."

"Did she tell you?"

I shook my head, wondering why my sister hadn't confided in me. That last night we spent in our home, when I combed her hair and held her until she slept, why didn't she say something to me? Give me some hint of what was going on. Although hindsight is a wonderful thing. Looking back on it now, I probably wouldn't have believed her either. I would have thought it was grief turning her head, looking for answers when there weren't any. Babies die, mothers grieve. The idea of a nun stealing a baby would never have occurred to any of us. After all, nuns were the handmaidens of Christ. Holy women whose purpose in life was to serve God. They couldn't do something as evil as steal a baby from its mother.

"Maggie came here," I looked around me, "to this very room. She asked the Haughtons for help. They thought she had lost her mind. She was sent away to Our Lady's Hospital. We never saw her again."

I gulped back a sob. The half-truth was better than the full truth. Evelyn didn't need to know that I'd witnessed her biological father ready to beat Maggie to death. Or that her grandmother had denied her existence. And especially that her grandfather ordered Maggie to be sent back to Our Lady's.

Evelyn looked around her, searching every corner as if Maggie's ghost would suddenly appear out of the woodwork.

"She's not here, Evelyn," I said. "Those ghosts were banished long ago. Maggie lives on in my heart and in Jimmy's. Hopefully now in yours too."

"Thank you, Lizzie, for being so honest with me."

Those words burned into my brain, yet I knew I couldn't tell Evelyn the whole truth. There was nothing to be gained in that. For anyone.

Chapter 54

Going Home

It was an eventful three weeks but all too soon it was time to go back to the States. After my initial meeting with Evelyn, we become quite close. She sought out my company. I brought her for walks around the woods and Primrose Cottage, making sure to avoid Ralph. We talked about Maggie and about Ma and Da and our lives on the estate.

Evelyn talked at length about her upbringing in the States. She had led a charmed life. Riding lessons, private school, designer clothes, the best education. I told her as much.

"I know what you're saying... but it was lonely. I was an only child. I don't mean to sound ungrateful. I realise I had a privileged upbringing."

"I hate to say it, but you had a much better standard of living than you would have had if Ma had brought you home to live with us. Don't get me wrong. Ma and Da worked hard to put food on the table. We had the best they could afford. Ma believed in education, so she insisted we stay in national school. Jimmy got a scholarship for secondary school otherwise he may never have got there. You went to private school. You even got a college education."

"But you did have a happy childhood?"

"Yes, without a shadow of doubt. We were loved. Ma and Da did the best they could for all of us."

"But they sent Maggie away when she became pregnant, didn't they?"

I drew a sharp intake of breath. How could I answer that question without telling her the whole story? I could feel my colour rise as I struggled to contain my annoyance at any perceived criticism of my parents.

"They didn't have a choice. It was different back then."

Evelyn didn't look convinced.

"Even now, life in Ireland and America is very different. You've lived in both countries. You know that. Well, believe me, Ireland before the war, before independence, was like nothing you've ever experienced. We were tenants on an estate owned by a British lord."

"I didn't intend to upset you, Lizzie. I suppose I want to understand the circumstances around my birth. It is all so confusing."

"It was a difficult time for everyone. But there's no point in dwelling on the past. What's done is done. Count your blessings. You've had a great upbringing and look around you. You own this lovely hotel. How lucky is that?"

Evelyn laughed. "You're right of course. It is a beautiful hotel. I fell in love with this place the minute I saw it."

I wondered about that. Was there something that drew her to the home of her biological parents? At that stage she had no way of knowing her connection to the estate. And even when she heard the old rumours about the master of the house and the daughter of the estate worker, she couldn't connect them to herself. Evelyn believed that she was born in the United States. She held an American passport, lived like an American, believed in American culture. Until the day before Robert

Boyle died, she thought her Irish blood came from her Grandfather Boyle.

On our last night Evelyn invited the entire family to dine with her in the hotel. We took up a very large table in the main dining room that night. Evelyn, Ian and Teresa, Jimmy and Kate, Nora and Fionn, Michael and Lori, Conor, Beth and me. The food was delicious, and the conversation flowed. We finished our meal with Irish coffees. I had never tasted one before.

"They were invented in an airbase in Limerick in the forties. Before Shannon Airport was built. The story goes that the restaurant chef had a planeload of Americans who had to turn back to Ireland because of bad weather. He invented the drink to warm them up, hot strong coffee, drop of whiskey, lots of sugar and a dollop of cream."

"Well, they are delicious," I said. I rubbed my arm. The pain that had started in my shoulder early that morning was working its way down my arm and getting steadily worse.

"Are you okay, Lizzie?"

"Yes, nothing a good night's sleep won't sort."

That was the cue for everyone to take their leave and retire for the night. We had an early start the following day. Evelyn and Jimmy were taking us to Shannon Airport. From there we had our flight to New York and then the train journey to Florida.

The following morning, we said our goodbyes at Shannon Airport in the pouring rain. It felt fitting somehow. I left Ireland on a rainy day, to start my new life in America. Here I was, leaving again on a rainy day, only this time I wasn't alone. I had my family travelling with me, away from my roots to return to theirs.

"I have a gift for you," Evelyn said. "Something to occupy you on your journey."

It was a tape recorder. I looked at her, grateful for the gift but I knew somehow that there was a deeper meaning to it.

"I'm hoping that you will record your story." Evelyn showed me the blank tape and how to use the controls. "You press record and talk into the microphone. When you've finished speaking you press it again. You can rewind it and replay everything you've just said."

"I'll help you, Gran," Beth said.

Her thoughtful gesture was touching but it also scared me a little. How much of our story did I want to record for posterity? For my story was also Maggie's story, was also Evelyn's story, was also Michael's story, was also Angela's story. All those intertwining circles that make up a life. No one person lives in a bubble. Everything we do affects those around us. We exist within a family, within a community. Even the recluses amongst us like Ralph.

Chapter 55

The Luck of the Irish

The tape recorder sat on the dresser in my bedroom for nearly a year. I picked it up several times and talked into the microphone, but I deleted every word. How much of my story should I tell? In the end I decided to tell everything. Warts and all.

It was Beth who made the decision for me. My granddaughter was such a free spirit. She reminded me of Maggie. Bubbly, outgoing, full of the joys of life. She was courageous in a way that I could never have been. And I told her so, one sunny afternoon on the veranda.

"Don't think so, Gran. You're the brave one. You left your family and friends and moved to a new country to start a new life with a man you barely knew. Now that's brave."

Beth gave me cause to think, to re-examine my opinion of myself. When I married my American sailor, it would never have occurred to me not to move with him to America. None of us even considered Ed staying in Ireland. There was nothing there for him. No job, no prospects and even if there was, he was my husband and as his wife it was my duty to leave my parents' house and go to his. There was no bravery involved.

That's the way it was done in those days. I said as much to Beth.

"Oh, Gran, you are so old-fashioned."

"Of course I am. I'm old, thank you very much. And privileged to get to this age. Your grandfather didn't. God bless him. I miss that man."

Beth hugged me. "I know you do, Gran. We all do."

I patted her hands and smiled. Beth could always make me smile. Since she was a small child, she had an infectious smile. You could see the mischief sparkling in her eyes. Beth went inside to fetch the pitcher of lemonade I kept in the fridge. I may be old-fashioned, but I made full use of all those new-fangled inventions that made life easier in the Florida heat. A climate I'd learned to enjoy.

From my vantage point on the veranda, I could see the sea in the distance. I'd grown to adore this house. Ed built a home for us here. In a country I had grown to love. My husband is buried here. My son and my grandchildren live here. It is my home.

Jimmy had asked me, more times than I care to remember, to move back to Ireland. He said I could live with him and Kate. That I would be close to Nora, to Angela. He even offered Michael a job, figuring if Michael moved to Ireland, then I would have to follow. Michael turned him down. My son was an American born and bred. Lori is American. Their children are here. They all live full and happy lives on American soil. None of them had any desire to move to another country. America is vast. It is the land of opportunity.

It's a wonderful country with gracious, friendly people who opened their arms to welcome me. Yes, America may have its troubles. The government abolished segregation a few years back and a lot of people weren't happy about it, but they would work it out. That Martin Luther King was a great speaker. With men like him motivating people to do the right thing, I'm sure this country would get even stronger. I've never taken an interest in politics. Ed used to get incensed when he read the papers. He'd fling the paper and pace the veranda when he read something he disagreed with. I'd continue my mending and let him rant. Once he got it out of his system, he'd pick up the paper and start reading again.

As for Jimmy, well, his last letter was full of the fiftieth anniversary of the Easter Rising. It's funny, neither of us remember much about the rebellion. I would have been sixteen, Jimmy was thirteen. Ma and Da talked about it but our Maggie was in Our Lady's Hospital. We had other things to worry about. The Easter Rising was in April. Maggie died in September. When the war for independence kicked off Jimmy was only sixteen but that didn't stop him joining the Irish Republican Army.

Jimmy sees Ireland from a different point of view than I do. He fought against the British. He was against the treaty and ended up on the rebel side in the Civil War. I'm grateful he survived it intact. Many didn't. He sees Ireland as a work in progress. A democratic republic that he loves and was prepared to die for. Me, when I lived in Ireland, it was owned by the British. The Haughton family were British. They owned my family. They owned land as far as the eye could see. Our village was theirs. Nothing was Irish. It was the country I was born in, the country I left at nineteen to make a better life for myself. And I did. Ed used to tease me, that I had the luck of the Irish, whatever that meant. I told him that my da called me Lucky Lizzie, that it was nothing to do with being Irish and everything to do with being Lizzie McCarthy.

Chapter 56

Home Truths

"My dearest Beth:

We had a wonderful time in Ireland last year. Being with family is so important. I had some reservations about seeing my childhood home, but it turned out to be a worthwhile experience. I hope you enjoyed it as much as I did.

The pain that started in Ireland has spread all over my body. I believe it is my time, but I am not afraid. The idea of meeting my beloved Ed again fills me with joy. I firmly believe that Maggie is there with Ma and Da and they will be happy to see me.

I've been to see my doctor and have had a battery of tests. He says I have four months at most. It's amazing how having a timeframe focuses the mind. I need to put my house in order. I've written to Jimmy and told him, so when the time comes it won't be as much of a shock.

Evelyn has been on my mind. She gave me the gift of this tape recorder, but I have been lax about recording anything. You are a smart girl, my Beth, *mo ghrá*. You are aware that each life ripples across the lives of others. To record my life story impinges on the life stories of other people. For the past year

Maria McDonald

I've debated the wisdom of telling my story warts and all. I've finally decided that is what I need to do.

It has been a difficult decision. How much should I tell? In the end I've decided to tell everything. Let those I love and who love me make of it what they will. At least you will all finally have the full truth.

I hope I have explained everything, and I pray that no one is hurt by anything I have done or failed to do. That sounds like a prayer from the Catholic Mass. And no, I don't mean to be flippant. I have been incredibly fortunate to know the love of my parents, my siblings, my wonderful husband, my incredible sister-in-laws, my beloved son and his gorgeous wife and my grandchildren. My da labelled me Lucky Lizzie and I have been just that all my life. Incredibly lucky to have lived and loved so many good people and to have that love reciprocated.

I decided not to say anything to your father yet, then realised that would be cowardly. It is only right that I should be the one who tells him the story of his birth. He is upset, justifiably so. It is a huge thing to be told that the woman you believed gave birth to you has no blood ties to you. He feels as if his whole life has been a lie. But it hasn't been. The only lie was in his genetics and even in that, he has the Anderson genes. Everything else was real. He was our child from the second he was born. We loved him as if he were our own blood. I don't think we could have loved him more. Angela loved him too but as an aunt. She would never have survived as a mother and by giving him to us to raise, she blessed our family.

I'm hoping that you can help him through this, Beth. Your father is a wonderful man, whose sense of identity has been shaken. I honestly feel he needs to talk to Evelyn. She may be able to put it into perspective for him. At the end of the day, the twenties were very different times. We all did what we thought was for the best. Maybe we should have told him as he got older, but the opportunity never presented itself. The older he got, the further his birth was buried under other memories; wonderful memories of feeding him and changing him, of teaching him to talk, holding him when he cried, smiling when he laughed, worrying about him at war, our pride when he married your mother. And then Conor and you. We were so proud of everything he achieved. So proud of both of you.

Maybe we were cowards. Me and Ed both backed away from ever telling him, afraid of hurting him, the way he is hurting now. I should have told him in Ireland. When we found out that Evelyn was my sister's baby, was the perfect opportunity. In fairness I was reeling myself after finding out that news. I don't think I could have coped with talking to Michael as well.

I have also written to Angela. It's only fair I let her know that Michael knows. I have no doubt he will contact her. They have always been close. Sometimes I wondered how people didn't guess they were mother and son. Especially Kate, but she didn't. Maybe because of how much we loved him. Try and remind your father of that unassailable fact. He was loved, is loved.

As for Evelyn. She deserves to know the whole story about her birth mother, my sister Maggie. When you play her these tapes, tell her I'm sorry I didn't tell her about her father. At the time we thought we were doing the right thing, for her more than for anyone else.

With hindsight I now realise that by keeping Maggie's story a secret I did her a huge disservice. She was a beautiful, feisty girl who could have gone places, been somebody. Instead, she is buried in a little cemetery in rural Cork, barely a mark in this world.

Although, in some ways, life has come full circle. The big country house is now owned by Evelyn Dennison, a woman who can claim the master of the house as her father, and the servant's daughter as her mother. By all accounts Evelyn has inherited her mother's traits.

I am happy to go to meet my maker. My da gave me the nickname Lucky Lizzie on the day I was born. I have lived up to that nickname my whole life and will die content in the knowledge that I have been lucky in every way possible."

Chapter 57

Beth, 1976

Conor was back a few days before I managed to get him alone to tell him about the tapes. I made him promise to listen to Grandma, then talk to me. I badly needed his opinion, but I let him digest the information first. He was always smarter than me. Conor can put all this into perspective. Our grandmother was the keeper of so many secrets.

I could hear the murmur of Grandma's voice behind Conor's bedroom door. So did Mom.

"You gave Conor Grandma's tapes?"

"Yes, I thought he should listen to her story."

"Good, I'm glad. We'll talk when he's got time to think about it."

It didn't take long. Two days later Conor knocked on my door and handed me the box of tapes.

"It's hard to believe this wonderful woman endured so much. Yet she called herself Lucky Lizzie," Conor said.

I agreed, relieved that Conor didn't appear to be angry with Grandma.

"I'm so glad you feel that way, Conor. I applaud her bravery.

To keep those secrets must have weighed heavily on her but she did what she thought was right for everyone," I said.

"At the end of the day Pops loved her, we all loved her."

Revealing the truth to our father must have been so difficult for Grandma.

"Our poor father. He must have been devastated. Why didn't he tell us? He carried that secret with him to his grave."

"Maybe he intended to tell us when the time was right but unlike Grandma, he had no warning. Grandma was sick for a few months before she died. She had time to put her house in order as they say."

We lapsed into silence, reliving Grandma's last words to us. Conor broke the silence.

"Let's talk to Mom."

We found her on the porch, rocking in her favourite chair. Conor brought a pitcher of lemonade from the fridge and filled three glasses.

"Can we talk, Mom?"

She started, nearly spilling her drink.

"Of course. Sorry, I was daydreaming, thinking about your grandma."

"That's what we want to talk about," Conor said.

She sighed then, before she settled back into her chair, gently rocking back and forth.

"You've listened to the tapes," she said, more of a statement than a question.

"We both have," I told her as me and Conor pulled up a seat beside her.

"Good. I'm glad. Your father and I listened to them a few years ago. It was just after you went to college, Beth. He packed them into that box in your wardrobe for safekeeping. Your father said you were too young to understand, that you would listen to them when you were ready."

Conor glanced at me, astounded. "So, Dad heard them?"

"Yes. Your father wanted to tell you both, but it was so difficult for him. It took him some time to adjust. Make no mistake, he always felt Lizzie was his mother. His feelings for her never changed. Maybe he saw her in a different light, but he loved her. You've no perception of how difficult life was back then for women. Your father told me that he believed that Angela had made the right decision."

"But he must have felt some resentment against Angela?" I asked.

"No, well maybe at first but once he thought it over, he realised that they did the right thing. All of them, your grandma, Pops and Angela."

"But she said herself in the tapes that she should have told him when they found out about her sister's baby."

"She was very open with your father about that. Your grandma was a good woman, but she wasn't a saint. She made mistakes, like all of us."

My mother looked at me over the top of her glasses and I blushed, wondering if she had somehow found out about my dalliance with a married man.

"Your grandma adored her son. To be honest she put him on a pedestal. At times he could do no wrong. Maybe part of her was always afraid that if he found out he wouldn't love her as much as she loved him. Who knows what went on in her head. But she was brave enough to tell your father in the end. He could have turned against her, but he didn't. He said that she was the one who had brought him up. She was his mother. It's as simple as that."

"Did Angela ever say anything to him?" Conor asked.

Mom hesitated as if unsure how much to tell us. She looked at us both, shook her head and smiled.

"After your grandma's funeral, your father and Angela had a

long talk. Don't forget, at that stage he had only found out a month or so earlier. She was completely honest with him which helped him come to terms with it all. She told him how lucky he was that Lizzie and Ed were prepared to bring him up as their own. Reminded him of how loved he was. Which he was. They idolised him. In Lizzie's mind he was theirs, the fact that she didn't give birth to him was immaterial."

"So why didn't he tell us?" I had to ask.

Mom shrugged.

"I think your father wanted to find the right time but when is the right time to tell you something like that? You both adored your grandparents. He was afraid in case it would change how you felt about them, and he didn't want that. Now it's too late."

Whether I am genetically related to my grandma or not, I know in my heart that I am like her. Listening to her story has made me realise that life is never black and white, that bad things can happen to good people, that learning how to live a good life despite its challenges makes you a better person. She was a strong Irish woman who made a positive difference to the lives of those around her. Lucky Lizzie will live on in all our hearts.

THE END

Also by Maria McDonald

The Devil's Own

Tangled Webs

Author's Notes

The big house

In Ireland in the 18th and 19th centuries, 'the big house' was the term given to the large country mansions occupied by the Anglo-Irish, the predominately Protestant ascendency class. These foreign landowners were given land and power in Ireland by successive British governments as rewards for their loyalty to the crown. As their wealth grew, the ascendency built large mansions signifying their elitist social status. The big houses were symbols of colonialism. Some landlords didn't even live in Ireland, having their permanent homes in England while others lived permanently in Ireland but were schooled in England.

During the famine years (1845-1852) many of these landlords evicted their starving tenants while exporting foodstuffs to the British Empire. During Ireland's War of Independence against England and subsequent bloody civil war, over 300 of these big houses were burned by Irish Republican forces. Many of the owners abandoned their houses and returned to their homes in Britain. The majority of the big house burnings occurred during the Civil War period. Some were rebuilt, using compensation from the new Irish

Author's Notes

government, but on a smaller scale. Many of those big houses that survived, were repurposed as luxury hotels.

Queenstown

Cobh was renamed Queenstown in 1849 after a visit from Queen Victoria. It reverted to its original name after Irish independence in 1922. It is the largest town in County Cork, sitting on Great Island, one of three islands in Cork Harbour. During the famine years, Irish migrants sailed from the port of Queenstown to America. From the same port the British authorities sent Irish prisoners to Australia and Van Diemen's Land, (the colonial name for the island of Tasmania). Their stories are recorded in *The Queenstown Story* in The Cobh Heritage Centre.

RMS *Lusitania* was a passenger liner owned by the Cunard Line. On 7th May 1915, she was sunk by a German U-boat eleven miles off the Old Head of Kinsale in Cork. Of the 1,962 passengers and crew on board, 1,198 died. 764 people were rescued by a flotilla of smaller boats who brought the survivors to Queenstown. They also recovered 289 bodies, 169 of which are buried in Queenstown cemetery. The sinking of the *Lusitania* caused uproar across the world, especially in America, who lost 128 citizens including millionaire businessman Alfred Vanderbilt. It eventually led to the entry of America into the war and their navy's arrival in Queenstown harbour. In Casement Square in Cobh, opposite the harbour, there is a monument to the people who died aboard the Lusitania.

In May 1917, the American navy sailed into Queenstown and stayed there until 1919. Over 10,000 doughboys passed through Queenstown. They were both welcomed and detested. Some married local women. When they left, the American Embassy issued visas to their Irish wives. These Irish war brides travelled to America leaving everything they knew behind them. Their stories have been recorded by historian Damian Shiels. www.shielsheritage.com

The character of Lizzie McCarthy is based on a mixture of the Cork women who met and married their American doughboys and moved to America after the war.

These days Cobh is a tourist destination and home to an international cruise terminal. Described by *Condé Nast Traveller* as 'one of the most beautiful small towns in Europe', it is worth a visit.

Child of Prague

Putting out the Child of Prague the night before a wedding was a tradition in Ireland for many years. If the little statue was headless, it was even better, although he must lose his head by accident not by intent. When I was younger every home had a Child of Prague, my mother's included, but these days you rarely seen them. It may be a purely Irish tradition. I had to google the origin of the statue and found that the original statue still exists and lives in the Church of Our Lady of Victories in Prague. This statue of Jesus as a child is 48cm high, carved out of wood, covered with linen and waxed. In 1556 a Spanish noblewoman named María Manriquez received the statue from her mother when she married Czech nobleman Vratislav.

Copies of it can be found all over the world but in Ireland, the tradition is that a bride-to-be puts it in her garden the night before her wedding to guarantee glorious sunshine on her wedding day.

John F Kennedy

John F Kennedy was revered in Ireland. His photo could be found in pride of place in the parlour alongside a photo of the Pope. The first Irish-American Catholic president, he travelled

Author's Notes

to his ancestral home in Wexford in 1963. The whole country turned out to welcome him. His death was mourned in Ireland as much as in America. His wife, Jackie was unable to accompany him to Ireland but after he was assassinated, she requested that the Irish army provide a guard of honour at his funeral.

Eleanor Roosevelt

Eleanor Roosevelt was a hugely influential woman who changed the role of America's First Lady. Married to Franklin D Roosevelt, the 32nd President, she was America's First Lady from 1933 until his death in 1945. She was a strong advocate for equality and social reform. After President Roosevelt's death, President Harry S Truman appointed her as delegate to the United Nations where she served as Chairman of the Commission on Human Rights 1946-1961. She had a major role in drafting the Universal Declaration of Human Rights in 1948. Eleanor Roosevelt played an active role in the Democratic Party all through her life. In 1961 she was appointed to President John F Kennedy's Commission on the Status of Women.

From 1936 until her death in 1962 she wrote a newspaper column, *My Day* which was extremely popular. There is a lot written about her by more knowledgeable people than me. She was outspoken, ambitious and a humanitarian who devoted much of her life to fighting for social equality for women and for people of colour.

Hurling

Hurling is a traditional Irish sport that is known to be the oldest and fastest field game in the world. The first references to the sport of hurling date back to Brehan law in the 5th century.

Author's Notes

It is an ancient Gaelic game played by men. The female version is just as tough but is called camogie.

The objective of the game is for players to use an ash wood stick known as a hurley to hit a small ball called a sliotar between the opponent's goalposts either over the crossbar for one point or under the crossbar into a net for three points. It is purely an amateur sport but played with passion and thrilling to watch.

Acknowledgements

It's a question usually retained for job interviews: 'Where do you see yourself in five years' time?' I have to be honest, if anyone had asked me that question, I never thought that on the first day of 2024, I would be writing an 'acknowledgements' page for my fourth novel. To be a published author is really a dream come true for me. For that, I thank my publishers. *The Keeper of Secrets* is my third novel to be published by Bloodhound Books. Thank you to all the team at Bloodhound; Betsy, Fred, Tara, Hannah, Katia and Abbie. A special word of thanks to my talented editor, Shirley Khan whose sharp eye for detail and solid encouragement I am extremely grateful for.

When writing historical fiction, it is important to keep the background facts accurate. Research is my favourite part of the writing process, and I am forever grateful to the experts who are so willing to share their knowledge. A special word of thanks to James Durney www.jamesdurney.com and Damian Shiels www.shielsheritage.com. It was Damian's research into the Irish war brides which sparked the inspiration for this book. I have tried to be as accurate as possible but please remember *The Keeper of Secrets* is a work of fiction.

I can never thank my family enough for their unwavering support.

A huge thank you to you, the reader. Thank you for choosing to read my book. I sincerely hope you enjoy it.

A note from the publisher

Thank you for reading this book. If you enjoyed it please do consider leaving a review on Amazon to help others find it too.

We hate typos. All of our books have been rigorously edited and proofread, but sometimes mistakes do slip through. If you have spotted a typo, please do let us know and we can get it amended within hours.

info@bloodhoundbooks.com

Printed in Great Britain
by Amazon